The Roses
of Constant

The Roses of Constant

BETHANY CAMPBELL

Five Star
Unity, Maine

Five Star Romance

Published in conjunction with
Kidde, Hoyt & Picard Literary Agency.

Cover photograph © Alan J. La Vallee

February 2000

Five Star Standard Print Romance Series.

The text of this edition is unabridged.

Set in 11 pt. Plantin by Minnie B. Raven.

Printed in the United States on permanent paper.

Library of Congress Cataloging-in-Publication Data

Campbell, Bethany.
    The roses of Constant / Bethany Campbell.
       p.   cm.
    Originally published: Toronto ; New York : Harlequin Books, 1989, in series: Harlequin intrigue ; 116.
    ISBN 0-7862-2352-9 (hc : alk. paper)
    1. Conspiracies — Arkansas — Fiction.   2. Arkansas — Fiction.   I. Title.
PS3553.A43954 R67   2000
 813′.54—dc21
                                             99-058250

For Meg and Pete

Prologue

April

For years he had been trying to impress her again the way he once had. He'd show her.

He'd walked out on her tonight, and she hadn't blinked an eye. That was Valery for you. She'd gotten so self-sufficient it was eerie. But he'd show her yet.

This time he had it all together. He was going to be a hero again. Only this time a different kind. This time they could keep the glory; it didn't last. This time he wanted money. He had a lot of it and he was going to get more. Valery didn't know, and money alone wouldn't impress her, but what he was going to do with it would.

He saw himself in a beautiful little twin-engine Cessna, flying between the islands, gliding high above a blue ocean slightly hazed with heat. He wasn't even sure which islands yet; that part of his dream was unclear. He just saw himself in the plane, his *own* plane, running his own charter service, invulnerable, independent, free as a god as he flew.

Nobody had ever said he wasn't one hell of a pilot. Nobody. And nobody ever understood that he wasn't meant for the plodding, earthbound life of ordinary mortals.

He would show everybody in this stinking little town: the Talmidges, the Perrys, the Upchurches, the whole lot, but most of all, Valery. He would show her he could take care of himself just fine, thank you. This time he had it all together. This time he knew all the secrets.

Even his mother was going to be proud. She would admire him again, the way she had that one magic summer so long ago. Before he threw everything away for Valery.

The light in Valery's eyes back then, he thought, the light in her eyes when she looked at him. He thought he could fly forever just on the light in those eyes. And then the light had died.

He stretched out on the bed of the motel. He was a big man of thirty-one years, whose blond good looks were becoming thick and faded. The motel was the Bed o' Roses Motor Inn in the central Arkansas town of Constant.

Outside his window, the cold wind rattled the dead rose bushes. He smiled to himself. He imagined himself again in the silvery Cessna, winging above the world like a free, immortal force.

The others were frightened. When he'd realized how frightened, he knew his fortune was made. Their fear would buy him a whole fleet of Cessnas. He knew all the secrets, and he knew what they were worth.

Soon he'd be island hopping, high in the tropical sky, the sun glinting off his wings. He wasn't going to worry about anybody turning on him, either. He had what he thought of as his insurance policy. He could use everybody against everybody else. It was clever.

They didn't know it yet, but if they touched him, he'd left a way to blow the whistle on them. He would tell them tomorrow: no funny stuff. He was covered. He was home free.

He reached for the glass of cheap Chianti on his nightstand. He opened his bottle of Seconal and shook out two capsules. He put them into his mouth and washed them down with a swallow of wine. Valery was always giving him hell for that: the booze and the pills. She didn't believe he could handle it. She said it was a rotten example for the kid.

Once she'd even hidden his pills when he'd been drinking. Could you believe that? He told everybody—the Talmidges, John Upchurch, Terry Perry—she takes my pills and *hides* them. My *prescription*. She *hides* my prescription, which is from the *doctor.* He'd made such a fuss he thought she'd never do it again.

But Valery, being Valery, didn't flinch. "It was for your own good," she'd said.

"I'm telling everybody you won't keep your hands off my stuff," he'd warned, "that you're interfering with my medication. Something goes wrong on the job, I say, 'Sorry, my wife is messing with my medication.' So back off, Valery. Back off and stay off."

"I don't care what people think," she'd said.

And that was Valery's whole problem, just like it had been her father's: she didn't care what people—

The poison hit him like a bolt of fire that flared through his stomach and up his throat. It hit him so hard that his arms flew out convulsively and then, just as convulsively, knotted around his midsection as he doubled up, silently screaming, on the bed.

He realized at once that he was dying. He was burning up rapidly from the inside out. It was like having an explosion within. Astonishing, astonishing.

He reached wildly for the phone. His fingers closed spasmodically around the receiver. The rest of the phone went crashing to the carpet, along with the wine and the pills and his flight maps.

A second bolt of fire went through him and straightened him out for a brief moment, like a man being tortured on the rack, then doubled him up again. He said a few garbled words into the receiver, then it fell from his clutching hands.

They betrayed me, he thought in wonder.

For a moment he saw things quite clearly, how he had thought everything worked and how it really worked. Wheels within wheels. He thought he was protected, and he was wrong, because he hadn't told them yet. They had moved too quickly.

An incredible agony welled up through his stomach and throat, swelled in his chest and shot down his arms. The joke's on you, it seemed to say. You always were a sucker, Charlie.

He knew, as certainly as he knew he was dying, that they were going to frame Valery for this. Or kill her. Or both. He hadn't proven anything to her after all. Instead he had betrayed her, right into their hands.

And she has no idea, he thought. *They'll get her, too. Nothing will stop them.*

Then the pain drove all thought from his mind, and a third jolt of fire surged through him, wiping away even the pain. Blackness ate up everything. His mind fell into the dark and disappeared forever.

Charles Lonnie Essex was dead, at age thirty-one, alone in the Bed o' Roses Motor Inn in Constant, Arkansas

Outside, the empty rose bushes chattered in the wind.

Chapter One

June

It was midnight in the town of Constant. Valery's phone rang, as it now did every midnight.

It can't be, she thought, her heart hammering. She'd had the number changed just yesterday. Nobody could know the new one yet. It wasn't possible. She prayed it wasn't.

She lifted the receiver. A wave of anxiety so strong it was almost nauseating swept through her. Changing the number had been useless. He had found her again. She heard the same muffled male voice she had been trying to escape. It was right on schedule, with its same nightmarish message.

"What ye sow, ye reap. The wages of sin is death," the man rasped. "You killed your husband. They know. They'll find you guilty. They'll take your son. They'll put you away. You'll be on death row, and then in a grave, and then in hell. You'll burn and burn in hell. And you know what else?"

Stunned, she said nothing. She sat as if frozen while the voice ranted its litany and finally began its inevitable descent into obscenity.

Damn! she thought, anger overriding fear. This was just what he wanted: to have her trapped, listening to his poison. She slammed the receiver down with all her force. But a few seconds later, the ringing started again.

Usually she unplugged the phone when the midnight harassment began. She set her jaw. Tonight she refused to give the caller even that much satisfaction. She didn't know how he had gotten her new number, and it almost didn't matter. He wasn't going to break her.

She set her jaw. He can sit and wait for me to pick up that receiver until Judgment Day.

The phrase was unfortunate. She didn't want to think about Judgment Day. It would occur in precisely two months. She would be on trial for murder.

None of this was possible, she thought sickly, none of this was happening. Yet it was true: Charles was dead, and she was accused of killing him. Worse, most of the town believed it.

Someone had tampered with the sleeping capsules Charles needed every night. Instead of Seconal, they contained parathionex, the pure and uncut base of a powerful insecticide.

He knew he'd been poisoned. He had tried to use the phone in the motel. The switchboard operator said he had moaned, "Valery killed me. My God, Valery killed me!"

Valery shook her head, remembering. Could Charles have believed that? Had he really said that? It couldn't be. But the switchboard operator swore he had said it. Valery hardly knew the woman; neither had Charles. Why would a near stranger lie about such a monstrous thing?

Others seemed eager to believe in Valery's guilt. Valery had been a pharmacist's assistant, the perfect person to empty a sleeping capsule and fill it with parathionex. Everyone Charles worked with had heard him complain that she had tampered with his medication in the past.

Like anyone in Constant, Valery could easily get parathionex. The Talmidge Corporation's main product was a rose dust containing the poison. Everyone knew that Valery's father, a chemistry professor, had kept quantities of it in the garage for experiments. Valery claimed she had thrown it all away, but the police didn't believe her. The chief of detectives found a jar half-filled with it buried in the backyard.

All the evidence was circumstantial. But all of it pointed directly at Valery. *Murderer,* it said.

The night air with its heavy scent of roses suddenly seemed to smother her. Spring had been late this year and passed too quickly into an oppressive summer. The filmy curtains stirred, fitful and ghostlike in the warm breeze.

The phone kept shrilling. Fiercely she tried to ignore it. But she got up and shut the window to lock out the perfume of the roses. The scent reminded her of funerals. Her hands were clammy. Someone had wanted Charles dead. Why? If she couldn't answer that question, she would end up in prison.

At last the ringing ceased. The silence echoed.

She sat alone in a small circle of light at her father's old rolltop desk and forced herself to study the papers before her. She shuffled through them for what seemed the thousandth time, looking for a clue to explain what had happened to her husband, what was happening to her.

Tall, slim, she was a woman of twenty-seven, with dark shoulder-length hair and hazel eyes. She had inherited this house and everything in it when her father had died a year ago. She and Charles and their son, Tony, had been living in Missouri then.

Valery had not wanted to return to the old house or the claustrophobic small town of Constant, but there had been little choice. Charles had quit his job again, this time as a pilot for a private aviation company. He wanted to go home. In Constant, he was still a hero. In Constant, nobody knew the truth about him yet. In Constant, they would take him in.

He had been right. The town welcomed him back with open arms. But now he was in a grave, and Valery was accused of killing him because he had left her.

Numbed as she was, she intended to fight with all her power. Tony was upstairs sleeping, and Valery would battle to the death to keep the child from hurt or from harm. Nobody could take Valery away and put her in prison; they would have to kill her to keep her away from Tony. She vowed it.

She ran taut fingers through her dark hair. She looked again at the names and dates on the papers before her, copies of Charles's flight logs as a pilot for the Talmidge Corporation, Constant's only major industry. She wasn't supposed to have the copies, but Sheridan Milhouse, the chief mechanic at Talmidge, had grudgingly given them to her this afternoon. She had badgered him until he'd complied. She didn't know whether she should have the copies, but she didn't care. She was desperate.

She had studied Charles's comings and goings in the company plane until they gave her a headache.

Dammit, Charles, she thought ferociously. She clenched her teeth and forced tears of weariness back. *What made somebody kill you? What?*

She had never understood her husband, she thought with frustration and regret. She hadn't understood him in life, and she understood him even less in death. She had been ridiculously young when she married him—a freshman in college, barely seventeen—and spectacularly naive.

He had been a senior, a star athlete, and the foremost golden boy of a campus full of them. He was also the town of Constant's one bona fide hero. When Paris Talmidge had her terrible automobile accident, it had been Charles who had braved the flames and carried her, unconscious, to safety seconds before the car exploded.

In reward, Paris and Amanda Talmidge promised him anything his heart desired. He said he wanted a pilot's license, and the Talmidge sisters granted his wish. He didn't even have to work that summer; all he did was fly. He was, after all, a hero. They even gave him a medal to prove it.

When Valery met Charles, she had hardly so much as dated before. She was one of the youngest freshmen on campus, and the daughter of the college's most difficult and rebellious professor, Arthur Donovan. She was swept away by Charles as if by a whirlwind. They were married six days after they met.

Charles rented a plane and they eloped to Reno. When Valery, happy, breathless and a bride of two entire hours, had called her father to tell him, he said curtly, "You've taken vows. I hope you have the character to keep them. You're not welcome in my house if you don't. You've made your bed. Now lie in it."

Professor Donovan was opinionated and stern, but he had watched Charles's progress through three years of college and he knew what Valery, young and in love, didn't suspect: she had married a man who was both unstable and dangerously weak.

Charles took umbrage at her father's remarks and refused to return to Constant. Charles's mother was so unhappy over the marriage that she disowned him. Charles said she was a terrible mother anyway.

During the early years of their marriage, Charles seemed merely immature, but when Tony was born, he grew worse—alarmingly so. Sometimes Valery felt she was all that stood between Charles and the darkness of mental chaos. She understood at last what her father meant about having the character to keep vows.

So she had stood by Charles. Until he left her—and died. Valery hadn't even been able to weep. The only good that had come out of the marriage was Tony, and Valery loved Tony with an intensity so great it hurt. Now the two of them were caught up in the horror of murder.

She shook her head and stared at the flight log again. The names and dates blurred together. *I'm not going to let them put me in prison,* she thought, biting her lip. *I'm not going to lose my child. I'm not. I'm not.*

She searched the logbook, looking for some answer, some hint of an answer, even the shadow of a hint. She had to save Tony. She had to save herself.

At precisely twelve-thirty the phone began to ring again. Repeatedly.

Go ahead, ring all night, damn you, she thought darkly. *You don't scare me.* She turned a page of the logbook, searching the entries with blind determination.

It was true. She wasn't scared.

She was terrified.

Valery was not being suitably docile about her fate. She was asking too many questions, poking her nose where it didn't belong, raising too many thorny issues with Judge Pike.

In a way, it was Judge Pike's fault. He hadn't thrown Valery in jail where she belonged and where she could have been appropriately supervised. Instead she was out, free as a bird, and disagreeably determined to stay free.

For this reason, it was necessary to prove her guilty beyond the proverbial shadow of a doubt, so guilty that no jury on God's green earth would ever let her go free again.

So thought Thelma Bellarion, Valery's mother-in-law. And there was, Mrs. Bellarion had been told, a certain man who could ensure that Valery was proven guilty. This man, she was assured, could be as relentless as the Angel of Death.

This man's services were specialized, his talent unique. He would not work for just anyone. Indeed, he did not wish to work for Mrs. Bellarion. But he would. Thelma Bellarion had made him an offer impossible to refuse.

Now he drove north through the June darkness, heading for Constant.

There, for the final time, he would do the kind of job he was sick of, the kind he had vowed never to do again.

He would do it for one reason only: to repair some of the damage inflicted by his last dirty job. He wanted to find that pathetic, fleshy woman called Penny Shaw and save her from her own destructive unhappiness. The unhappiness he had created so expertly.

Poor, hurt Penny Shaw had disappeared from the face of the earth as completely as if she had never existed.

Thelma Bellarion claimed to know where she was. The old lady would tell him for a price, but the price was not money. The price was revenge. He would acquire it for her in an obscure little Arkansas town named Constant.

Nikolas Constantine Grady was half-Irish, half-Greek, and despite the years he had been headquartered in Washington with the FBI, he was 100 percent Texan. He had returned to Dallas two years ago as a private investigator, an exclusive one, with a Texas-size price tag on his services. He was worth big money, and he knew it. He liked law, he liked justice, he liked truth, and he was good at serving them.

What he was sick unto death of, he thought, hands tightening on the wheel, was how law and justice and truth always got tangled up with women. It was like a curse.

It had started in Vietnam, when a Saigon bar girl nicknamed Sun had gone gage for the tall, big-shouldered Texan soldier with the curly black hair. All he'd done was smile at her. Sun's normally hard little face went soft and vulnerable as a child's, and she couldn't keep her eyes off him.

The next thing he knew, he was unofficially drafted by Intelligence, with orders to win Sun's confidence. Intelligence suspected Sun was an enemy agent. Intelligence, Nikolas found, was right. She told him one night as she lay in his arms. She wanted to recruit his assistance.

He hadn't felt much when she was arrested. Already Vietnam had taught him it was safest not to feel. He had saved a lot of lives by helping bust Sun, Intelligence said. Truth, law, justice and country had been served.

Intelligence kept him. They moved him on to Hanoi, disguised as a lieutenant and ordered to win the trust of the wealthy Madame Phan. Madame Phan was taken by his easy charm. She also proved to be a spy, and was also arrested. Nikolas was again commended and told he should feel proud, but he allowed himself to feel nothing. It was war, and he'd done his job.

His work for Intelligence led naturally enough to working for the FBI when he came home. But always, somehow, women got mixed up in it. If the Bureau needed someone to get next to a woman, the someone was Nikolas. His code name was Casanova, which he despised. Still, sometimes the work had to be done and he did it.

Then two years ago, during a cocaine bust, he'd gone face-to-face with an ex-football player turned drug runner. They'd tangled, and the gorilla threw a crab block on Nikolas, knocking his knees out of joint. And Nikolas had been permanently disqualified for active fieldwork; his knees made him too big a disability risk for the government.

Instead of taking a job as desk jockey with the Bureau, he went back to Dallas. He had little family left, but there was family money and family connections, and he started his own practice. He never lost his outward charm, but he had a lot of miles on him, and he'd become as cynical as it was possible for a man to be.

Then the Fields case had come along. The Fields case had made him feel mean, lean and hungry again. If Fields was running an investment scam, Nikolas knew it was one of the biggest in Dallas's history. Unfortunately, the quickest way to get information on Fields was through his efficient, refined, but painfully colorless secretary, Penny Shaw.

It had been easy to make Penny Shaw fall for him. She gave him access to any information he wanted. And when things started breaking and she learned how he had used her, she tried to kill herself. Not succeeding at that, she had vanished.

Just as bad, Fields somehow got wind of the impending bust and disappeared himself, along with all his records and about twenty-million dollars in cut gems. Fields liked to keep his assets in the portable and international currency of jewels. He left behind him a wasteland of ruined investors.

Losing as big a fish as Fields made Nikolas slightly crazy. He supposed he would give his immortal soul to catch the man but it was Penny Shaw who haunted him. She had been an innocent bystander. She weighed heavily on what was left of his conscience, and as much as he wanted to find Fields, he wanted to find her.

Other women Nikolas had misled had been on the wrong side of the law. Penny Shaw had done nothing criminal whatsoever. But he had destroyed her. She had lost her job, her reputation, her self-respect, even perhaps her will to live. Nikolas owed her, and if she was still alive, he would find her.

Now the rich and brittle Mrs. Bellarion said she knew where Penny was. Nikolas had checked the woman's story. It was true. She was distantly related to Penny Shaw. For clinchers, she had all of his correspondence with Penny, the notes, the florist cards, even the stupid greeting card that said, "Hi, Funny Face." He'd felt slightly sick when he'd seen that.

He was driving north through the dark because Mrs. Bellarion wanted him to do what he did best: get next to a woman. He was to prove beyond all reasonable doubt that Valery Donovan Essex was guilty of the murder of the old lady's son, Charles Essex.

Nikolas's lip curled in a slight sneer. It was, he reflected blackly, a fair trade: one woman for another. Valery Essex for Penny Shaw. More than fair, for Valery Essex sounded as guilty as hell, and Penny Shaw was blameless, a victim. His victim.

He felt bad about Penny, but his motives for finding her weren't all noble. His motives seldom were. He narrowed his black eyes and flexed his fingers against the steering wheel.

Valery Essex was small-time, at the sleazy center of a family scandal. But Penny Shaw, if he could find her, just might know something about where Fields had gone—and the whereabouts of those twenty-million-dollars worth of gems.

Twenty-million dollars—all bagged by Fields through his investment scam. Twenty-million dollars that had to be somewhere. It hadn't floated off into outer space.

Yes, it was essential to get to Penny Shaw. Compared to her, an ordinary and common household-variety murderer like Valery Essex was of no importance. None. She was just one more guilty woman to beguile, then trap. But she would be the last one. After her he was through with that particular dirty trick for good.

He drove on through the darkness.

The mockingbird's song rippled across the morning's summer air. Valery dropped Tony off for his ten-o'clock session with his math tutor, then went to her lawyer.

Keep fighting, she told herself as she walked into Osgood Perry's office. A quarter of the lawyers in Constant were related to the Perry family, one way or another. It was her misfortune that Osgood happened to be the dimmest star in that constellation of otherwise bright legal minds.

"What do you want, Valery?" Osgood Perry asked. He looked crabby, because she had just wakened him from a nap. He was a skeletal little man with a bald freckled scalp and bony freckled hands. He peered at her irritably through his trifocals.

He'd been about to make a particularly tricky trout fly knot just before he dozed off. He resumed tying after his secretary disturbed him with the irrelevant news that Valery Essex wanted to see him again.

His walls were hung with the stuffed corpses of fish. Fishing was his passion. He had only a year until he officially retired, and he wanted only to doze and tie flies until it happened.

Valery, who had known Osgood Perry from the time she was a child, reached over and gently but firmly took the fishing fly from his hands.

"I beg your pardon!" Osgood said, staring at his captured trout fly with irate resentment.

"I'll give it back," she promised, sitting down uninvited,

"but right now I want your full attention." She used the cool, fearless stare she had learned from her father. Inwardly, she felt neither cool nor fearless.

Osgood Perry crossed his arms irritably. "And what," he demanded sternly, "do you want to talk about *this* time?"

Valery forced herself to remain calm. "About being on trial for murder," she said between her teeth.

"Oh," replied Osgood pettishly, "that."

Valery nodded. *Yes,* she thought ironically, *that little matter murder.*

"Valery, I'll contact you if any developments occur. The case against you is disturbing, but not ironclad. Nobody has proved you bought that poison. But I wish you'd honestly tell me how the jar came to be buried in your backyard. I'm your lawyer, you know."

Valery sighed harshly. Osgood was her lawyer, but not by choice. She had hardly any money. She couldn't benefit from Charles's will because she was under suspicion of his murder, and she'd lost her job at the pharmacy as soon as she'd been charged. She and Tony were living on her meager inheritance from her father.

Since she couldn't afford a lawyer, the court had appointed Osgood to defend her. Since court-appointed lawyers worked on a rotation system and she'd had the bad luck to draw him, there was absolutely nothing she could do about it. She had tried to petition the court for a different lawyer. Judge Pike, although kindly, had said rules were rules; if he made an exception for her, there'd be no end to people asking him for exceptions. For now, Osgood was all she had.

"I don't *know* how the poison got buried in my backyard," she told him for the dozenth time. "If I was going to put poison in Charles's sleeping capsules, do you think I'd bury the rest in my own backyard? With the lid sticking out of the ground? Good Lord, Osgood, I'd have flushed it down the drain, thrown it in the river—anything but bury it in my backyard."

"Well," Osgood said, folding his knobby fingers together and giving her a superior stare, "I hope a jury believes that. Because if you didn't bury that jar, who did?"

"That's what you should be finding out," she retorted in exasperation. "It's obvious whoever put it there must have killed Charles and tried to incriminate me. I've been racking my brain for six weeks trying to figure out who. Or why. I've got no idea."

"Well, you'd better come up with something," Osgood said prissily. "Right now, you're the only one with a motive. If somebody else did it, I suggest you figure out who. It's not my job. I'm a lawyer, not a detective."

Valery bit back the impulse to speak sharply; it would do no good whatsoever with Osgood. Nothing did any good with Osgood.

She placed a folder on his desk. "I went to a lot of trouble to get these. Osgood. I nagged Sheridan Milhouse for five weeks. They're copies of the records of the flights that Charles took in the company plane. I can't find anything unusual, but then, I don't know what would *be* unusual. All I know is he was doing more flying than usual toward the end. For the last month he was making flights to Newark—I don't know why. On his last flight there he was carrying all the royalty: the Talmidge sisters and their lawyer, their niece Dahlia Lee, and John Upchurch."

Osgood pursed his wrinkled lips. "Do not," he said, "try to implicate the Talmidges. They gave Charles a job when he needed one. Both sisters have expressed concern about you. Those women are saints. As for their lawyer, Terry

Perry's reputation is spotless, and he's my first cousin twice removed. Dahlia Lee is an important young woman and she's been through hell, losing her husband—"

"Osgood," Valery said between clenched teeth, "I'm not accusing the Talmidges of anything. Or Terry Perry. Or Dahlia Lee. Or John Upchurch. I just said everyone who's anyone was on that last flight. Look at this log. It may indicate something I don't understand. Especially this Newark business. Charles didn't used to fly that far north—at least not that I knew. He was closemouthed about it. What were they all doing in Newark?"

"Dahlia Lee was having treatments. To help her recover from the accident," Osgood said coldly. "Also, Paris and Amanda were considering investments in Newark. And the police know it all." He cast a disgusted glance at the duplicated flight log. "The police already have copies of these records," he added contemptuously. "John Upchurch has talked to them about everything."

John Upchurch was the executive vice president of the Talmidge Company and the right-hand man of the Talmidge sisters. Paris Talmidge was almost an invalid nowadays. Although Paris was still the brains of the family corporation, it was John Upchurch who kept affairs in order.

"Each of these flights has a logical explanation," Osgood stated. "I just told you."

"But—"

Osgood cut her off. "No," he said tartly. "You're grasping at straws. Relax, Valery. Dress nicely, act like a lady, avoid scandal, and everything should go fine. If it doesn't, you can appeal the decision. You shouldn't have these records. It doesn't look good. I think it's illegal. You'll get yourself and Sheridan Milhouse in trouble."

Valery clenched her fist on the desktop. Didn't Osgood

The Roses of Constant

even *know* if it was illegal for her to have the records? He was supposed to be a lawyer, for God's sake.

"Word is out all over this town that Charles's mother wants my son," Valery said, her passion rising. "I hear she's assembling lawyers in Vicksburg to get custody of Tony once this trial is over. And she's never even *seen* Tony—she just wants to punish me because I married Charles. I get strange phone calls in the night, even though I changed my number. The police and the phone company won't help because the situation isn't 'threatening.' But I feel threatened. Osgood, I can't fight everybody at once. Not by myself."

Osgood sighed. The phone calls didn't interest him, but Charles's mother, Thelma Deems Essex Oxbridge Bellarion, did. She could be a formidable enemy, and he didn't want to think about her, so he refused to do so.

"We will cross that bridge when we come to it," he said. "Relax, Valery. Just be quiet and behave yourself. Now give me my trout fly."

Not trying to disguise her disgust, she slapped the fly before him on his desk. She looked at her hand. When she had clenched her fist, she had jabbed the hook deep into her palm. A drop of blood bloomed from her skin.

"Thanks, Osgood," she muttered. She arose, and turned, not trusting herself to say anything else. *I'm charged with murder and Thelma Bellarion wants my child,* she thought. *Every night I get crazy phone calls, and all you want to do is tie flies. The best legal advice I can get from you is "act like a lady." Thanks for everything, Osgood. Thanks a lot.*

She strode from his office. She would try again to get the judge to give her another lawyer. She knew she would be pushing his patience; he had raised eyebrows all over town by letting her out on her own recognizance. Well, she thought grimly, she was already accused of murder. She hardly needed to worry about being thought a pest.

She tried to ignore the anxiety that welled in her chest. It was her constant companion these days. She couldn't afford to surrender to panic. She had to hang on for Tony. She had to think straight.

Six weeks ago Charles had come home from a flight to Newark for the Talmidge Corporation. He had told her he wanted a divorce. He was going to start over. He had already told his co-workers that he was quitting and that he was leaving her, as well.

He was tired of their marriage, tired of Constant, tired of working for the Talmidge Corporation. He had always wanted his own flying service, he said. Now he was going to start it. He would go to a motel that very night. He had already told the higher-ups; he was not even giving notice, just quitting. She should tell Tony goodbye for him. He was sorry about Tony. The boy was a good kid, but he just had never been able to take to him.

Valery had simply stared at him. She had felt nothing, nothing whatsoever. She wondered, numbly, curiously, where he'd get the money to buy a plane.

Then, when he actually walked out of the house, she felt a great, cool, cleansing wave of relief. It was over. By his choice. She asked him before he left if he had found another woman, but he'd only looked at her "No," he'd finally said. "Never again." And then he'd left.

She'd felt dazed. And yet it was as if he'd been gone for years. She hadn't been able to leave him, because he was sick, and his endless failures weren't his fault but that of his sickness. He had never been able to cope with his own emotions. But now he had left her and she was free. He had freed her.

Five hours later he was dead.

The clue to who had killed Charles had to be contained somewhere in the flight log. If it wasn't, then Valery didn't know where to look—she had exhausted every other possibility. She would be cornered, caught, trapped.

Her worst fear rose again, clutching her heart like a cold spectral hand. Charles had traveled all the time, flown many places. He knew dozens of people she didn't, in dozens of places that were strange to her. If one of those people was the killer, she had almost no chance to discover who.

Unless, she thought desperately, *unless I get lucky.* No, she couldn't count on luck. She would have to be smart. Somewhere there was a clue. There had to be. She had to find it. She, alone.

Alone, she thought. She was alone and the odds against her were rising all the time. If she had to, she would fight those odds until they killed her. Nobody was going to separate her from Tony. Nobody.

She swallowed hard. Her father had always taught her that when trouble came, one simply kept the trouble to oneself and walked taller. Valery kept trying to live up to that dictum. She stiffened her spine and walked on alone. She clenched her fist to hide the fact that she was bleeding.

Chapter Two

Tony sat in the front room slumped in front of the television set, watching a rerun of *Star Trek*. Rather, he seemed to be watching. Valery could tell he was eaten up with anxiety, wondering what was going to become of them. She was sick with apprehension herself, but she could not let him know. Her hardest job was trying to appear calm and cheerful for his benefit.

She sat beside him, wearing her oldest cutoffs and a gray T-shirt. Concern for him made her giddy, almost slightly hysterical. Tony was only eight years old, but since Charles's death, he seemed to be going on eighty.

He had flunked every subject in school this past spring, and he seemed sad all the time. Valery worried incessantly about him.

Neither of them ever talked of the possibility of her going to prison. In fact, they barely mentioned Charles. Alive, he had been only a peripheral part of the household: the moody, silent man who was usually gone and wanted only to be left alone in his garage workshop when he wasn't.

Now Charles's absence haunted the house. Valery bit her lip in dread. Six weeks had passed since Charles had died, and she was no closer to knowing who killed him than she was that terrible night. Eight more weeks remained before the trial. She'd pinned all her hopes on finding something in the flight log, but it told her nothing. Nothing at all.

She had been going through its entries, as well as old bills, the mail of recent months, searching for some bit of information that offered a glimmer of hope.

Today she had a third and absolutely threatening card from the public library about a book Tony had checked out. It was the final notice, the postcard said, and the police would be notified if the book was not returned.

Again Valery felt giddy. She was accused of murder—and an overdue library book? The police would take her off for *two* crimes? Tony swore he'd never checked the book out, and *Best-Loved Poems of the English and American People*, didn't sound like anything he would be vaguely interested in, but the library wasn't buying that story. Turn over the book, growled the library, or face The Police.

She couldn't stand it any longer. She pushed all the papers to the floor with a reckless flourish, then she pounced on Tony and began tickling him. She wanted to touch him, hold him, be near him, feel emotion, even silly emotion, pouring through both of them.

"Mom!" he cried with affronted dignity, but soon he was tickling her back. For a few seconds everything was as it used to be. She felt alive and joyous, her child in her arms.

The moment was brief. It ended when an awkward rattle shook the lock of the front door. "Aargh," Tony groaned, straightening up, "Charmian." He rolled his dark eyes.

"Shh." Valery tried to retrieve the scattered papers. "She means well." She stuffed the library notice between the pages of the log, along with Charles's bank statements.

The front door gave one last rattle and swung open. Valery's Aunt Charmian, who had lived in Constant all her life, peered around the corner dramatically. She was Arthur Donovan's sister, a tall, gaunt, unmarried woman of considerable eccentricity.

Charmian's wide blue eyes always looked alarmed or accusing, and her hair was a wild wealth of silvery white curls.

She was famous for walking into places uninvited; she seemed to enjoy it. She was a supervisor at the telephone company, a position she held as if it were the most sacred of trusts.

During her brother's final illness, Charmian had duplicated his key so that she could look in on him. After his death, she'd kept the key, and now felt free to walk into the house any time day or night.

Valery would have objected, but she knew it would break Charmian's heart. She and Tony were the only relatives the older woman had left, and Charmian was ferociously possessive of them.

Tony had stiffened again, staring stonily at the television. Valery gave him a discreet motherly elbow in the side. "Say hello, Tony."

"Hello," said Tony.

Charmian had just come from work. She wore a brilliant blue dress and several strands of large red, purple and blue African beads. "I've come to warn you," she said ominously. "You have a new neighbor. A *man*."

She waited for the impact of this statement to register, sitting herself down in the old oak rocking chair and looking at her niece expectantly. Valery didn't respond, so undaunted, Charmian repeated the news. "Did you hear me? You have a new neighbor. A man. Watch out."

Valery stacked her papers neatly and set them on the coffee table. "I'm not afraid of a man, Charmian."

The house next door was a rental property. In a college town with its ever shifting population, she was used to an unending stream of new neighbors. Both houses sat on the edge of town, isolated, and Valery felt safest when the property next door was occupied.

"Maybe you *should* be afraid," Charmian said sagely.

"What does that mean?" Valery asked. Lately Charmian was a compendium of warnings, prophecies and sinister hunches. The charges against Valery had made the older woman more eccentric than ever, and Valery was worried.

"I mean watch your step. I heard some of the girls at the telephone office talking about him—this new neighbor. He's apparently very attractive. Don't get involved with him. You can't afford to. Not with your t-r-i-a-l coming up."

"I can spell," Tony said out of the side of his mouth, but kept watching the television screen.

"I don't intend to get involved with anybody," Valery objected truthfully. "And I doubt anybody wants to get involved with me. Relax, Charmian."

"You never know," Charmian muttered, fluffing her silver curls. "Upchurches own that house. And the Upchurches and the Talmidges are like *that*." She held up two bony fingers entwined. "The Talmidges and Thelma Bellarion used to be like that, too. How do you know that Thelma didn't send that man here expressly to ensnare and entrap you?"

Valery tried to keep from smiling. She was not completely successful. "I have enough trouble without conspiracy plots."

"I have suspected the Talmidges all along in Charles's d-e-a-t-h. I would put nothing past Paris or Amanda Talmidge if it came down to saving the family dynasty. Nothing. I'll bet that Charles found out they were smuggling d-r-u-g-s or something—concealed in the body of the plane. Have you ever seen *Miami Vice*? It shows you precisely how these things are done. Paris, in her everlasting gadding about, probably got involved with a Colombian d-r-u-g ring."

And Charles was murdered by space aliens who are now

hiding out in Atlantis with Elvis, Valery thought ruefully.

Still, Charmian had hit on two unpleasant possibilities that nagged Valery. Was someone from the Talmidge Corporation mixed up in this? Could Charles have somehow gotten involved with drugs or some other kind of smuggling?

"Well?" Charmian demanded. "Well? *Well?*"

"Paris Talmidge is in a wheelchair half the time," Valery said dryly. "It's hard to imagine her running drugs from Colombia and dodging the Miami vice squad."

"Valery," Charmian asserted, her eyes narrowing, "wake up. Someone in this town is a-f-t-e-r you."

"I don't want to talk about it now," Valery said shortly. She didn't, not in front of Tony. And she wasn't even sure that whoever killed Charles was in Constant. She would be relieved if she could know that much.

"I can spell," Tony repeated resentfully. He thrust out his lower lip, but it was trembling. The phone rang, and he jumped up to get it, rather than listen to any more of Charmian's dire scenarios.

"Tony, don't!" Valery cried, rising, but he was already halfway to the little alcove between the living room and dining room. She had told him not to answer the phone. Her sinister caller usually phoned only at midnight, but such a man was unpredictable. She wanted to make sure Tony was protected against him.

Charmian's thin hand shot out and grasped Valery's arm. "Valery," she said hoarsely, "listen to me. You're being framed. Charles was involved in something terrible. You've got to find out what. Your life depends on it. So does Tony's."

Valery set her teeth in frustration. She knew that better than Charmian did. Tony stood, listening to the phone, his face oddly blank.

"Charmian, stop!" She pulled her arm free. "I won't discuss this in front of Tony. He's only a child. He can't cope—"

"How will he cope if they take you away?" Charmian demanded, once more seizing Valery's arm. "It's no secret. Thelma Bellarion wants him. How are you going to fight all this?"

Valery shook her head, desperately attempting to clear it. She knew Tony belonged with her. Charmian was too flighty to take care of him, and Thelma Bellarion didn't even know the boy, but Valery was doing all she could, and—

Tony crashed the receiver down blurting out a shocking word. He stood glaring down at the phone as if it were a snake he needed to kill.

"Tony!" Valery said, shaking off Charmian and rushing to him. She put her hand on his shoulder and felt the tension radiating from him. "What—?"

"Some nut," he said with disgust, his voice trembling. "Some sick puke." He refused to look up at her.

So now the caller was terrorizing her child, Valery thought angrily. It had descended to that. "Listen to me," she said, tipping his face up to hers. "It *was* a sick person. You can't pay any attention. You can't mind—"

"Valery!" Charmian descended on the two of them. "You're still getting those calls? Why didn't you tell me? I work at the phone company. What is wrong with you?"

Tony tried to pull away as Charmian thrust her face into Valery's. *I'm going to go crazy,* Valery thought fatefully. *Will somebody please help me? If there's a God in heaven, will somebody please come help?*

A knock sounded at the front door. All three of them froze, looking apprehensively at the entranceway. Tony went pale under his tan.

It's the police, Valery thought wildly. *Come to take me away for murder and an overdue library book.*

The knock sounded again. She pulled herself together with difficulty. Somebody had to be in control, and the somebody was her. She went to the door and opened it.

A man stood there, a tall man with curly black hair and a deep tan. He wore a blazing white polo shirt and white tennis shorts. His shoulders were broad and his sinewy arms were crossed on his chest. His eyes were incredibly dark. He was handsome enough to jolt her through.

She stared up at him in consternation and surprise. What an attractive man, she thought in confusion. She couldn't get over the blackness of his hair and eyes, the whiteness of his clothing. If she had a guardian angel, she thought irrelevantly, he would look a great deal like this.

"Yes?" she said.

"You live here?" the man asked. "You own that white Mercury Lynx in the driveway?"

"Yes," Valery replied hesitantly, not comprehending who he was or why he was there.

"I just moved in next door." He nodded his dark head toward the east. "I'm afraid somebody's vandalized your car. Slashed two of the tires."

Valery's guardian-angel fantasy vanished as reality crashed down again. "Oh, no," she moaned. She ran to the porch railing and stared into the driveway. The Lynx sat with a decided list on the driver's side, as if it were sinking into the earth.

"Oh, no," she breathed again. What was happening now? she thought tensely. She half ran down the front stairs and to the other side of the Lynx. She stared helplessly at the slashed tires. The twilight seemed to close in around her.

The stranger was beside her. His presence rattled her even more.

He smiled with wry sympathy. He had a strong jaw, deep

dimples in both cheeks, and a cleft in his chin. Although his smile was boyish, there was something almost dangerously masculine about him.

"I'm sorry," he said. "This is a crummy way to meet you—bringing bad news. The least I can do is help."

Charmian and Tony had followed her outside. "What? What? What?" Charmian was demanding. Tony looked stricken. He suddenly seemed very small to Valery, a shriveled old man, no longer a child. She put her arm around his shoulders and pulled him to her tightly.

"Somebody slashed the tires," the man explained. He stared at Valery, at the way she held Tony. She felt her skin warming and tingling under his scrutiny.

"Slashed the tires?" Charmian screeched. "I am appalled!"

Things couldn't have come to this, Valery thought in despair. But the tilted car proved her wrong. The man kept his black gaze on her, his face sympathetic.

"Why can't everybody just leave us alone?" Tony asked bitterly. Tears welled in his eyes and he put his fist to his eye and ground savagely, in anger and humiliation.

Valery felt sick with pity for him. She hugged him more tightly.

"Tony, Tony, Tony," Charmian admonished. "You must be a little man for your mother. You must be her rock in the time of her adversity. You must—"

Valery gritted her teeth. She gave silent thanks when the dark stranger interrupted Charmian before she could embarrass Tony more.

"Hey," he observed, cutting Charmian off nimbly, "the big guy here got something in his eye, that's all. Somebody should take him inside and get it out. He could scratch his retina."

He gave Charmian a significant glance. The authority in his voice seemed to make the older woman realize how upset the boy was.

"Of course," Charmian said. "Of course. Come along, Tony. Stop rubbing your eye. Stop this instant."

Tony managed to walk back to the house with a semblance of dignity, Charmian fussing behind him.

"Thank you," she said to the man, grateful to him for saving Tony's ravaged pride.

She stood, her hands on her hips in stoic helplessness, staring at her car. She wasn't sure she had enough money for a new set of tires. "I guess it's good I like to walk," she said philosophically. The stranger was still studying her with a thoroughness that made her feel vulnerable, almost naked.

"You won't walk," he said with the same air of authority. "We'll put on your spare. Then we'll put on my spare. I've got the same kind of car." He nodded toward the driveway next door. His garage door was open.

Valery saw that his car, too, was a Lynx, twin to her own, except it was black.

"Really," she said, unsettled, "you don't have to bother—"

"No bother," he said with a finality that cut off protest. "Who knows? Maybe it's fate. I'm your new neighbor. Just moved in. The name is Nikolas Grady." He offered his hand. It was tanned and strong.

She took it and would have smiled if he hadn't made her so peculiarly nervous. He held her hand a moment longer than necessary, and his eyes studied hers.

"I'm Valery Essex," she said, her hand still in his.

His dimples appeared again. "And I'm lucky—" he smiled "—to be living next door to Valery Essex." His thumb grazed her knuckles provocatively, exploring their peaks and valleys.

36

He gazed at her a moment longer, with such dark intensity that she thought with alarm: *a woman could get lost in those eyes.* Then he released her hand, as if he had suddenly become aware of what he was doing. "Have your car keys?" he asked, clearing his throat in apparent embarrassment. "I'll get out your tire—and jack."

He gave her a slightly chagrined half smile. For a moment she felt a thrill of pure awareness, aliveness.

She reached under the bumper where she kept a spare key in a magnetized case. She handed him the case and forced her face to be blank and rigid. Why, she asked herself, would this tall man who looked like an urbane Greek god be interested in the likes of her? She glanced at Nikolas discreetly and felt oddly jarred that he was smiling at her again.

It was as if he were saying, "We're both adults. We're attracted to each other and we know it."

No, she told herself, he couldn't have looked at her that way. It had been a trick of the failing light.

"You look so in control of yourself." A note of teasing played in his deep drawl. "What are you? A professor at the college?"

"No," Valery said shyly, not feeling in control of herself at all. "I'm . . . nobody."

"Don't underestimate yourself," he said with a smile that made her look away so she wouldn't blush. "Me, I'm back to being a student. Did twenty years on the L.A. police force. Thought I'd come back to the South and get an education degree. Guidance and counseling. Help kids."

His calm announcement that he had been a police officer startled Valery. It made her uneasy. He didn't look like the type to teach, she thought. He had too much of the aura of a man of action. And, she thought wryly, teenage girls would fall out of their seats if he walked into a classroom.

But she said nothing. She felt suddenly tongue-tied.

Nikolas opened the trunk and took out the jack and the spare. Expertly he raised the car and removed the cut tire. He got his own spare from his trunk and started to mount it on the back wheel.

"Nice-looking boy you've got," he said casually. "You're married, I suppose."

"A widow," she said tightly.

"Sorry," he returned gently, but he didn't look sorry. Again he gave her *that* look.

Damn! thought Valery. She didn't have the strength to deal with this. The last thing she needed was to feel attracted to a man, any man.

"I saw somebody cut across your yard earlier," he said, adjusting a hubcap. "You should call the police."

"No!" Valery almost cried, then bit her lip. She had seen enough of the police. Her fear of them was deep and it was real.

The stranger looked at her, his dark curly head cocked. "You've had trouble before?" he asked.

She reminded herself again that he had been a policeman, one of the enemy. "Yes," she said, her voice slightly choked. "We've had some trouble." *And I get this year's award for understatement,* she thought.

He shrugged. "If I can help, remember I'm next door. My motto is still To Serve and Protect."

"Thanks." She watched the play of his muscles as he moved the jack to the front of the car. He seemed admirably suited to serve and protect—but not the likes of her.

"I'm alone myself," he said, expertly twisting the wrench. "I'm glad to meet you, even if the circumstances—" he wrenched a lug nut into place "—could be happier. I hope your insurance covers this."

Valery crossed her arms in an age-old gesture of self-protection. The man threatened her usual self-possession. "We'll see."

Nikolas shrugged. "You're sure you don't want to call the authorities?"

"I'm certain," she said sharply.

He frowned slightly, dark brows drawing together. "I should have paid more attention to that guy I saw crossing your yard. I hope this hasn't upset your boy too much. He seemed disturbed. The woman, too. Your mother?"

"My aunt," she said. "Tony, my son, has been taking things hard lately. I'll get everybody calmed down. It'll be fine."

He gave her a sideways smile as he finished changing the tire. It made his dimples deepen, and she thought once more how disarming they made him look. He must be nearly forty, but there was something perennially youthful in the way he carried himself, and his body looked strong and fit.

"Is that your job?" he teased gently. "Taking care of everybody?"

The man was flirting with her. Desperately she retreated behind a facade of coolness. As heady as his interest felt, she knew he had been in Constant only a day. By tomorrow he'd know all about her and wonder if he really lived next door to a murderer.

"They keep me busy," she said tonelessly.

He put the jack back inside the trunk and returned her car keys. His fingers grazed hers, their touch almost imperceptibly light, yet hot. When she flinched at the slight contact, he raised one brow. "No time for people besides family?"

"Not really." He was making her heart dance strangely

again, and she resented him for it.

"I'll pick up another tire for you tomorrow," he said.

"No—please don't bother," she said, fighting a rising panic. "I can do it myself. You've already been too kind."

"Maybe if I keep it up," he said, his dimples deepening, "you'll finally smile. I'd like to see that. And I insist. A woman shouldn't lug tires around. They're dirty and heavy."

"No," Valery protested, unused to chivalry. "Really—"

"Yes," he said, hoisting up the vandalized tires. "Really." He carried them with ease to his own car and put them in the back. When he returned, she noticed that he had badly smudged the pristine white shirt.

"Oh," she said, "your shirt. I'm sorry!"

"It's okay." He smiled. "You have a washer and dryer?" She nodded.

"Good, I don't. You could wash this for me."

She was nonplussed, but could think of no polite way to refuse. Even if she could, it was too late. With one fluid movement he drew the shirt off and handed it to her.

The evening was nearly dark now, but by the light of the street lamp, Valery could see the power of his chest and shoulders. She had felt alone for so long that this man's size and muscularity seemed almost menacing. Reflected light gleamed from his shoulders. His chest was shadowed by a thick cloud of dark hair. It narrowed into a line that ran down his flat stomach and disappeared beneath the waistband of the white shorts.

She looked away as she took the shirt, still warm from his body. She felt suddenly only half-clad in her skimpy shorts and thin T-shirt.

He stared down at her for the space of a heartbeat. "Look," he said, "I know what it's like to be alone. I'm a widower myself. If you should need me . . . well, like I said, I'm right next door—to serve and protect."

He gave her a long look, then walked away. She gazed down at the grass. The warmth of the shirt in her hands disturbed her somehow, and she could smell the subtle scent of his cologne on it.

She felt he had just issued her a frankly sexual invitation. Or had he? She was unsure of what exactly had happened, except that her heart was beating too hard.

Desire, she thought with bewilderment. For the first time in years, she felt the awakening of desire. Perturbed and guilty, she turned back to her house. Tony was upset. She would take refuge in comforting him.

Nikolas Grady stood in his darkened living room by the window. Through the fluttering curtains, he watched her retreat.

She was prettier than her photographs. She was a stunner, in fact. But she tried to be unreadable, as if for years she'd made that lovely face into a mask.

He rubbed his bare shoulder meditatively. He was slightly stiff from driving that cramped Lynx all the way from Dallas, but he'd leased it because it was what she drove, and he wanted the connection.

The woman was more self-contained than he'd expected. He knew much about her, but he was unaccountably disturbed by how alone she seemed, except for the child. She was strong, but not in a hard way. That surprised him, too—the way she seemed both vulnerable and unbreakable at the same time.

She, in turn, was in darkness about him, a darkness he had spun and would continue to spin. Everything he'd told her was false. He had no intention of either serving or protecting her. He was in Constant to help convict her. That would make Mrs. Bellarion happy enough to tell him where poor, dumpy Penny Shaw had gone, and maybe, just maybe, he could clean up one part of the bloody mess that was the Fields case.

No, Valery Essex knew nothing about him. She did not even suspect, for instance, that it was he who had slashed her tires.

He hadn't particularly liked doing it. He was, however, used to doing things he didn't like for the sake of truth and justice and law.

It was his job, dammit, he reminded himself. Charles Essex was dead and all evidence pointed to his widow's guilt. He had no choice. He had to find Penny Shaw, whose life might be at stake. And who just might know where that bastard Fields had gone off to, with his twenty million in jewels.

Still, he felt uneasy, profoundly discontent. Something else troubled him. From the moment he saw Valery Essex, he had wanted her. It had never happened to him before, a genuine surge of desire for his quarry.

It was that simple, that primitive. He wanted her. He wanted to know the feel of her bare skin beneath his hands. He wanted to see that face looking up at him from a pillow, framed by the spilling fan of her dark hair. He wanted to strip her restraints away, then explore the emotions beneath, slowly and completely.

Too bad. He ground his teeth. He wasn't here for pleasure. He was here to deceive and entrap.

When darkness fell completely, he would go out and slash her tires a second time.

Then he'd have her. It would be almost a sure thing from there.

Chapter Three

Valery sipped her morning coffee, trying to keep frown glancing out the window at the house so recently rented by Nikolas Grady.

She struggled hard not to dwell on the slashed tires. She had told Tony that there was no proof the incident was even directed at them personally. It could have been a random act of vandalism, meaning nothing. It could have been; she wished she believed that.

The evening before, a tight-lipped Charmian had kept silent for once, at least until Tony was in bed. But when Tony was asleep, she confronted Valery. "You aren't taking this seriously, miss. I told you to be careful of that man. How do you know you can trust him?"

"Never mind the man," Valery had replied impatiently. "How did somebody get my phone number when I'd just changed it to an unlisted one? Did you give it to anyone?"

Charmian looked offended. "*You've* given it to almost everyone," she accused. "Your fool lawyer, Tony's tutor, Judge Pike. To say nothing of the police."

"I had to give it to those people."

Charmian shook her silver curls. "I tell you, Valery, someone is after you. Trust *no one*. Especially strangers."

Charmian had left at last, grumbling ominously. Valery had unplugged the phone, then again pored over Charles's papers. She stayed up past midnight, studying them until her eyes burned. Desperate, she still believed her last chance lay hidden in Charles's flight log. But it told her nothing.

Now the morning was already warm, the scent of roses heavier than usual. Valery shook her head to clear it. She wished she could forget Nikolas Grady, too.

His white shirt lay in the laundry room, and she avoided it as if it were radioactive. When she touched it, fine tremors coursed through her. She remembered his naked torso in the dim light, and the warmth of his body still clinging to the shirt.

She had no business thinking of any man. She was fighting for her survival and Tony's. If she could only prevail, they would be free to go, to escape Constant and its memories.

"Hi, Mom." She turned and saw Tony, his face still crumpled by sleep, his straight brown hair unruly. He wore a mischievous smile she was glad to see. "Charmian didn't stay all night? She actually went home?"

"Let's not be awful about her," Valery said guiltily. "She *is* fond of us—she just shows it in strange ways."

"*Real* strange," Tony said wryly. He yawned, then drifted to the dining-room window and stared with frank interest at Nikolas Grady's house.

"Tony, don't spy."

"I'm not," he said, stifling another yawn. "I'm just looking. That guy seemed nice. He's big. What is he? A basketball coach or something?"

She took Tony firmly by the shoulders and steered him toward the kitchen. "He's going to be a teacher. He used to be a policeman in Los Angeles. Sit down. I'll get your cereal."

"A policeman." He stretched and scratched his tousled hair. "Hey, he could help you."

She looked quizzically at her son's sleepy face. "Help? How?"

Tony sat down. "I mean he knows how to find clues and

44

stuff. The cops here only know about giving traffic tickets and piddly junk like that. They really don't know anything about . . . you know."

He couldn't bring himself to say *murder*. Valery's face clouded. Out of the mouths of babes, she thought. The Constant police didn't actually have any experience investigating murder, but Nikolas Grady might.

"No." She shook her head. "He probably gave out traffic tickets himself."

But Tony stared dreamily out the kitchen window toward Grady's house again, as if the man really were a knight in shining armor who had appeared to save them.

A shuffling sound from the letter slot in the front door told her the mail had arrived. She went to gather it up. A bill, a bill, and another bill, she noted darkly. And a notice addressed to Charles from the MacGregor post office.

Puzzled, she opened it. It was another bill, announcing that the rent on Charles's post-office box was overdue.

His post-office box? she thought numbly. What post-office box?

Her heart seemed to stop beating. Her hands shook. She hadn't known Charles had a post-office box. And why would he have one in MacGregor, a town at the other end of the county?

This could be important, she thought, her hands shaking harder. Her heart came back to life and thudded painfully. Whatever was in that post-office box might tell her who killed Charles—and why.

She should tell her lawyer. No, Osgood would be no help. She would find out herself. But what, precisely, would she find? What could be in the box? And why had Charles kept it secret?

"What's wrong?" Tony asked. He watched her apprehensively as she returned to the kitchen.

"Nothing," she said, and thrust the notice into the pocket of her denim skirt. "Nothing at all."

Maybe, she thought with a surge of hope, she had a chance at last to clear herself, to save herself and Tony. She would take Tony to his tutor's, then head straight for MacGregor.

But when she and Tony went outside to get into the car, her heart sank, cold and hard and dead as a stone.

Her tires had been slashed again. All four of them. And this time, her windshield had been smashed, as well. A long crack ran down the driver's side, surrounded by a thick web of smaller cracks.

She stood, staring in helpless horror. *Somebody really is after us,* she thought sickly. *It's getting worse.* Instinctively she pulled Tony closer.

Almost immediately the helpful and sympathetic man from next door, Nikolas Grady, appeared and competently took charge. He insisted on driving them to the tutor's. Valery accepted his help numbly, too stunned to protest. Who could have vandalized her car with such savage thoroughness?

Thank God Nikolas was there, she thought with desperate gratitude. He really did seem meant to serve and protect. Maybe, just maybe, a little bit of her luck was changing at last.

Wasn't this just too damned cozy for words, Nikolas thought darkly, driving Valery and the kid across the sunlit town. He was keeping up a stream of comforting small talk, because the kid looked scared half to death, but behind Nikolas's easy manner his thoughts were grim. It would take some tricky maneuvering from here on out, but he was certain that Valery was as good as his.

The pain in Valery Essex's eyes bothered him, though. She was putting up a good front for the kid, but she couldn't keep the hurt and fear completely hidden. He had a sudden, deeply instinctive doubt that this woman was a killer.

But, he reminded himself, somebody killed Charles Essex. Somehow, half a jar of poison had turned up in Valery's backyard. He'd checked on Charles thoroughly. He had been a troubled man without anything resembling a close friend—or an enemy. There was no trace of anyone with motive to kill him. Except Valery.

Still, Nikolas felt a small wave of self-loathing. He was deceiving and manipulating Valery expertly, almost automatically. How in hell, he wondered, had things come down to his serving the law by conning women? But he kept right on smiling and charming and conning. And she was so desperate she seemed to be falling for every false word.

Tony got out of the car and Valery walked him to the door of his tutor, Willadene Davis. She told Nikolas she would wait for Tony and walk him home, but he insisted on taking her for coffee. She refused, but he wouldn't leave.

He opened the door on the passenger's side. "Get in," he said. "I'm not leaving without you. If you try to walk away, I'll follow you like a bloodhound. I might even bay."

Valery looked at him. His curly hair shone almost blue-black in the morning sunshine. Humor and seriousness were mixed in his face, but the concern in his eyes seemed deep and kindly, and most important, it seemed real.

Wordlessly, almost against her will, she got into the car. He smiled.

"You really should call the police this time," he said, putting the Lynx into gear.

"No," she insisted. She turned so she could look at him. She couldn't tell him why she feared the police so deeply; nobody believed her. "Listen," she murmured, "you've been very kind. But you don't want to take me for coffee. You don't want to be seen with me. There are things you don't know."

"Yeah?" he said with friendly skepticism. "Like what?"

"Like I'm accused of murdering my husband," she said bluntly. She waited for the shock to register on his face. It didn't.

He merely shrugged. "I heard that. From my charming landlady. Mrs. Hughy Upchurch. It doesn't bother me."

Valery looked at him, amazed. His reaction had genuinely astonished her. "It doesn't bother you? I might be a murderer and it doesn't bother you?"

He gave her a calm glance. "Did you do it?"

"No," she said. "But I'm accused."

"I've seen a lot of people accused," he returned. "Some weren't guilty. Mistakes get made."

"Yes," Valery said, nonplussed by his unflappability. "Well, this mistake happens to be a doozy, and it happens to be happening to me."

"Have you got a good lawyer?" He knew she didn't.

"My lawyer is more interested in fishing than felonies."

"Then you could use a friend, at least. Where's the major coffee-drinking place in this town?"

"The Rose Café," she said numbly. "Downtown. Why?"

"We'll go there. I'll walk in with you on my arm for all the world to see."

"Are you crazy?" She gave a small laugh of disbelief. "Everybody thinks I'm guilty. What makes you think I'm not?"

He gave her another concerned glance. "Twenty years as

a cop. Twelve of them in homicide. A man learns to trust his instincts. My instincts say, no way. Every time I see you with the boy or look into your eyes, I hear that voice in my head again. 'No way,' it says. 'No way.' "

My God, I should be struck dead by lightning, he thought, slightly sick to his stomach. But he gave her his best I'm-so-sincere-I'd-die-for-you look. "Could you use an old homicide cop on your side? If nothing else, knowing I'm around might keep the mad slasher away from your tires."

Valery could only stare at him, her mouth slightly open.

This was it, he thought grimly, this was the moment, when she either went for the bait or didn't.

"I—I don't know what to say," she murmured at last.

"Then just nod," he said. "And maybe give me a smile?"

She nodded without quite understanding why she did so. She tried to smile but couldn't. Tears stung her eyes, and hurriedly she wiped them away.

"I'm sorry," she said, her voice shaky. "I'm not used to people being kind. Thank you."

"Let's go get some coffee," he said gruffly. The knot in his stomach twisted a little more evilly. "You can tell me the details of the case they've got against you. Mrs. Upchurch was fairly comprehensive, but not convincing."

When they walked into the Rose Café, he took her arm protectively under his. Every head in the place turned to look at them, and Valery felt bold and embarrassed at the same time. Nikolas simply squeezed her arm and smiled a friendly smile at all of them. Even at Amanda Talmidge, who was having tea with her lawyer, Terry Perry, and John Upchurch, the Talmidge sisters' chief adviser and administrator.

Of the crowd, Amanda Talmidge alone smiled back. "Good morning, Valery," she said brightly. Amanda Talmidge was considered the town's most gracious lady. Her sister, Paris, who was the business brain of the pair, was blunter and cooler.

"Good morning, Miss Talmidge," Valery said self-conscious. "How is Dahlia Lee?"

"She's much, much better," Amanda said with the same determined brightness. "She's still grieving for the Count, of course. That's the worst part. She still has to rest from the accident. But she's more like her old self every day."

"Send her my best," Valery said, trying to smile. Amanda nodded, clearly dismissing her. John Upchurch and Terry Perry stared at Valery and at Nikolas, as well. But Nikolas kept his arm linked with hers as if he were guarding her from all harm. He led her to a booth.

"Who," he whispered, "in the name of all that's unholy, is Dahlia Lee? And who's that woman? Who was the late lamented Count? Dracula?"

"That," Valery said with a discreet nod toward Amanda, "is Amanda Talmidge. She and her sister are major stockholders in the Talmidge Corporation. Dahlia Lee is their niece and *the* major stockholder. She was married to a count, but he was killed in a car accident a couple of months ago in Colorado. Dahlia Lee came home to recuperate."

"How did she ever recuperate from being named Dahlia Lee?"

His sheer irreverence made her laugh in spite of herself.

"There," he said, cocking a brow in satisfaction. "I finally got it."

"Got what?" she asked, feeling suddenly self-conscious again.

"A smile. It was worth waiting for."

You, Valery thought in wonder, *are too good to be true.*

God really should strike me dead, Nikolas thought. *I'm probably going to die a really horrible death as punishment for all this.*

"This whole case against you sounds trumped up," Nikolas said as they drove back toward the tutor's house. "Do you have any idea how that jar of poison got in your backyard?"

"None," said Valery.

"Or why your husband would say that you'd killed him to this—what's her name?—switchboard operator at the motel?"

"I don't know why he'd say it. I can't believe he'd say it. Her name's Milhouse. Melissa Milhouse."

"Could Melissa Milhouse be lying?" he asked. "Is she related to the Milhouse that gave you the copy of the flight log?" She shouldn't have gotten the flight log that way, he noted. It could count as another point against her.

"Melissa has no reason to make anything up," Valery said. "None. She and Sheridan are cousins, I think. Almost everybody in town is related one way or another. My father used to say if the town got any more inbred, people would start being born with two heads."

Nikolas nodded, feeling bleak. The town was a confusing morass of Talmidges, Perrys, Upchurches, and now Milhouses. The number of Thelma Bellarion's marriages compounded things even further. It was enough to make a man's head ache.

"What about his sleeping pills?" Nikolas asked, his brow wrinkling. "You had access to them. Did anybody else? Could anybody else?"

Valery took a deep breath. This man was actually listening to her. It was a heady sensation and a comforting one.

"Well, he took the pills with him whenever he'd be gone overnight. He'd been gone the night before. A lot of people were on that plane. They went to Newark. Theoretically any one of them could have had access to the pills, I suppose."

"Who all?" he asked, even though he knew

"The whole power structure of the Talmidge Corporation." Valery listed them by name. "Half the people on that plane were in the café just now."

"Which ones?" he asked. He didn't yet have faces attached to the names.

"John Upchurch," she replied. "The executive vice president. He was that tall, good-looking man with the beautiful white hair. And of course, Amanda herself. And Terry Perry, the Talmidge Corporation lawyer—the redheaded man with the pipe."

"Could any of those people have wanted your husband dead?"

"None," she said emphatically. "None at all. Paris and Amanda adored Charles. He had saved Paris's life once, years ago. They loved him."

"He said he was leaving and starting his own charter company? But you don't know where he was going to get the money?"

"I have no idea. And he never mentioned the charter service to anybody but me. I don't know if the jury will believe he said it. He had no money—or very little. And none ever turned up."

She thought again of Charles's mysterious post-office box. She stirred nervously. She needed to get to MacGregor; perhaps some clue about the money lay hidden there. It was imperative she find out. But she had no car.

"Look," he said gently, "I don't want to bring up anything painful, but could he have been seeing another woman? One with money?"

Valery turned and stared out the window. They were passing Talmidge Park, where the roses bloomed lavishly this time of year. She didn't want to tell Nikolas that Charles had been incapable of having sex for the past two years of their marriage.

"He told me there was nobody else—he sounded almost bitter about it," she answered. "He said 'Never again.' " She shrugged helplessly. "But that's apparently not what he told other people."

"What other people?" he prodded, concern in his voice. "And what did he tell them?"

"Sheridan Milhouse. Tammi Smith—she's a secretary at the corporation. Cameron Carter—he and Charles had a few beers together from time to time. And Cameron Carter is a police officer. They all say he told them he'd met a woman in Newark."

"No name? No details?"

She shook her head. "Just a woman. He'd been taking a lot of trips to Newark."

"So, he could have met this woman?"

"He could have. He never stayed at the same hotel as the others. He stayed close to the airport. Nobody knows what he did that last night."

Nikolas frowned again. "He told a police officer he had another woman?"

"Yes." She sighed harshly, remembering Cameron Carter. She didn't know why Charles would say such a thing if it wasn't true, except to boost his suffering ego. He had admitted to her once that he had tried to be unfaithful but couldn't. He had wept bitterly when he told her.

"What's this guy's name again?" he asked, frowning harder.

"Cameron Carter. He and Charles went to college together for a year. Cameron's a detective now." And he had questioned her, roughly and endlessly. She remembered him with fear and anger. Cameron Carter had been brutal.

The list of witnesses contradicting Valery was impressive, Nikolas thought grimly. "None of these people have any reason to lie, I suppose," he said.

"No conceivable reason." Valery shook her head. She had agonized long hours over this same question. There was no reason for anyone to lie. About anything.

"Everything against you is circumstantial and hearsay," he pointed. "A good lawyer would pound away on that."

"I don't have a good lawyer," she stated simply.

"Well," he said with a self-deprecating smile, "at least you've got yourself a detective—me. I hope that's better than nothing. But you don't have any clue about any of this? Nothing at all?"

She was silent a moment. She felt guilty and vulnerable. She knew little about this man. She was unsure what to do or say. Yet she wanted to trust him. Suddenly it seemed like the most desirable thing in the world to trust someone, to believe there was someone she could depend on.

"I have one clue," she said slowly, and drew the post office notice out of her skirt pocket. "Maybe. I don't know what it might mean."

He looked at her, careful to keep his face friendly, but otherwise blank. He withdrew the notice from the envelope and read it quickly.

Pay dirt, he thought with triumph. He wasn't even sure what he was hoping to find in the post-office box. He realized he half wished it would be something to clear her.

That, he told himself firmly, was stupid. If Valery Essex was innocent, he was in trouble. Forget innocence.

"I think we'd better pick up Tony and get over to MacGregor," he said. He kept his voice calm, reassuring.

She nodded, looking frightened now that she had shared the information with him.

He kept his face friendly, but otherwise blank. She had trusted him. She was his now. Her neck was in the noose.

Chapter Four

Willadene Davis was a thin, no-nonsense woman who looked every inch the mathematics teacher she was during the school year.

Valery was pleasantly surprised when the tutor met her at the door and offered to keep Tony for the afternoon.

Willadene explained that her twin nephews from Little Rock were visiting this week. Might Tony stay and play? The swimming pool was repaired, and the three children could swim all afternoon.

Valery swallowed hard, taken aback. Tony stood in the hallway behind Willadene, mute appeal on his face. One of the twins stood expectantly beside him. They looked like such normal little boys, Valery thought with a wrench of the heart. More than anything she wanted Tony's life to be normal again.

Touched, Valery tried to give her consent and could not. The words choked in her throat. She nodded numbly. "Thank you," she managed to say at last.

Tony gave a small whoop of joy and disappeared with the redheaded twin.

"I'm a widow myself," Willadene said matter-of-factly "I know what it's like, being alone. And for the record, Valery, not everyone in this town thinks you're guilty. I don't. Take an afternoon for yourself. I'll drop Tony by your house at about six-thirty."

Valery returned to the car, filled with a fluttering warmth. Willadene had gone out of her way to be kind. And

Nikolas Grady had appeared from nowhere, determined to serve and protect. Perhaps her luck, and Tony's, really was changing a little.

"What's the matter?" Nikolas asked as he swung the door open for her. "You look pale. Where's Tony?"

Valery got into the car. "She . . . she invited Tony to stay and play with her nephews," she said, her voice trembling with emotion. She turned and stared out the window so that he couldn't see the tears rising. She struggled to regain her self-control.

My God, Nikolas thought with a sinking feeling, *somebody asks her kid to spend the afternoon and she nearly dies of gratitude. What have people done to this woman?*

He wanted to reach out to touch her hand, lying motionless in her lap. But he did not.

It would be too easy to touch her now, as vulnerable as she was. It would be pushing his advantage too relentlessly. Besides that, he realized he wanted to touch her so much it was dangerous. She was still staring out the window, determined to fight back the tears.

He had a sudden, almost savage desire to take her into his arms and hold her, kiss her until she forgot that tears existed. He had an irrational urge to protect her, keep her safe, make her happy.

Instead, he thought about punching his steering wheel. What was happening to him? He'd played this Casanova scam almost a dozen times, and no other woman had ever seemed anything to him other than a job, a mission, a target.

"I'm all right," she said, facing him. Her expression was unreadable, masklike. He felt a muscle in his jaw jump in exasperation. She had too much self-control, he thought. What really was going on behind those unreadable eyes?

He put the car into gear with a smoothness that belied his turbulence. "Let's go to MacGregor and see what's in that post-office box."

Valery nodded. "Can we get into it?" she asked, her voice still slightly unsteady. "It's in Charles's name. Aren't there laws about that?"

He had regained sufficient control to give her his most reassuring smile. He wasn't worried about getting around whoever controlled the mail in a one-horse town like Mac-Gregor.

Whatever was in that post-office box would be in his hands within an hour. He would have bet his life's blood on it.

It took Nikolas only five minutes to charm, dazzle, and finally persuade the plump little postmistress of MacGregor to hand over the mail that was gathering dust in Charles's box. He rewarded her with a flashing white smile, then returned to the car, where Valery sat, nervously waiting.

"Don't open it yet," he warned. "Wait until we get out of town. Someplace where nobody will see us." He was worried. One glance at the envelopes had told him that the news they bore might be bad. He suddenly wanted out of MacGregor, as if its empty streets hid innumerable spies.

He shifted his wide shoulders impatiently. He was getting hinky. That's what cops called it when things started feeling strange, wrong, warped, and the old instincts started stirring uneasily. Hinky. This assignment was suddenly making him edgy as hell. He didn't like it.

Disturbed, Valery hardly noticed as Nikolas headed out of town and toward a shady old graveyard they had passed on the way in. Most of the envelopes looked bland, harmless, nothing but junk mail.

But the bottom two seemed to be personal letters, addressed in a feminine hand to Charles L. Essex. They bore no return address. They were postmarked Newark, New Jersey.

Valery's heart speeded up with painful force. There was no question; the flowing lavender script on the envelope was a woman's writing. Had Charles had another woman, after all?

She willed her hands to stay steady. She started to open the first letter. She bit her lip.

"Wait!" Nikolas's order rang with unexpected sharpness. She looked at him apprehensively. He frowned as he slowed the car to pass through the cemetery gates, then drove down the road that led deep within the grounds.

"Wait," he repeated, deliberately forcing his voice to be milder. "If those letters say anything that clears you—anything at all—you want a witness to see you open them."

She nodded. The law, it seemed, was always shadowing her, watching her, judging her.

He drove slowly under the arching branches, until the car was out of sight from the road. He parked near a grove of cypress trees and across from a particularly depressing marble monument. On it, a grieving stone woman wept as she contemplated a broken flower in her lap.

Valery looked around in alarm, realizing for the first time that she was in a graveyard. The monuments were old and weathered, the graves mostly unkempt. Nikolas leaned back against the seat, dark eyes resting on her. "Now," he said kindly. "Now read them."

Her eyes met his. "I think," she said hesitantly, "that they're from a woman."

"It's all right," he encouraged. "Read them. Maybe they'll tell us why he was killed. Or give us a hint."

Valery's face had paled. So much might depend on these two letters. Tony's security, his future, his whole life. And her own.

Nikolas nodded encouragement. "Go on, Valery," he said. "Read them. It's all right."

He looked so strong, so reassuring, that she believed him. She opened the first letter carefully.

She was catapulted back into the darkest center of her nightmares. The letter was dated two days before Charles's death, on the day he was to have flown from Constant to Newark.

Dearest Chuck, my Darling,

Although I know I'll be in your arms tonight, I can't stop myself from writing. I want to touch you with my mind if I can't with my body. I can't wait until we can touch all the time. My body is never so alive as when you make love to me.

Soon we'll be together and the ugly past will be gone. I am not afraid of your wife, Chuck, no matter what you say. Her anger can't be stronger than my love.

Truly, Chuck, I can't blame her for being jealous. But only a sick person makes the kind of threats she's making, and you must not let yourself be trapped by a sick person. Only sick, insecure people talk about killing.

Together we will triumph. Our love was meant to be. I love you. I can't wait to hold you in my arms.

Love, kisses,
Chrissy

This was crazy, Valery thought desperately. She felt as if she'd been struck in the stomach.

Nikolas, silent as a waiting predator, observed her most minute reactions: she was even paler than before, yet patches of hectic red stained her cheek; her breathing had turned irregular, her breasts rising and falling spasmodically.

"What is it?" he asked, keeping his voice just kind enough, just gentle enough.

Her eyes met his. She was too stunned to think of lying. She handed him the letter. "It's crazy," she murmured, her voice strained. "Just . . . crazy."

He took it and read it, while Valery opened the second envelope fearfully.

She was shaken when she unfolded the letter and found $2,000 in five-hundred-dollar bills. They fluttered into her lap, crisp and green. She stared at them a moment, then let her eyes fall to the written message. Like the first letter, this one was written on a typewriter. Only the signature, "Chrissy," was handwritten, in the same flowery script as on the envelope.

The date was the day following Charles's death. "Chrissy" apparently hadn't got the news yet.

Dearest Chuck, my Dearest Darling,

I still feel warm from your lovemaking. I treasure the memory of your touch.

Darling, here is the $2,000 we talked about. I'm sorry I couldn't get it for you while you were here. Now you can go to Savannah and check out the job with the aviation school. Savannah! Palm trees and flowers and warm blue sea! And you and I making love all night long, the way we were meant to.

I love you, Chuck, and I'm not afraid of Valery, no matter what she threatens. I will help you fight to keep

Tony if you think she's a danger to him. I'll love him because he's part of you. I promise to make him a wonderful mother. And you a wonderful wife.

Savannah soon!
Chrissy

Nikolas had finished the first letter. His face was stony. He saw the crisp money lying in Valery's lap and he watched her expression as she read the second letter. She was reading her death warrant, he thought, and she knew it.

Suddenly she bolted from the car. The money fluttered to the car floor as she slammed the door. He watched as she made her way, almost stumbling, between the tilted, broken tombstones. Almost convulsively she crumpled the second letter in her fist.

Like a shot he, too, was out of the Lynx. She had stopped beside the monument of the weeping woman and she stared unseeing out across the shadows cast by the swaying, shaggy trees.

He strode to her side and placed a hand on her elbow. Her skin was cold. She refused to look at him, her head down, her dark hair blowing around her pale face.

"Leave me alone," she muttered. "I need to be alone."

"Valery," he returned between clenched teeth, "what's wrong? What did she say? It can't be any worse than the first one. Valery?"

His hand felt like a brand on her flesh. She let her gaze sweep wildly up to his. The breeze tossed his thick black hair. If his expression hadn't been of such intense concern for her, she couldn't have spoken at all.

"It is worse," she managed to choke out. "She . . . she . . . she sounds as if I'd hurt Tony. Tony! My own child!"

The shock suffused her with a sudden jolt of energy and

she seized the letter with both hands and began to tear it.

"Valery!" Nikolas's hands whipped up, grasping hers hard to stop her. "No, don't. That's destroying evidence. If anybody ever finds out, it could tip the scales against you. It could send you to prison. Don't!"

"This is full of lies. I don't know why Charles would tell her such things, but he did. I can't keep this! I can't show it to anybody. None of it's true, dammit!"

He kept her hands imprisoned in one of his. He used his free hand to pry her fingers from the letter. "Let me see," he ordered. "I'm the lawman, right? Just let me see, for God's sake."

He wrenched the letter from her at last. It was crumpled, torn, a corner missing, but otherwise whole. He kept hold of her wrists, although she had stopped struggling. Quickly he read the words.

Oh, Lord, he thought, a sick feeling wrenching his stomach. This was exactly the kind of thing Mrs. Bellarion had hoped he'd find: this crumpled, damning sheet of paper.

But the whole thing made him edgier still. Edgy as hell. *Damn,* he thought. *I don't like this.*

"Don't you see?" Valery demanded, staring up at him defiantly. "It says I might hurt Tony. What kind of lies was Charles feeding her? And why?"

He kept her wrists in his grasp. "I don't know," he answered quietly. "What kind of lies are they? Why do you think he told them?"

"It's *all* lies," Valery insisted, tossing her hair. Her eyes flashed. "That I'd be a danger to Tony. That I was jealous of Charles. That I ever threatened him. He never said anything about an aviation school—he told me he was buying a charter service. And it sounds as if I knew he was having an affair. I didn't. I didn't think he was capable of it, for heaven's sake. But that I'd ever hurt Tony . . . Why, if that ever came out in court—"

"What?" More roughly than he meant to, Nikolas drew her nearer. He folded the letter and thrust it into his shirt pocket. Then he grasped Valery's upper arms and held her fast, staring down at her. "What?" he repeated, his voice harsh. "What do you mean, you didn't think he was capable?"

The strength of angry protest that had flooded her so suddenly drained away. She felt weak, as if she might sink to the ground if Nikolas wasn't holding her. She turned her face from his. She hadn't meant to speak of sex. Nikolas knew too many of her secrets already. "Nothing," she murmured. "I didn't mean anything."

He sensed that the shock of the letter was sinking in now, starting to paralyze her. She had gone so white he wondered if she was going to faint.

He shook her, trying to make her pull herself together. "What do you mean?" he demanded again, bringing his face close to hers. "Are you saying he didn't make love to you? Or that he *couldn't?*"

Valery had closed her eyes, shaking her head as if she could shut out reality. But at Nikolas's question, her eyes snapped open again and met his. She had never discussed this subject with anyone. Anyone except Charles, who was so humiliated he could scarcely talk about it.

"He couldn't make love to anybody," she said slowly. "He'd been to a doctor about it. Two doctors. They couldn't help him. I guess she—this Chrissy person—could."

Nikolas didn't blink when she told him of Charles's impotence. But he became uncomfortably aware that the woman he held was young, warm, desirable—and had no one in the world to depend upon except him.

"For how long?" He forced himself to grip her arms more gently, yet somehow he brought her closer to him still. "For how long hadn't he been able to . . . go to bed with you?"

Her white face flushed slightly. "Almost two years," she admitted at last.

He set his jaw, studying her face. He could tell she was frightened and ashamed. He could also tell that her courage was coming back, and that was good.

She was still breathing hard, but now the rise and fall of her breasts was regular beneath the whiteness of her blouse.

"Two years," he muttered, his voice low. "He went two years without making love to you? Why didn't you leave him?"

She raised her chin. "He was sick. He had problems. Emotional problems. I couldn't just walk out."

"Why not? He could walk out on you." His right hand had moved to her back, preventing her from stepping away from him.

She was suddenly conscious of how near he was, the fact that he was nearly holding her in his arms, and that his fingers seemed to burn tingling imprints on her flesh.

"I don't walk out on people," she said, "or responsibilities. My father didn't raise me that way."

"Didn't he raise you to have feelings, either?" he mocked, his mouth quirking in disbelief. "You weren't interested in finding somebody else?" He brushed a tendril of breeze-tossed hair from her cheek. "You didn't mind living like a nun for two years? No sex? No affection, even? Nothing at all from this man?"

Valery tried to move away from him, but he held her fast.

She no longer wanted to look at him. "Of course, I minded," she said bitterly. "Of course, I have feelings. But I took a vow, dammit."

He put a finger under her chin, forced her to look at him again.

"You took a vow," he repeated, his fingers framing her jaw. "Women take vows all the time. They don't always keep them. Why did you?"

She tried to shake off his hand. His touch only became more demanding, more possessive. Something in his dark eyes made her tell him the truth, as ugly as it was.

"I was afraid. Afraid he'd do something to himself. I was never afraid for myself or Tony; Charles wasn't dangerous that way. Charles was mostly dangerous to himself."

God help me, Nikolas thought, his fingers tracing the silky outline of her jaw, *I believe her.*

He found he was gazing at her lips and wondering how Charles Essex could ever want another woman. If he couldn't make love to this one, he was a very sick man indeed.

"What that letter says is a lie," she said, her voice fearful again. "I'm not like that."

"I know," he muttered. He bent, lowering his face to hers. He let his lips brush hers only slightly, only briefly. "I know." He drew back, although the touch of her mouth had shot through him like fire.

She drew away quickly, for the contact had shaken her. He let her nearly escape him, but not quite. He stayed at her side, his arm around her companionable, protectively.

Valery was torn, both wanting his nearness and not wanting it. His kiss, the firm warmth of his lips brushing hers, had riven her through, like a bolt of lightning, shaking her down to her heels.

But, she cautioned herself, she was still too stunned by the letters to think clearly. She wanted human warmth, a man's touch, but that didn't mean she should have them. An accused murderer, she reflected nervously, shouldn't allow herself to be swept away by passion in a graveyard. Some might think it altogether too fitting.

Yet she did not resist the strong arm coiled around her waist. She let him walk her back to the car. The weathered monument loomed behind them like an omen, the stone woman forever bowed and weeping.

He opened the car door for her. She paused before getting in. She looked at the money lying on the car's floor, and she looked up into Nikolas's eyes again.

"The letter," she said tightly. "You took the letter."

Wordlessly he reached into his pocket. He handed it to her. He knew she would never trust him if he didn't. "Don't destroy it," he said.

She said nothing. She took it and thrust it into the pocket of her denim skirt.

"If you'd let me keep one of the letters," he offered, his words sounding stiff even to himself, "maybe I could do something. Trace her—the woman—somehow."

He didn't have a snowball's chance in hell of finding a woman named Chrissy in Newark, and he knew it. Mrs. Bellarion would want the letters, and he should get his hands on them if he could. But he knew that what mattered was that he had seen them. They existed, and so did the two thousand dollars, and he could swear to it in a court of law.

Valery, willing herself into even greater self-control, shook her head. "No," she said. The letters were shameful, and they were weapons that could hurt her, and worse, Tony. She trusted them in no one's hands but her own.

Silently he watched her get into the car, gather up the

bills and the other letter, and put them into her pocket.

A change had come over her, and he sensed it. He got into the car.

He turned to face her. His face was kind, but solemn. "Don't," he warned.

She straightened in her seat, eyeing him in apprehension.

"Don't keep the letters secret. And don't think about running. Two thousand dollars could take you and the boy a long way, Valery. But not far enough. They'd find you. And if you run, they'll take it as a sign you're guilty. You'll never beat the charges if you run."

She bit her lip and looked away. "Did being with the police give you the power to read minds?" The man was disconcertingly perceptive, she thought, confused again.

"Yeah, I read minds. And I read fears. You're afraid those letters will prove you had motive to kill Charles. He was cheating on you, he was leaving you, and he was going to try to take the kid. Right now it seems more than you can fight, so you get the bright idea to take the money and run."

She shrugged unhappily. She wasn't sure that running wasn't the only chance she and Tony had. She stared out the window at the cypress trees, not wanting to meet Nikolas's dark gaze.

He watched her carefully. A nerve twitched in his jaw. "Listen, Valery. The best thing you can do is go to the police. Turn over the letters. And the money. Be up-front. It'll be in your best interests when the trial comes up."

She turned and gave him a disbelieving look. "Turn over letters that practically call me a homicidal maniac? That say I'm a danger to my child? That's in my best interests?"

"Look," he said, trying to sound reasonable. "The letters might not even be admissible evidence. What if nobody can find out who this woman is? If you turn them over, it'll show you're not afraid of the truth, because the truth is that you didn't kill Charles. Somebody else did."

Valery shook her head. "I can't take the chance. What if they could be used against me?"

"You can't withhold evidence," he argued. "If anybody finds out, your neck is in a noose."

"It's in a noose either way. And I can't tell anyone about this." She blinked hard. Her heart sank. Someone already knew about the letters. He did. He could ruin her. The power was his.

"Will you tell?" she asked, trying to sound calm. "After all, you're supposed to serve and protect. Don't you need to serve the public? Protect it from the likes of me?"

He shook his head. He started the car and gunned its motor. "Believe me," he said, his patience straining. "For your own good—"

"Are you going to go to the police?" she demanded, her eyes wide and accusing. He sensed her trust in him dissolving into nothingness. "Aren't you guilty of something yourself if you don't tell them?"

He was silent as they drove through the leafy shadows. It was of paramount importance that she trust him. Yet what he'd told her was the absolute truth. Her safest course was to give the letters to the authorities. He edged the car back onto the highway.

At last he said, "You're too shaken to think straight. So for now, I won't say a thing. I'll give you time. But I don't know why you won't trust the police. If you give them the letters, maybe they can find this broad and maybe their case against you will fall apart. She could have a jealous husband. Or dangerous playmates. It's suspicious as hell that she'd send that much cash through the mail. But if you don't let somebody—me or the police—look into it, nobody's going to find out. The worse thing you can do is hide evidence from the police."

"I don't like the police," Valery retorted. "I'm scared of the police. They've acted like I was guilty from the start. Cameron Carter even hit me, for God's sake."

Nikolas stepped on the brakes so hard that the car skidded to a halt at the highway's edge. He turned on Valery, black eyes alight with skepticism. "Carter? The detective? He did what?"

"He hit me," she repeated. "We were alone in the interrogation room, or whatever you call it. The other detective left. For just a minute. Cameron switched off the tape recorder and said, 'Admit you killed him. Or I'll make you admit it. I can hit you so it won't show.' And he did. He hit me hard. Twice. But he didn't leave a mark. He said I could be hit like that every day when I was in jail. But Judge Pike let me out until the trial. I hate Cameron Carter. Do you think I want him to have these letters?"

She trembled in rage at the memory. Cameron Carter was a big man, as tall as Nikolas, but beefy and heavy-fisted. She had wanted to hit him back, but knew she couldn't. She'd had to sit and take it. Her only satisfaction was that she'd never flinched. She had sat and stared at him as if he were an insect.

"That's illegal," Nikolas said between his teeth. He suddenly really doubted her. Any detective who roughed up a suspect—especially a woman—was either a fool or an incompetent. "Why didn't you report him?"

"I did," she almost cried. "To the chief of police. He called me a liar. I told my lawyer. Osgood Perry. He wouldn't do anything. He said I was overimaginative and just trying to make trouble." *And you don't believe me, either,* she thought fatalistically as she watched the doubt flickering across his features.

She made an impotent gesture. What could she say? Why should he believe her? She turned away and stared out the window once more. She could feel his eyes on her.

"Valery," he said at last, "you know what this sounds like, don't you?"

She nodded numbly, still not looking at him.

"Everybody's lying—except you," he said bluntly. "That's what you want me to believe, and what you hope a jury will believe. Everybody, including the police, is lying."

"I never said that," she muttered helplessly.

"That's what it sounds like," he returned, almost biting the words off. "Listen. You want a favor from me. You want me to keep quiet about the letters. All right. Do me a favor in return. Make me a list. Write down the names of everybody you think is lying or spreading one of Charles's lies. Because according to you, so many people are lying about you, I can't keep them straight. It sounds like a damn conspiracy."

"I never said that," she retorted. She knew she sounded paranoid.

"Just make the list, all right? And don't tear up those letters. Promise me. And don't run. You're done for if you run, I guarantee you."

"Is that all you want?" She still stared out the window.

A beat of silence pulsed. "No," he answered. "That's not all I want."

She stiffened slightly. She had heard it clearly, the undercurrent of passion in his voice It left her trembling on the brink of an abyss of new threat. She said nothing.

"I want more. You've known that from the first. You know what I want."

She turned back to face him. Yes, she thought, frightened, she knew. Somehow she had known from the first.

He wanted more. He wanted her. The desire that flashed from his eyes was so strong it blazed through her. It was as if in his mind he was making love to her right now.

Her lungs seemed to stop functioning. She couldn't breathe. In spite of everything, he awoke desire within her. It was as if he had breathed on a spark buried, deep and secret, within her. He made the spark flare, and its heat flowed through her, tingling and languid at the same time.

He made no move to touch her, nor she him. Still, the air between them crackled, almost shook with primeval energy. *I won't betray you*, his eyes seemed to promise. *I won't let anybody hurt you, because you're mine.*

Her own eyes sent a message: *I want you, too. But I'm afraid. You could destroy me.*

I won't, he said without words.

How can I know? she wondered, searching his eyes.

Then, with lightning rapidity, as if to quell her fear, his expression softened. His old demeanor, quizzical, kind and patient, came back. He looked away, sighed, then smiled.

"Make me a list." His manner was suddenly easy, nonchalant. He eased the car back on the highway.

Valery nodded. She felt numbed again, unsure of what had happened between them.

Nothing, she told herself.

Nothing. They had looked at each other for a moment. He had asked her for a list. That was all.

He smiled to show her everything was okay. He started joking about missing classes because of her. But inside he was not smiling. Too many things were wrong with the situation.

He was getting emotionally involved with a suspect. He actually wanted to help her, which was crazy, because her story was full of holes.

There was no way that everybody except Valery was lying. The world didn't work that way.

Yet, things were falling into his hands a little too easily, a little too fast, a little too smoothly.

The letters, for instance.

Something about the handwriting on the envelopes, the signatures, troubled him. When he had seen the writing, it had looked oddly familiar. At first he couldn't place it. Now he could.

Chrissy's writing reminded him of Penny Shaw's.

The writing wasn't really the same at all, yet the similarity was there. But Penny Shaw couldn't be Chrissy.

She couldn't be. The plump, shy, slightly suicidal secretary in Dallas couldn't also have been Charles Essex's sexy mistress in New Jersey. It was impossible.

Wasn't it?

He glanced at the woman beside him. She made something inside him stumble and fall. Maybe he wanted to believe in her enough to warp his perceptions, to make him imagine things.

He couldn't afford that. He had to remember what she was. She was prey.

Chapter Five

"Look," he said when he parked the car in front of her house. He put his hand on her shoulder. His touch made her nerves leap. "Come out with me tonight."

Her heart beat thunderously. "I can't. Tony and I—"

"I'll take Tony, too." His hand moved to cradle the back of her neck. "We'll go to supper, a movie."

She edged away, frightened of the emotions he awoke. "Tony and I have to go to Charmian's. She has us over once a week for supper and games and things. I'm sorry. I have an appointment with a fried chicken and a Monopoly board."

"Sounds wonderful." Nikolas toyed with a silken tendril of her hair.

"I can't ask you," she said abruptly, moving away from his contact. "My aunt doesn't like strangers. She's already warned me about you, in fact."

Damn, Nikolas thought with irritation. Since the discovery of the letters, he didn't trust his tenuous hold on Valery. The aunt could be damaging. The old girl might be a crank—or one of those women twice as smart as anybody ever suspects.

"Afterward?" he suggested, his voice intimate.

"No," she said more sharply than she meant. "I have to think."

He refused to let her elude him. He reached for her again, this time touching her face, framing her jaw with his large hand. "Valery, promise not to do anything foolish. Just make the list. And trust me, will you?"

She eyed him warily, but she nodded.

"I had a wife once," he murmured, his face serious and earnest. "I loved her, but she said I loved police work more. So I lost her. Do you know how?"

She shook her head, wisping his fingers weren't so gently sensual against her face.

"We were at a party one night," he told her, the line of his mouth harsh. "Friends gave a surprise party for our anniversary. Nothing fancy, a backyard picnic, really, with all the friends and everybody's kids, but drinks were flowing. Right in the middle, I got a call about a break in a homicide case. I left. I left her there, at our own anniversary party."

His hand moved downward slightly, his thumb resting on the pulse that leapt in her throat. He spoke bitterly. "She didn't want me to go. I did. She drove home alone. She shouldn't have. But she slipped away from the party before anybody could stop her."

He took a deep breath. He looked into her eyes. "Valery she'd had a little too much to drink. It wasn't like her. She didn't think she'd be driving. On the freeway she met another driver, one who'd drunk a lot too much. He swerved into her. Her reaction time wasn't fast enough. She died. So did our son. His name was Brian. He'd be Tony's age now if he'd lived. Ever since that night, it's like I have a hole through me the size of a train tunnel."

Her body tensed with horror at the pain he must have felt. To lose both his wife and child must have plunged him into an unspeakable hell of loneliness and guilt. The thought of such suffering made her suffer herself.

"I'm sorry," she managed to say. She no longer tried to draw back from his touch.

"You can trust me," he told her, his eyes dark with emotion. "I'll never put the law before a woman again. I'll never hurt another woman. Ever. And certainly never another child. Give me the chance to help you. Trust me. Co-operate with me. Please."

Tentatively she put her fingers against his. Her touch was as hesitant as a butterfly's.

"Please."

Her fingers clasped his, tightened slightly. "All right," she whispered, her throat tight. She gave his hand a shy squeeze, then released it. She unlocked the door of the Lynx and quickly let herself out, before he could stop her.

He leaned across the seat, looking out the window at her. "I mean it," he said, his voice taut with conviction. "Let me help you. And the boy."

Unable to reply, she nodded. She tried to smile, but couldn't. She nodded again. "I'll try," she said. She turned, walking away quickly, filled with conflicting emotions.

Nikolas watched her go, his face stony and bitter. He pulled into his own driveway, slammed the car door and strode into the house.

He made it to the living room, then spun around and hit the wall so hard his fist went through the plaster and he cut his knuckles. He swore savagely.

He wanted nothing so much as to go out and get roaring drunk, so drunk he was oblivious. Instead he called the garage and made arrangements to get Valery's windshield and tires replaced.

He had her again, he knew it. Of all the lousy lies he'd ever told, he was sure the batch he'd just laid on her was the lowest and the lousiest.

There had been no wife. There had been no kid named Brian, or anything else. There had been no accident. The only grain of truth in the whole spiel had been that he didn't want to hurt another woman. But with Valery he had no choice, and the damnable part was that somehow he still didn't want to believe she was guilty. Somehow he couldn't.

Valery locked the door behind her. She was almost as frightened of Nikolas Grady as of the letters. He offered a confusing combination of safety and danger. He made her feel things she had no right to feel. All her energies should be concentrated on preserving Tony and herself.

She glanced at the mantel clock. It was almost four. Tony would be home in a few hours. She needed to regain her balance, get control of herself.

She sat at her father's desk. Shoulders squared, she took out the folder containing the copy of Charles's flight log, his canceled checks, every scrap of paper she had studied in hopes of finding an answer to the riddle that ensnared her.

Reluctantly she withdrew the two letters from her skirt pocket and laid them atop the stack of papers. The five-hundred-dollar bills she locked safely in a desk drawer, then she sat and read the letters from Chrissy again. She wanted to read them until they lost their power to hurt.

She couldn't afford to be emotional about the letters. She must be able to think about them clearly.

Lies, she thought doggedly. The letters were full of lies. Charles had told the woman a mountain of lies. Why?

To make himself seem dramatic and interesting, she decided. That was the only answer. She leaned her forehead on her fist. A pain was knotting up behind her eyebrows, hammering at her mind, trying to shatter her line of thought.

Charles had liked to dramatize things, to distort them so that he stood center stage, the hero that he so desperately wanted to be again.

Yet something wasn't right. She knew Charles. He might have lied, trying to make the failure of their marriage seem her fault, but he would never have said he was frightened of her or what she might do. It would have made him sound weak. Charles couldn't have stood that.

Unless, she frowned, Charles really *hadn't* wished to marry the woman, had wanted only the woman's money, and needed an alibi to keep her at a distance.

No, Valery thought. Charles had craved admiration too much. This Chrissy obviously adored him. She believed in him, lusted after him, wanted him, and had given him money. More than that, she had given him back his manhood. If Charles had found such a woman, he wouldn't want to drop her. He would want to show her to the world, flaunt her.

Valery sat up straighter. The thought startled her. That was precisely what Charles would have done—if he had found such a woman. If.

If.

If he had found such a woman, he would have told Valery. He couldn't have helped himself. He would want her to know he was a hero to somebody. Oh, yes, he would have made sure she knew.

She stared at the damning letters one more time, slightly stunned.

Perhaps Chrissy wasn't simply spreading lies. Perhaps Chrissy herself was a lie, an audacious one designed to incriminate Valery.

She smoothed out the letter she had crumpled. The thought was nearly mad. If there was no Chrissy, then who had written these letters and sent the money?

Nikolas was right. She couldn't win her case simply by claiming everyone else was lying or wrong. But *why* were there so many lies about her? Why did they keep increasing and growing stronger, like a great teeming nest of venomous snakes?

She ran her fingers through her hair in frustration. She didn't know how Nikolas could believe her any longer, either, not after seeing the letters. But if she could just prove the letters were false . . .

She shut them up in the folder. She set her jaw and took out a clean sheet of paper.

Nikolas was the lawman. She would follow his advice. She needed to trace the path of all these intertwining lies. Perhaps they could lead her to whoever had written the letters.

At the top of the paper, she wrote neatly: People Saying Damaging Things About Me.

The ultimate exercise in paranoia, she thought ruefully. But she forced herself to write down every name. The list, finished, was depressingly long.

She shook her head. On the other side of the paper, out of a sense of self-preservation, she made another list, headed: People Who've Offered Support.

It was depressingly short. Nor was it cheering to realize that the person on whom she counted most was the one she'd known the least time: Nikolas.

Nikolas Grady, standing in his darkening living room, watched through the fluttering white curtains as Valery and Tony left to walk to Charmian's that evening. When she and the boy disappeared at the end of the block, his black mood returned. He tried to shrug it off and couldn't.

The woman didn't stand a chance. He knew that. He felt dirty all over, used and corrupted. The only reason he'd come to this rotten town was so he could put a guilty woman behind bars, then trace an innocent one and save her from herself. It had seemed simple.

It was no longer simple. For years he'd bent the law to enforce it, he had cheated so justice could triumph, and he had lied so the truth would come to light.

Lies had become second nature to him, a line of work at which he excelled. He had been sent to make sure Valery Essex was convicted of the murder. But the job was almost too easy. It gnawed at him.

He'd like to leave town, never mention those damned Chrissy letters to anybody. The kindest thing he could do was let Valery take her chances, maybe even bolt with the kid and try to escape.

But he couldn't do that, because he had to find Penny Shaw. Penny Shaw and the Fields case had made him so crazy he was starting to hallucinate, see ghosts in strange handwriting. Why did he sense a resemblance between Penny's staid handwriting and Chrissy's florid script? The intuition troubled him.

Again he had the impulse to go out and get skull-banging, blackout drunk. Not yet, he thought, the knot in his stomach tightening again. He had to make a phone call.

He dialled long distance. A husky, drawling woman's voice answered.

"Mrs. Bellarion?" he asked, the nerve in his jaw jumping with distaste.

"Mr. Grady? You're late. I expected your call an hour ago. Promptness is a virtue I exalt. Cultivate it."

"I don't keep a lady waiting without reason," Nikolas lied, his teeth clenched. He hadn't called because he couldn't stand the old woman or the business she had involved him in. "I was doing surveillance on your daughter-in-law."

"She's not my daughter-in-law," Mrs. Bellarion snapped. "I have no son. I can therefore have no daughter-in-law. She killed him. Have you wriggled into her confidence? Have you found anything out?"

"I'm in her confidence, Mrs. Bellarion. But I don't give away information. I trade it. I want to know about Penny Shaw."

Mrs. Bellarion didn't miss a beat. "Penny is currently safe. Currently. But she is depressed, deeply. Over you, Mr. Grady. I fear for her, I truly do. What have you found out about Valery?"

"Mrs. Bellarion," Nikolas said, his voice still silky, "where's Penny? How can I be sure you can put me in touch with her once I've . . . taken care of Valery?"

Mrs. Bellarion sighed deeply. "I just talked to Penny. She cried. She said you used to say her eyes were like blue diamonds. She thought you meant it. Now she knows you were just interested in Fields and the money."

Nikolas swore inwardly. It was true he had told Penny that damnable foolishness about her eyes. She had pale blue eyes with a kind of desperate sparkle. It hadn't seemed like a bad line at the time. Now he wished he'd choked on it.

"How can I be sure she's all right," he demanded, "or that you know where she is?"

"I know she's all right because I'm family," Mrs. Bellarion answered acidly. "I know where she's at for the same reason. You'll never find her without me. No matter how hard you try. So you may as well give up and do things my way."

The nerve in his jaw jerked again. She was right. A person determined to stay hidden could remain hidden for years. Police and FBI files were full of such people. He would like to crawl through the phone wire and shake Mrs. Bellarion until the thick makeup shattered off her face.

He decided to hurl his crazy long shot at the woman. "Penny hasn't been hanging around Newark, New Jersey, has she?" he challenged. "She didn't try to console herself with another man, did she? Like your son?"

There was not even a pause. "Don't be ridiculous," Mrs. Bellarion snapped. "If my son had another woman, it wouldn't be Penny Shaw. He never saw her. He never met any of my late husband's relatives. Besides, my son was a handsome man. He appreciated a beautiful woman. Penny is a frump, poor creature."

Nikolas decided to press the woman anyway. "Did your son have a mistress?" he persisted. "Is that a fact you left out when you sent me after Valery Essex? That your son was cheating on her?"

"People say he was. If he cheated, he had reason," Mrs. Bellarion almost snarled. "Valery wasn't good enough for him. She never was, and she knew it. If he found someone else, more power to him."

Nikolas swore to himself again. Mrs. Bellarion was tough, rock hard. He tried to bluff. "I think your son was getting it on with a bimbo in Newark, Mrs. Bellarion. A woman whose handwriting resembles Penny's. But you don't know anything about that, I suppose."

"I know nothing," Mrs. Bellarion returned in her most aristocratic tone. "If Charles found solace in Newark, then bless Newark. Heaven knows he had little enough happiness with Valery. Is she the source of this story? If so, she's changed her tune. The last I heard she had no idea why Charles would want to leave her. I sense you've found something, Mr. Grady, I hope, for poor distraught Penny's sake, that you're being completely honest with me."

Nikolas swore to himself a third time. "There's evidence that Charles was involved with a woman in Newark. Your daughter-in-law just found out herself."

"I told you once, Mr. Grady: I have no daughter-in-law. All I have is a grandson. Tony. I want him. I want his mother in prison and the boy to be *mine*."

The way the woman said *mine* set Nikolas's teeth on edge.

"Precisely what have you found?" Mrs. Bellarion demanded. "Have you physical proof of this Newark woman's existence? Is it proof that damages Valery?"

He took a deep breath. He felt the familiar sick dissatisfaction twisting in his stomach. "Certain items may be damaging."

"How lovely," Mrs. Bellarion returned sweetly. "Keep up the good work. The closer Valery is to prison, the nearer you are to Penny. Poor Penny. How lucky you were her first suicide attempt failed. Let's hope there isn't a second."

Nikolas inwardly cursed Thelma Bellarion to eternal hell. Penny Shaw was valuable to her, and if he guessed correctly, the girl was hidden somewhere in an exclusive rest home under an assumed name. But he'd checked and rechecked, and her whereabouts had eluded him. She had little family. If anyone besides Thelma Bellarion knew where she was, they weren't talking.

"I'll keep you informed," he told Mrs. Bellarion tersely. He wasn't giving the old bat any more information than he had to. He hung up.

Again he felt a wave of disgust for the whole situation and for himself. He really did want to get blackout drunk, something he hadn't done since Vietnam. Not since the night they arrested Sun and he hadn't allowed himself to feel anything when they took her away. That first woman he'd betrayed. So long ago.

"Valery," Charmian said angrily, "I told you not to trust

that Grady man. And what do you do? Spend half the day gallivanting with him. Haven't you got any sense?"

They were drying dishes in Charmian's cluttered kitchen while Tony sat in the living room, pecking at the keys of Charmian's piano.

Valery set her jaw. She had sensed her aunt's simmering displeasure all through supper. She had suspected the source was Nikolas Grady.

"The man's a policeman," Valery countered. "Or was. In Los Angeles. He thinks he can help me."

Charmian's blue eyes glittered angrily. She slapped her dish towel down on the counter. "The man *says* he was a policeman. How do you know? Why would he help you? He's a handsome man, Valery. How do you know Thelma Bellarion didn't send him here to seduce you? To make you look like an unfit mother?"

Valery gave her aunt a look of sorely tried patience. The letters from Chrissy were one more hideous complication in her life. She didn't need Charmian's everlasting suspicions as well.

"Charmian, he's a nice man."

"There are no nice men." Charmian crossed her arms stubbornly.

"My father was a nice man. At least he was a good man. He stood up for what he believed. He always did the right thing."

"Your father," Charmian countered ominously, "was far from perfect. Men tend far too much to have s-e-x on their minds. I've seen this Grady man. Valery, don't trust him, and don't get involved. Charles has been dead less than two months. Do you realize how it looks, your taking up with this man?"

"I haven't 'taken up' with anybody," Valery replied, but it

was true. Nikolas had penetrated her defenses to an amazing degree.

"Well," Charmian warned, eyes narrowing, "if you do get involved, you can bet it'll be dragged into court. Why can't you think of Tony?"

Valery flushed guiltily. Charmian's words were the hellfire and damnation version of Osgood Perry's staid admonition to act like a lady.

Worse, Charmian's warning contained a kernel of truth. Valery's marriage had been a hollow thing for years, but how many people knew the truth of that? How would it look if she took up with Nikolas Grady so soon after Charles's death?

She dodged the unpleasant subject by switching to another one, equally unpleasant. "Charmian," she asked, "why are there so many lies about Charles and me? Why do so many people say things that aren't true?"

Charmian jerked irritably at her beads. "I told you, Valery. People are after you."

Valery sighed. She dried the last cup and put it away. "Somebody killed Charles. Somebody tried to throw the blame on me," she said, shaking her head. "But I can't believe a whole bunch of somebodies killed him and are trying to blame me. That's too farfetched."

"Life is farfetched," Charmian countered, tossing her white curls. "I suspect those Talmidges. Amanda and Paris—they're up to something. They deal with chemicals, and it's a short step from legal chemicals to illegal ones. Somehow Paris got her company caught up in the drug trade. She's probably queen of the drug world—underworld connections everywhere. Charles found out, and she poisoned him."

Valery suppressed another sigh. She sat down at the

kitchen table. "The Talmidge sisters have never said a word against me," she argued. "Nobody high up in the company has. John Upchurch even called to see if there was anything they could do for me. It's not them. It's other people."

"Precisely the advantage of being high up in a company," Charmian retorted with satisfaction. "Your underlings do the dirty work."

Valery gave her aunt a skeptical look. "You mean Cameron Carter is willing to perjure himself to convict me? He doesn't even work for the Talmidges."

"Fiddle." Charmian snorted. "He *is* a Talmidge. On his mother's side. He's first cousin once removed from Paris and Amanda."

"Charmian, we're related to the Talmidges, too. Aren't you a second cousin to Paris and Amanda yourself?"

"That's different," Charmian said darkly, although Valery didn't see how it was. "What have you got there? What, what, what?"

Valery had opened her purse and taken out her list headed People Saying Damaging Things About Me.

"Nikolas Grady told me to make a list of people who'd said things that could be used against me," Valery said. "I did. I just can't understand why any of them would lie."

"Let me see," Charmian ordered, sitting down. She commandeered the list. "Melissa Milhouse—the switchboard operator at the motel. She claims Charles said you killed him. Hmmph! That's simple. Her first husband was Cameron Carter's cousin."

Valery struggled to keep from rolling her eyes. The connection between Melissa and Cameron was too slight to note. Nevertheless, Charmian whipped a pen from her blouse pocket and scribbled "Cousin!" beside Melissa Milhouse's name.

"Tammi Smith," snorted Charmian, gazing at the next name. "That bubble-headed secretary who claimed Charles had a mistress. She's another one."

"Another what?" Valery demanded.

Charmian frowned in concentration. "A Talmidge. On her—let me see—great-great grandmother's side. Which would make her a second cousin once removed from Paris and Amanda." She scrawled the tenuous relationship beside Tammi Smith's name.

"Charmian," Valery said grimly, "this won't work. Practically everyone in this town is related. Tammi Smith's also related to *us*. Me more than you. My mother's mother was a Smith."

"Hush," Charmian muttered. "This gives me a migraine. Who else? Oh, that dreadful Sheridan Milhouse. He said Charles had a mistress, too. Which means he's helping to set you up."

Valery shook her head hopelessly. "He told the police what Charles told him, that's all. Besides, he got Charles's flight log copied for me. He could get in trouble for that. He went out of his way to help me, really."

"Sheridan Milhouse is in this up to his neck. He gave you those flight logs just so you'd get in *more* trouble. Let's see . . . he's a second cousin to Paris and Amanda—and a second cousin to that silly would-be Sherlock Holmes, Cameron Carter. So there!"

Charmian furiously scribbled the relationships beside Sheridan Milhouse's name.

"Sheridan Milhouse is Charles's first cousin," Valery practically wailed. "He's as closely related to Tony as he is to the Talmidges."

Charmian ignored her. She went down the list, finding similar slight relationships, blithely ignoring Valery's protests.

Charmian flipped the paper over, frowned at the second list and said, "What's this? People who've been supportive? Well, I'm glad to see *my* name. But what's Judge Pike's name doing here?"

"He could have thrown me in jail without bond," Valery explained. "Instead he released me until the trial."

"I don't trust him," Charmian said. "He has an ulterior motive. He's an Upchurch on his mother's side and a Talmidge on his grandmother's. He'll throw the book at you. Cross him right off."

The older woman vigorously blacked out Judge Pike's name. Really, Valery thought wearily, if she herself was paranoid, the trait must have come from Charmian.

"Willadene Davis? The math teacher?" Charmian sneered. "I wouldn't trust her farther than I could throw her. She's Milhouse on her mother's side and a first cousin once removed from—"

"Charmian, please! Stop! Willadene's related somehow to Charles, too—"

"She's mathematical. I don't trust mathematical women," Charmian grumbled. "They're an aberration of nature. I can't do math, and I'm a lady and a normal person." She scratched Willadene's name off the short list of friends. She looked at the last name, furrowing her brow. She narrowed one eye and peered up at Valery accusingly.

"Nikolas Grady?" Charmian queried, shock in her voice. "You're already counting this Don Juan as an ally? Valery, Valery, I am astounded."

"Why? Is he a nineteenth cousin to Paris and Amanda? Twice removed?"

"Don't get smart, miss." Charmian scratched out Nikolas's name. "You know nothing of this man. He could be the devil himself. Look at this list. You have no friends you can trust. None but me. But do you listen to me? No."

Valery felt a small unwarranted shudder. Charmian was shaking her fragile confidence. Perhaps, her aunt was right on this point. Who, after all, was Nikolas Grady?

Across town, in a house far more splendid than Charmian's, a man paced across the Oriental rug in the library. He hoped for a peaceful night. Paris and Amanda Talmidge had escaped to Nantucket for a few days. They wanted the solace of cool ocean breezes and island isolation. Amanda was jumpy and weepy these days, Paris cross and demanding. They were both frightened by what was happening.

He sipped his scotch and stared at the leather-bound volumes of Shakespeare. He was frightened himself. What had Shakespeare said? Something about wading so far into a river of blood it was easier to go forward than to turn back?

The phone jangled discreetly. Its flashing light told him the call was from within the house. His innards contracted. He picked up the receiver. His stomach twisted even more nervously when he heard the voice at the other end. He hated it.

"I'm hurt and I'm lonely," said Penny Shaw. Her voice was flat, depressed and mournful. "I know Nikolas is in town. I know he's seeing that Essex woman."

"He has to see her," the man said, trying to sound patient and reasonable. "It's the plan."

"I don't like it," Penny said petulantly. "I want to see him myself. Why can't I see him? I want him to know exactly what he's done to me. He nearly killed me. He can still destroy all of us. You, too."

The self-pity in her tone made the man wince. "He'll pay, Penny. I promise."

"What good if he pays and doesn't know it's for me?" Penny asked querulously.

"He can't know it's you," the man said wearily. "You have to stay hidden. You weren't going to talk to anyone, remember? You shouldn't be using the phone. It's dangerous for you to use the phone."

"I'm a person, too. I have needs. I have rights."

"Of course, you have rights," the man soothed. "But right now you can't be seen—or heard from. It's dangerous. Is Dahlia Lee there? Let me talk to Dahlia Lee."

"Dahlia Lee's sleeping," Penny Shaw said contemptuously. "She's still recovering—ha! As if *she's* been through anything. I'm the one who's been through hell. Dahlia Lee's almost well. What about me?"

"I know you've suffered. But you mustn't use the phone. It's dangerous. I thought you understood that. Get off the line, Penny."

"I don't want to. I'm tired of being cooped up. Sometimes I just want to end it all—"

"Stop it!" the man ordered, his heart racing in panic. He hated it when she got this way. She scared years off his life. "Stop!" he repeated with surprising authority. "You'll ruin everything. You have to trust us. Do you understand? You have to go along with this, or you're lost, along with everything else, dammit. If Dahlia Lee isn't there, let me talk to your friend."

"She's not my friend," Penny said sulkily. "She's bossy and she's cold. She thinks she knows everything. I wish I'd never let—"

"She's the best friend you've got," the man said acidly. "I said let me talk to her. Now."

"I hate this," Penny wailed. "I hate it here. I hate everything—"

"Penny!"

"All right! All right'" She set down the receiver with such a bang that he winced. There was a long silence at the other end. At last he heard the receiver being taken up again.

"Hello," said a woman's voice. It was deep, firm, possessed of an icy calm.

"Is that you?" he asked, relief mingled with apprehension in his voice. He put his hand over his eyes, as if they pained him. There was no longer any peace in this house. No wonder Paris and Amanda had fled.

"Sorry. I slipped away for a minute. I didn't expect Penny to act up."

"She's got to be kept under control. She's dangerous— weak and self-destructive. Do you know the damage she can do?"

"I know the damage already done," said the voice, cold with control. "She's been extremely unhappy ever since Grady's been in town. She's right, in her way. This is dragging out too long. End it. Then we can all have some peace."

Damn, thought the man. This woman scared him. He spent all his time in a hell of fear because of her. She had taken control of all their lives.

"Did you hear me? It's time. End it."

"Everything in its time," he argued. "We have plans. Let it take a week, a week and a half. We have more letters to plant—"

"Forget the letters. Damn the letters. A week and a half's too long," the woman snapped. "I want it sooner! So does Penny—only for different reasons. Let's do it now. Then we can all finally rest easy."

"It can't be any sooner," the man replied, hoping he didn't sound frantic. "We planned this carefully. Grady just got to town—it's too early. Don't even talk about it. We can't be hasty again. Let me talk to Dahlia Lee. Please."

"Dahlia Lee's resting," the woman said. "She's emotionally worn out by all this. This is grinding everyone down. It's killing the two old ladies."

"Please don't call them old ladies." He was fiercely protective of Paris and Amanda. "They deserve more respect than that."

But he knew what she said was true. Ever since this woman had entered their lives, Paris and Amanda were almost undone, and Dahlia Lee, weak silly Dahlia Lee, was at her mercy. She could destroy all of them if they resisted her wishes.

The woman spoke with her same relentless calm. "I say now. Tonight."

"No," the man returned, trying to keep the panic out of his voice. "Absolutely not tonight. We can't do this without consulting Paris and Amanda. They don't get home until tomorrow."

"Then tomorrow," the woman demanded imperiously. "Tomorrow. At the latest."

The man paused. He couldn't afford to anger her. "We'll see," he said. His voice was conciliatory, reassuring, kind, reasonable.

He didn't sound like a man talking of murder. Double murder, at that. That he spoke of it so calmly terrified him.

But he had known all along that this must happen. This, after all, was why Nikolas Grady had been brought to Constant. Not to convict Valery Essex. No. He had been brought here to die with her.

Violently. And soon.

Chapter Six

A small television set perched among the rows of bottles behind the bar. Nikolas watched, nursing his scotch, his mood darker than ever.

The news was on and it was about the damned Fields case. More federal investigators had been called into Dallas because the financial scandal kept growing like some evil fungus.

Fortunes, large and small, continued to vanish. Bankruptcies multiplied. Every day more innocent people discovered that they were ruined.

Nice work, Grady, he said to himself. All this disaster, yet Fields himself had slipped away, and a suicidal Penny Shaw was out there somewhere, lost and ashamed. He thanked God that the news didn't mention his name. Once the case started cracking, the feds had rushed forward to seize the limelight. They could have it.

"Disgraceful business, this Fields thing," muttered a slightly drunk man who had sat down next to him. "How many will go down in flames before it's done?"

"Who knows?" Nikolas replied blackly. He glanced at the man. He was a stout professorly type with a graying goatee. He seemed determined to be friendly in his own pompous, self-centered way.

He asked Nikolas's name and his business in Constant. Nikolas gave him an evasive song and dance that satisfied him.

"I'm Dr. Cato Davis Pike," the man said, extending a

plump hand. "Professor of Classics."

Inside Nikolas's head, a bell went off. Pike was also the name of the judge in Valery's case.

"Any relation to Judge Marcus Albert Pike?" he asked with elaborate casualness.

"My brother," the professor replied grimly. "My rich, successful, well-respected brother. He chose the field of law. I chose education, and thus am penniless. Of course, Marcus also had the foresight to marry money."

Bingo. If the judge had any secrets, they weren't going to be safe with his red-nosed and resentful brother. Nikolas signaled the bartender to bring the professor another beer.

"The judge married money? Judicious. Some of that Talmidge money I hear about? They're the fat cats in town, right?"

"Oh, this town," Dr. Pike said contemptuously. "My brother married *real* money. Miss Betsy Crocket of the fried-chicken franchise Crockets. The Crocket money, sir, is money. Not that Talmidge money wouldn't be good enough for me. I might have had my share. But, alas, my mother sold my birthright. Took the money and invested it in Studebaker—gad! Right before it went belly up. Leaving me to be naught but a poor professor. Damn the luck."

Nikolas studied Pike carefully. The man drank his free beer greedily. "You're related to the Talmidges?" he asked. "But your mother sold her company shares?"

"My mother," the professor returned bitterly, "was an Upchurch—a Talmidge on her grandmother's side. The Talmidge Corporation owns this town. It owns the most important bank and it owns the college—or at least endows it—and therefore, my friend, it owns me. When, but for a terrible whim of my mother's, I might have owned myself."

Nikolas thought grimly of Mrs. Bellarion's hooks sunk

into his own flesh. "Maybe nobody owns himself."

"Ah," sighed Pike, his tone still bitter. "I once admired a man who I believed did." He raised his glass in salute. "I dedicate this beer to Professor Arthur Donovan. The guy ruined me with his rotten idealism."

Nikolas's senses went on full alert. Arthur Donovan—Valery's father. "Donovan?"

"Donovan. He influenced me greatly. My brother, too. Donovan kept his principles, all right. But he lost what meant most to him—his daughter. What kind of choice is that, sir?"

Nikolas went as still as a hunter who has his quarry in his sights. "Lost his daughter? How?"

"By ignoring her, sir. And ultimately by letting her run off with an idiot. Arthur Donovan was so busy fighting evil in every form, he forgot to keep it off his own doorstep. He allowed his daughter to ruin her life by running off with a moron when she was hardly more than a child."

Nikolas shrugged, as if he found the story of slender interest. "What kind of evil does a guy fight so hard that he loses his kid?"

"The worst kind of evil," Pike answered firmly. "The sort no one intends."

Nikolas sipped his scotch and shrugged again. "You're too deep for me, professor."

The stocky man stroked his beard. "The worst sort of evil looks ordinary. It creeps up quietly and takes over before anyone notices—except the most alert. Arthur Donovan noticed. The evil he saw was in the Talmidge company. It was polluting the air. It was polluting the earth. It was polluting the river. Merrily and without shame—the way a lot of companies used to pollute."

"So?" Nikolas prodded.

"So he kept taking them to court. When the dust cleared,

he'd won all his victories but lost his daughter. He'd been too busy fighting to see he'd neglected her—how she was ripe for any young twerp with a gleam in his eye."

Nikolas's dark brows drew together. Valery's father had taken on the Talmidge Corporation, not once, but repeatedly? And had won? Thelma Bellarion had never mentioned this. Neither had Valery. But it was an intriguing fact. He saw that the professor's beer was almost finished and signaled the bartender for another.

"How did people feel about him, about this Donovan?" Nikolas asked.

"Most of them hated his guts," Pike stated flatly. He stroked his goatee. "He cost the company—and the town—a bundle. But to a few of us, he was a hero. Never have a hero, my friend. It's a damned expensive commodity."

"Meaning?"

"Meaning that I admired him enough to follow in his footsteps and teach. As for my brother, he admired the impartiality of the law and made it his field. But he had the good sense to marry money. He can afford principles. The rest of us haven't the luxury. Bah. Damn idealism."

Pike stared down into the amber depths of his beer, lost in unhappy memories. Nikolas urged him on. "And Donovan himself? What became of him?"

Pike shrugged indifferently. "The Talmidge Corporation knew they had encountered a man who couldn't be bought. So they simply bought everyone around him. Nobody dared be Arthur Donovan's ally. He died lonely and embittered. He had nothing left except his good name. Now even that's being filched."

Nikolas frowned again, sipping the last of his scotch. "How do you take away somebody's good name after he's dead?"

"By ruining that of his only child." Pike drained his beer with relish and wiped his mustache. "She's accused of murdering her sullen twit of a husband, you know. And she'll probably be convicted. The irony is that my brother himself will preside at her trial. If the woman can get a fair trial in this town, Marcus will see to it. She can thank her father for that. And, of course, the Crocket chicken money."

"Why shouldn't she get a fair trial?" Nikolas probed, signaling for yet another beer for the professor.

Pike thought it over. He waited for a fresh mug to be set before him. He sampled it and nodded. "A man was murdered. To purge the sin, someone must be punished. As far as most of this town is concerned, Valery Donovan Essex is expendable."

Nikolas felt a chill grip the back of his neck. "Expendable?"

Pike nodded beerily. "Expendable. Nobody of importance in this town cares what happens to her. Except my brother. He'll see justice is done. If it can be."

Nikolas fought back the rising desire to shake a straight statement out of Dr. Cato Davis Pike. "What are you saying? Do you think the woman's guilty?"

Pike took a long pull from his mug. The more he drank, the more philosophical he became, and the less direct. "Guilty is a legal term, sir," Pike droned, starting to lose himself in professorial complexities. "Can one ever say that one truly receives justice? Now take the case, years ago, of Freda Bloch. Freda Bloch was a young friend of Dahlia Lee Talmidge. She was seriously hurt in an accident when Dahlia Lee was driving. Her family tried to take Dahlia Lee to court, but Dahlia Lee was still a minor, to say nothing of being something of an hysteric, the sort of creature who always needs protection, absolutely incapable of standing on her own feet for more than two minutes at a time. So her aunts—"

Nikolas had no patience for stories of Freda Bloch, whoever she was, or of Dahlia Lee Talmidge's early indiscretions. He cut Pike off more sharply than he intended. "Do you think Valery Essex is guilty?" he demanded.

Pike looked irritated at being interrupted. "What I think doesn't matter. That's what I'm explaining. Valery has one chance: the justice system. If it can't save her, nothing can."

Justice, Nikolas thought without enthusiasm. He cracked his knuckles, but he kept listening. Listening and asking, and buying Pike beer. The man was a human sponge. The more he drank, the vaguer his answers became. When Pike finally lurched off into the night to stagger home, Nikolas stayed and finished his scotch to clear his head.

He had actually learned a good deal from the gaseous old booze hound, if he could only sort it out. But his head ached from too much smoke-filled air, and from a conversation that had rambled too widely for him to keep his edge on Cato Pike.

He sipped his drink and frowned at a series of framed pictures on the wall next to him. His glass stopped, midway to his lips. He could swear Thelma Bellarion stared back at him from one of the photos.

She looked young, beautiful, innocent, and was half-hidden in a group of other beautiful young girls. Still, he was sure it was she. She sat on a rose-covered parade float, a princess's crown on her head. She gave no indication she would someday become a monster of cold vengeance.

He waved the bartender to his side. "Who's the broad in the crown?" he asked, pointing at the photo. "The one on the far right?"

The bartender squinted. "Thelma Deems. I think it was

Deems. She got married so many times I lost track."

"What was the occasion?" Nikolas asked. "Or do all the women in town wear rhinestone hats every so often?"

The bartender shook his head. His name tag said Freddy.

"She was one of the Roses of Constant. That's a sort of beauty contest they used to have. Five girls got chosen to be the rose princesses, and one, she'd be queen."

"Who are the others?" Nikolas asked idly. He was still having trouble coping with a young and smiling Thelma Bellarion.

Freddy, a fair-haired man in his thirties, traced his finger across the picture. "This was a special year. Both Talmidge sisters were in the court. There's Paris, there's Amanda . . ."

Nikolas stood and moved closer to the picture, drink in hand. Paris Talmidge, a sharp-faced girl, reminded him slightly of a young Katherine Hepburn. Amanda Talmidge was shorter, rounder, softer, sweeter—and looked less intelligent, more emotional.

The bartender's finger moved to a fourth face. "Charmian Donovan," he said. Nikolas blinked again and stared harder. He hadn't recognized Charmian, but should have. She was less stringy, more curvaceous, and her wild curls were dark and tamed into a chignon. Her eyes gave her away—dramatic and staring off at something no one else seemed to see.

The man pointed at the girl at the center, standing on a dais, higher than the others. "Claire Smith Cartwright," he said. "The queen of roses."

Nikolas studied her. She was the most beautiful of the five—tall, blond, her hair falling freely to her bare shoulders. She was not smiling. She looked shy, almost frightened. There was something vaguely familiar about her. He was struck by a sudden suspicion.

"What happened to her?"

Freddy shrugged, lit a cigarette. "Got married. Died. Been dead for years."

Nikolas shot him a questioning look. "Who'd she marry?"

"A professor. Named Donovan. He's dead, too."

Nikolas sipped thoughtfully at his drink. He studied the picture of Valery's mother. Although Valery was beautiful, her resemblance to her mother was slight. She must take after her father, the combative Professor Donovan.

Nikolas gestured at the row of pictures adorning the wall. "These are all the girls, over the years?"

The bartender nodded. Nikolas moved farther down the row. He found what he was looking for. Another float, another set of girls, and in their midst, Valery. She looked young enough to break a man's heart. She was lovely. He swallowed hard.

"Why wasn't this one the queen?" he asked Freddy. He pointed at Valery. She wore the crown of a princess and stood in the background.

The bartender had moved beside Nikolas. "Because *she* was," he said laconically, and rapped his knuckles on the glass over the figure of a young woman in an elaborate white gown. "Dahlia Lee Talmidge was queen that year."

Nikolas frowned at the photograph. Dahlia Lee Talmidge was so slender she was almost cadaverous, but she held herself regally. She had a nose that was too long and a chin that was too short. Lank bangs nearly covered her eyes.

"Not much of a looker," Nikolas observed dryly.

"She improved with age," the bartender said sardonically. "Got her nose fixed. A big improvement."

"How the hell did she get to be queen?" Nikolas muttered. "She's a scarecrow."

The bartender gave him a knowing look. "Her aunt was on the committee that year. Amanda Talmidge. Amanda always thought the sun rose and set on Dahlia Lee. She saw that Dahlia Lee got everything she wanted. Almost."

"Almost?"

"Except for men. Dahlia Lee had unfortunate tastes in men. She liked ones she couldn't have."

"Like who?" Nikolas asked, scrutinizing Dahlia Lee's unfortunate nose, her hollow cheeks.

"You ask a lot of questions."

"I got a lot of curiosity." Nikolas reached into his pocket. He handed the man a folded fifty-dollar bill.

Freddy tucked it into his vest. "A guy named Charles Essex, for starters. He married one of these other girls." He tapped Valery's picture "But that's another story. Then Dahlia Lee quit school and started traveling. She decided she was in love with some guy in politics. But he was married. Then there was an English actor she met in California—this was a guy who could have any woman he wanted, and he didn't want Dahlia Lee. There was a golf pro. He had other plans. And then finally, after a lot of others, she found the Count, and he could be bought. So, the story goes, Amanda bought him for her. Until then Dahlia Lee's relationships weren't what you'd call stable."

"You mean with men," Nikolas said.

Freddy adjusted a gold cuff link. "I mean with anybody outside her family. She'd come home with some real cuckoos sometimes—men and women. Some very strange folks. Always needed somebody to take charge of things for her. But she'd pick the damnedest weirdos. There was this Austrian woman once—Never mind. But then she got the Count. Everything changed. Money's nice stuff. Does wonders."

"Yeah," Nikolas said, looking at Valery's photo again. God, she looked so young. She had no idea what life was going to throw at her. He handed the bartender another ten dollars.

So Dahlia Lee Talmidge had once been in love with Charles Essex, had she? And she was a flighty, emotional type. Maybe after the Count died, she'd come home to find a different Charles, one who realized her worth at last. Only maybe she didn't want him once she could have him. It was an interesting possibility.

Nikolas set his unfinished drink down on the nearest table. "Thanks," he muttered. He turned and headed for the door. He wanted to talk to Valery. Now. Even if he had to drag her out of bed. The thought of hauling her, warm and drowsy, from her sheets and into his arms struck him more forcefully than he wanted.

The bartender waited several minutes after Nikolas left. Then he went to his office, closed the door and dialed a local number. He lit another cigarette.

"Hello," he said when the other end answered. "This is Freddy Perry. At the bar. The Grady guy was here. Pumping old Cato Pike, then me.

"Naw, Cato couldn't tell him anything. Cato doesn't know anything.

"Me? Hell, I did what I was supposed to. I fed him a bunch of lies. Of course, I'm not going to tell him the truth. I tell you, I fed him lies. How's Dahlia Lee? Well, tell her to keep getting better. And tell her not to worry. When Grady's in my place, he'll hear exactly what you want him to hear. You can always count on me."

Freddy hung up the phone. He took a long drag on his cigarette. He didn't give a damn who was in danger. He was safe. And that's what mattered most in the world to Freddy. Himself, and nothing else.

★ ★ ★ ★ ★

Valery had just fallen asleep when knocking at the front door awoke her. Her first reaction was fear, her second irritation. Whoever was out there was making an ungodly racket. She pulled on a pink-and-white striped cotton robe and ran barefoot down the steps.

Be quiet, she thought angrily, *you're going to wake up my son.* But she was frightened, too. What if it was the police? They had beat on the door just this way the night Charles died.

What, she thought, edging close to panic, *if they found out about the letters from Chrissy? Will they arrest me again? This time, will they keep me locked up?*

She took a quick glimpse out the peephole in the front door. Her shoulders sagged with relief. But she was still exasperated. Nikolas was out there, pounding loudly enough to wake the dead.

She turned on the light in the foyer and swung the door open. She looked up at him through the screen door. He stood there, tall and shadowy in the moonlight. "What do you want?" she whispered, troubled. "Why are you beating on the door like that?" She glanced down at her watch. "It's past midnight. You'll wake Tony. You'll wake up the whole neighborhood."

"I am the whole neighborhood," he returned dryly. "I want to talk to you. Let me in."

She remembered Charmian's warnings and felt a frisson of alarm. "No," she replied. "It's too late. I told you I couldn't see you tonight. What if somebody saw you coming in at this hour?"

"We need to talk. Let me in."

"No." She reached up to make sure the screen door was hooked securely. "Go away. Please."

"Let me in, dammit, or I'll let myself in." He put one big shoulder against the screen door and pushed. "I mean it, Valery. If I want to get in there, believe me, I'll get in. And wake your kid. And probably scare the hell out of him. I don't want to, but if I have to, I will."

The screen door shuddered against his weight, and Valery watched, horrified, as the hook began to pull loose. "Stop," she ordered. "You can come in. But only for one minute." She unhooked the door, then took two steps backward.

He came inside.

"Your minute's already started," she said, taking another step backward.

He reached for her, grasping her upper arms. He bent his head so he could look into her eyes. "I said we have to talk."

His touch sent bolts of tremulous emotion through her. His eyes were stern, almost relentless, and the set of his jaw uncompromising. She smelled scotch and it terrified her.

"You've been drinking." She tried to struggle out of his grasp.

"Not enough that I can tell," he retorted. "Settle down, Valery. I'm not drunk and I'm not irrational, although I've heard a couple of irrational things tonight."

His words barely registered. She had let him in, and now she wished she hadn't. She tried to squirm away.

He suddenly realized the source of her panic and shook her slightly. "Valery," he ordered, "trust me. I'm not like Charles. I've had a few drinks, that's all. There's nothing wrong with me except I'm concerned about you. If that's a crime, I'm guilty."

She stared up at him. In the dim golden light of the foyer, the planes of his face looked hawkish, yet sincere and sober. His hands on her arms became gentle, almost caressing. His face drew a fraction of an inch nearer to hers.

"I'm going to count to five, then let you go, all right?" he breathed. "Then stand there and listen to me. I don't want to scare you. It's the last thing I want. Understand? All right. One, two . . ."

Her heart rattled in her chest as if it had somehow come loose and lost its mainspring. But his eyes and voice were so compelling, she willed herself to breathe evenly again. He didn't look like a man who'd come to do her harm. He looked like a man who would walk through fire for her if he had to.

". . . five," he said, letting his hands fall away from her. He took a step backward to give her space.

Or perhaps he took it to give himself space. Her normally fair skin was rosy with sleep, her hair tousled and shining in the dim light. The flimsy cotton robe was open, and the low-cut white nightdress beneath showed the velvety shadow of her cleavage. He allowed his eyes to linger a second too long on her full breasts.

Valery saw his gaze and gathered her robe together self-consciously. Her blood was starting to course too swiftly. She knotted the belt more tightly and tossed her hair back out of her eyes. "What do you want?" she demanded, her voice shaking. "I told you earlier I didn't want to see you tonight, but you force your way in. You almost break into my house—"

"I tried calling. I couldn't get you." His words were clipped.

"I unplug the phone. I get crank calls. And I've just spent an evening listening to my aunt lecture me about getting involved with you. I see her point. I don't like your coming here like this, Nikolas. I don't like it at all." And she didn't. He was reviving all the dangerous and forbidden feelings he had aroused that afternoon.

"Ask me to sit down. Talk to me for an hour. Half an hour. Then I'll go away. Forever if you want."

Go away forever, she thought fatefully. No, she didn't want that, not really. She looked up at him searchingly. His black curls were falling onto his forehead and he, too, breathed hard.

His white shirt made his skin seem more deeply golden, his eyes more remarkably black. The right shoulder was smudged where he had pushed it against the screen door. He seemed to always be getting his white shirts smudged, she thought. She wanted to put out her hand and rub the mark away, feel the hardness of his muscle beneath the fabric. Instead she kept her arms at her sides.

"Just talk a while," he offered, his tone husky. "Then I'll go. I'll do anything you want. Anything."

She took a deep breath. It was impossible to distrust him. She cocked her head toward the living room. "Come in."

Wordlessly he followed her. He watched the sway of her rounded hips beneath the striped cotton robe. She stood while he took a seat on the couch, then sat down herself, in the chair farthest away.

She crossed her legs primly, but not so primly that he couldn't see the fine curves of her ankles, the delicacy of her bare feet. She had truly beautiful feet. It was amazing. He couldn't remember ever noticing a woman's feet before.

"Look," he began awkwardly, "you want a drink or something? I didn't mean to alarm you."

"I don't want anything," she returned. "And you've already had your fair share for the evening."

He put up a hand as if to ward off her accusation.

"You're accused of murder, Valery. I wouldn't moralize, if I were you. But then you're your father's daughter, aren't you?"

She stiffened in her chair. She raised her chin. "What's that supposed to mean?"

He looked at her sitting so motionlessly in the old oak rocking chair. She looked so self-possessed he found it hard to believe she had been scared half to death of him a few moments before. Her natural dignity was back and it was formidable.

No wonder people might suspect her, he thought grimly. They didn't see the emotions that tumbled and roiled behind that cool facade she could erect. He took a deep breath.

"You didn't tell me you had enemies in this town. Powerful ones," he said. "You didn't tell me your father fought the Talmidge Corporation."

She raised her chin another fraction of an inch. "You broke in here to talk about that? That was years ago. It's ancient history."

"Time is relative. Some people hold grudges. They hold them a long time." He leaned back against the sofa cushions and succeeded in looking casual, even relaxed. Inside, the tensions twisted and clashed. He kept his voice calm. "Tell me what happened."

Valery shook her head. Her sleep-tousled hair swept her shoulders. That simple unconscious moment stirred him more powerfully than he'd thought possible.

"It started when I was a child, for heaven's sake," she said with an uneasy shrug. "It's been over for years—at least ten years. My father didn't do anything wrong. He stood up for his beliefs. The Talmidge Corporation was polluting. Someone had to speak out."

The only emotion he allowed to escape was cynicism. He

raised an eyebrow skeptically. "Noble. But it cost people money. Important people. A lot of money. Don't you think that could be relevant?"

"No, I don't." She linked her hands around one knee. She jiggled one bare foot rebelliously. She stared at the floor so she wouldn't have to meet Nikolas's eyes, which had a disturbing intensity. "The Talmidges never held it against my father. They recognized the matter for what it was—business, not personal. They made it a point to greet my father on the street when other people weren't even speaking to him—"

"What other people?" Nikolas demanded, his dark brow rising higher.

Valery shrugged again. "Other people. Employees. People who just didn't like my father. But as for the Talmidge sisters—or any of the company's executives—no, there was never bad blood."

Nikolas exhaled harshly in exasperation. Did she have any idea how beautiful she was in that simple robe, her shining hair all in a tumble? He forced himself to keep his mind on business. "Valery, how much did your father cost the Talmidge Corporation by the time it was all over?"

She shrugged a third time, jiggled her bare foot more nervously. "I don't know. I heard half a million dollars. I heard three quarters of a million. I don't know."

"And you think that everyone is just going to forget that? Tell me, did people lose their jobs along the way?"

She looked up briefly. His eyes drilled into hers. Uneasy, she dropped her gaze again.

"I said, did people lose jobs because of your father?"

"Yes. Some," she admitted reluctantly. She wished he wouldn't look at her that way. He made it hard to think.

"How many?" he persisted. "In high positions or low?

Were there other jobs open to them?"

"I don't know." Valery was shaken by his tenacity. "I was a child. When it started I was younger than Tony. I didn't understand what was going on—"

"That's what I'm telling you," he almost snapped. "You didn't understand. Your father made enemies, Valery. He probably made a lot of them. Powerful ones. Which may be why you're sitting there so prim and proper and calm, with a murder charge hanging over your head."

She flinched. She squared her shoulders, but still refused to meet his eyes. She felt anything but calm. But she forced herself to sound icily logical. "Are you trying to say that somebody murdered Charles—and is trying to frame me—because twenty years ago my father decided the Talmidge Corporation shouldn't pour arsenic into the rivers and the soil? I'm sorry. You're imagining things."

"I didn't imagine your husband's murder. Or the fact that you might lose your kid."

Again she flinched. She laced her fingers more tightly together around her knee. "Are you finished?" she asked, then set her mouth so that her lips wouldn't tremble.

"No, I'm not." He knew he was puzzling her and frightening her, but he had no choice. "You said your mother-in-law wants your son. How's she mixed up in this? Did she lose any money because of what your father did? Is her money tied up with Talmidge money?"

"No," Valery answered with a coolness she didn't feel. "Thelma Bellarion married money. She married it quite a few times, but it was never Talmidge money."

"In this town?" Nikolas scoffed. "How could she help it? Are you sure?" Good God, he thought, he was starting to sound like the Grand Inquisitor.

"She never married Talmidge money," Valery repeated

emphatically, determined to be as resolute as he was. "Thelma and the Talmidge sisters were friends once. They had a falling out, long ago. Charles was always proud that the Talmidges liked him in spite of his mother. Thelma has nothing to do with the Talmidge Corporation. Nothing. Now will you leave me alone? I feel like I'm back in the interrogation room at the police station."

She kept her eyes trained stonily on the fireplace, and Nikolas knew that for a bad sign. When she wouldn't look at him it was because she was afraid of crying. He rose swiftly and went to her. He knelt down on the floor next to her chair.

"Valery," he said gently. He tried to take her hand, but she refused to let him. Instead he put his hand on her thigh. His warmth seemed to burn through the thin robe. "Valery," he repeated, "I don't want to hurt you. I want to help."

His touch ran up her thigh, made both her legs tremble. The lower half of her body seemed to be going weak and fluttery. Anxious, she pushed his hand away, drawing herself up more tightly.

"Look," he said, "you never told me that Dahlia Lee Talmidge was in love with Charles once."

"That's ridiculous," she replied tautly. She wished Nikolas would move back across the room, keep his distance. "Dahlia Lee was never in love with Charles. That was a rumor. It lasted all of three months one summer. It wasn't true. Amanda may have had her eye on Charles as a good match for Dahlia Lee, but there was nothing between the two of them. Ever."

Nikolas shook his head in frustration. He looked down at the carpet because he didn't trust himself to look up at her. "Are you sure?"

"I don't know who you've been talking to," Valery continued, her voice strained, "but Dahlia Lee was *not* in love with Charles. Do you think if she were he wouldn't have reminded me of it night and day? No. He was Paris's and Amanda's fair-haired boy for a while. But then he ran off with me."

"And Dahlia Lee didn't give a damn, is that right?" He shook his head again. The bartender had sounded savvy enough. Now he wasn't so sure. Valery sounded just as certain of her version.

"Dahlia Lee," she answered emphatically, "had more important things to worry about than Charles or me. She was an heiress. She ended up marrying a Count, for heaven's sake. Are you implying she consoled herself with Charles after the Count died? That's ridiculous."

It was ridiculous, Valery told herself. Once again she wished Nikolas would move away. She wished she had never let him in.

"Maybe she wanted to prove she could have him," Nikolas offered softly. "Maybe she was jealous of you."

Valery's mouth opened slightly in surprise. She met his eyes at last, and her own were filled with disbelief. "Me? How could she possibly be jealous of me?"

"Because," Nikolas said, his hand encircling her ankle, "Because you're so mind-blowing beautiful."

She went as still as a statue at his touch. He felt the wariness coursing through her, but he kept her ankle firmly in his grip.

"How did she ever get crowned queen of roses when she was up against you?" he breathed.

She shifted uneasily, trying to ignore what his touch was doing to her. "I—I never should have been in the court, even. I wasn't popular . . . because of my father. It was

111

Amanda's doing that I was there at all. That's what I mean—she wanted to show there were no hard feelings. It was very gracious of her."

"I saw Dahlia Lee's picture," he said. "She looked like Ichabod Crane. You look at her face and all you see is that nose. And you looked almost as beautiful as you look now. How could she not have been jealous?"

"Dahlia Lee worried about how fashion models looked— not about me," she answered, her heart pounding. "I was nothing. A nobody. And nobody noticed me. I wasn't anybody to be jealous of."

"Darling," he said, caressing her instep suggestively, "you're somebody to be jealous of, believe me. But none of this adds up. Somebody's lying." He nuzzled her ankle and she shivered. It was as if he were shooting both fire and ice through her system.

"Nikolas, stop that," she said desperately. "I'm not lying. Whose side are you on?"

Good question, thought Nikolas. But he didn't answer. Instead he stood. He bent and clasped her around the waist.

"Come here," he said, drawing her up to him.

"No," she whispered, but he had her in his arms now, and her knees felt weak, incapable of holding her.

"Yes." He drew her more tightly to him. Her breasts ached against the hardness of his chest.

She looked up at him, dizzy with perplexity and with yearnings she hadn't ever wanted to feel again. He was going to kiss her. She knew it. And she knew she wanted it. His mouth descended on hers, making hot demands, his tongue darting against hers, daring it to answer.

He tangled his fingers in the silk of her hair. He ran them over the white satin curve of her throat.

She managed to draw back for one long second. "No,

Nikolas," she said, almost pleading. "I can't do this. I can't afford to."

"We can't afford not to," he said against her lips and before she could protest, he kissed her again.

It was a convincing kiss because he was a convincing man. It was his business.

But this time it was different. When his mouth met hers, something deep within him suddenly seemed to explode, either into life or out of it. He kissed her and knew that now he was either hopelessly broken or finally made whole. Whether this change would bring good or evil, he could not say. So he ignored the question, and kissed her still again.

Chapter Seven

He supposed it was bound to happen some day. He would play a part and it would swallow him up. It would consume him, and he'd end up crazed with wanting some woman he'd been supposed only to pretend to want.

Valery Essex's lips tasted like some addictive elixir to him, and she felt like warm silk and satin crushed against him. He wanted to make love to her. He wanted it badly, almost desperately.

He had her pinioned in his arms, determined to kiss her until she wanted him just as desperately. He had pushed the robe from her smooth shoulders, and when he pressed his mouth against her throat, he could feel the velvet hammer of her pulse. He kissed it, willing it to pound even harder, to keep time with his own.

Valery gasped. Nikolas was trying to bear her off to another world, another level of being. She suddenly knew how the women of the myths felt, when some Olympian swooped down upon them, intent on love. Nikolas was determined to take her beyond the ordinary bounds of the physical.

She wanted to go with him, but was afraid. There was something too powerful about him. He could overwhelm both her mind and body. She drew back in panic. "Let me go." It was as much a plea as an order.

"No." He kissed her throat again. His hands explored the smooth planes of her back, the curves of her waist.

She broke from him, knowing if she did not do so now, she would be unable to. His touch was too intoxicating. She

114

stepped away, turning her back on him. He came up behind her, one arm coiling around her waist, and kissed the nape of her neck.

"No!" She shuddered out of his embrace again. She moved to the fireplace, then turned to face him. She could not allow this to happen. Not with her trial coming up, and Tony's future and her own at stake. She had to think, be careful, stay in control.

Her cheeks were fiery, her hair a stormy cloud about her face. He took a step toward her, but something in her stance, her eyes, stopped him.

"No," she breathed again. She fumbled with her robe, drawing it around her shoulders again. She pulled it together and held it shut. She eyed him warily, but kept her head high.

He stood, muscles taut, watching her. He understood the fear in her eyes. He was disquieted himself. Nothing resembling this had ever seized him before. He could tell that she, too, was shaken.

Both of them were used to relying on their total self-possession. She brought him perilously near losing that iron restraint. That should never happen. To him, of all people.

He forced himself to relax, to smile. "Well," he said, his eyes still on hers. "Well, well, well."

She pulled the collar of her robe more tightly shut. She clasped her other hand protectively to her midsection. She felt vulnerable, threatened, too tempted for comfort or safety. "Nikolas, you'd better go," she said raggedly. "I never meant for this to happen. It mustn't."

He nodded and inhaled sharply. "Well, it's happened. It's happening." He ran the back of his hand over his mouth, as if thinking hard about a difficult problem. "So what do we do now, Valery? Call each other on the phone? Become pen pals? Send valentines? Look, but don't touch?"

She felt her cheeks grow hotter. "We don't do anything. We pretend this never happened."

"Oh." He nodded again. "We pretend. Well, let's pretend to face reality. We can't ignore this. I don't think we've got a prayer of ignoring it."

She took a deep breath. "We have to. I can't get involved with you. I'm about to be on trial for my life. I have a child to think of."

She watched him carefully. He had her if he wanted, and she knew it. He could blackmail her about the letters to Charles. He could simply say, "You want the letters kept secret? Sleep with me." He would reach for her and she would have to go to him.

He knew it, too. She could tell from his eyes. But he said nothing. He didn't speak for a long moment.

He sat on the arm of the sofa. He ran a hand through his dark hair in exasperation and sighed. He suddenly looked all forty of his years. "You're right."

He cast a derisive glance at the ceiling, as if God were mocking him. "I'm supposed to protect you. But who protects you from me?"

She turned away. He was a fair man, after all, an honest one. But they would be better going separate ways. Something was happening here that could flare out of control at any moment. "I didn't ask you to protect me. Don't think you have to."

"I volunteered."

"I'll take care of myself. I can, you know."

"Yeah. You're doing a great job. Congratulations."

She shot him a disbelieving look over her shoulder. How could he joke? But his face was as tense as her own.

"We're in big trouble, darlin'," he said.

She turned to face him again. She shook her head. "No. *I'm* in big trouble."

He smiled. His smile was wry, but weary. "If you're in trouble, we are. That's how it is. Your trouble's mine."

Heaven help me, how can I resist this man? Valery thought. She gave him a weak smile, yet felt a wave of pure hopelessness sweep over her.

"Look," he said, rising, "I think we'd better sleep on this. Alone, unfortunately. I'd kiss you good-night, but it'd be counterproductive. I'll see you tomorrow, okay?"

Valery was too shaken by her own emotions to agree. "Maybe we shouldn't see each other again." She looked away from him guiltily.

"Let's not decide that now. Good night, love."

Love, she thought fearfully. She had no right to thrill at that word on his lips. Not until her name was cleared—if it ever was. If she were ever free again. "Good night" was all she could manage to say.

He let himself out. He loped across her darkened lawn, then his own. He had the odd fleeting feeling that he was being watched. He let himself into his house.

He didn't turn on the lights. He moved to the front window and pushed the curtain aside. He stared out into the blackness but saw no one.

He turned away. He put his hand to his forehead, massaged his temples. He had made all the right moves, said all the right things. He had succeeded, he knew. Valery Essex was falling in love with him. She was his.

There was just one problem. He was hers.

He was caught in his own damned trap. If he tried to save Valery, he lost Penny Shaw. If he saved Penny Shaw, he lost Valery.

And if he somehow, against all odds, managed to save

both women, he could still never possess Valery. She would despise him when she learned the truth. For the truth was that he was still the servant of her enemy. Bought and paid for by Thelma Bellarion. He had deliberately deceived Valery, every inch of the way.

There was no good way out of this for him. None at all. He swore and threw himself down on the couch. He stared at the ceiling a long time. Valery was innocent. He knew it. He supposed he'd known it from the first. And where did that leave him? Damned, that's where. Plain and simply damned.

Outside, a darkly dressed figure watched the two houses for a long time. Thick woods still stood at this end of town. They provided excellent cover.

Nikolas's lights were the last to flick off.

Good night, Nikolas, thought the watcher. *Sleep well and deeply. And Valery Essex, too. And may you both have sweet dreams in this, your last earthly sleep. Your next sleep lasts forever.*

Valery dreamed that the letters from Chrissy multiplied. Every time she looked, there were more. Soon they spilled from the folder. Then they overflowed the desk itself, mounting until they threatened to take over the living room. There was no way to hide them. There were too many.

That dream faded into nothingness. She tossed uneasily. The curtains bloomed in the night breeze and she inhaled the scent of dying roses. After an indeterminate period, the same dream came again. This time, it was worse. She was caught in the letters up to her chest, as if in quicksand, and more kept raining down on her. She couldn't see Tony. She couldn't breathe, but she tried to scream his name. Nothing would come out.

She sat up with a start. She hugged herself to protect herself from the image of the letters crushing her and Tony. She looked around her room. The curtains billowed. Light was beginning to break. It was dawn.

She got out of bed and padded, barefoot, to Tony's room. It was ridiculous, she knew, but she had to reassure herself that he was there in his own bed, in his own house.

She gazed for a long moment at his motionless form. Then she turned and went downstairs to the kitchen to make coffee. Sleep would not come again, nor did she desire it. It brought dreams that disturbed too deeply.

She stood, sipping coffee and looking through the dawn's hazy air at Nikolas Grady's house.

A light in his house went on, and her heart took an irrational jump. He couldn't sleep, either. Perhaps she had been in his thoughts.

No. She couldn't indulge fantasies. She had a fight on her hands, more desperate than any her father had ever fought. It demanded all her energy, all her attention. She went to the desk, took out her folder and the list of people saying things against her. She sat down at the kitchen table with a fresh cup of coffee. She knew it was possible that someone on the list had killed Charles. It was probably that same person who wanted her out of the way, as well.

But who? And why?

She knew of no one who truly hated her except Thelma Bellarion. But Thelma had loved Charles. She might have loved him in all the wrong ways—coldly, possessively and in anger—but she never would have killed him.

The one straw at which Valery might grasp was that Chrissy was fictional, that the letters had been planted.

If that was true, her only chance to pierce the mystery was to find who had actually written the Chrissy letters.

She took the letters from the folder and studied them again for a clue, any clue.

None revealed itself. A knock at the back door interrupted her futile thoughts. Tightening the belt of her robe, she rose. She opened the door to find Nikolas standing there.

He looked tired, as if he had slept less than she. But he was clean shaven, and his hair shone with water from the shower. His smile, as always both kindly and satiric, was in place.

He held out an empty cup, as if for alms. "Coffee?" he said piteously. "Coffee for a poor, middle-aged man?"

She tried to keep from smiling, but could not. She let him inside. He paused and wound one arm protectively around her waist. He kissed her, gently but sensually, on the corner of the mouth.

He glanced significantly at the papers spread on the kitchen table. "Working already?"

She nodded, her eyes shining up at him in spite of all her troubles. At least she was not working alone. Nikolas would try to keep her from prison and her son from Thelma Bellarion's grasp.

He squeezed her. His touch seemed to infuse her with new strength. "Then fill up my cup so I can help. Let's get you out of this mess, baby. So we can get on with our lives."

During the long night, Nikolas had reached a grimly determined conclusion. He would get it all, by God. He would clear Valery. He would find Penny Shaw. Perhaps he would even find Fields and the missing millions.

He would figure out a way to explain his connection to Thelma Bellarion so Valery could understand and forgive it. Then he and Valery and Tony would all live happily ever after. He had no choice but to make it happen. Otherwise, they were all going to hell, and he was the Pied Piper leading them there.

Yes, by God, he'd have it all. Or die trying.

Across town, in the Talmidge mansion, John Upchurch stood in a square of sunshine falling through the big window of the exercise room. His white hair gleamed in the morning light.

Dahlia Lee Talmidge worked laboriously on a rowing machine. Her hair was freshly tinted a delicate red. She was so lean that her collarbone threw shadows. But still she kept obsessively working on the rowing machine.

"Stop," John Upchurch said. "You're going to hurt yourself."

Dahlia Lee kept rowing. "I'm too heavy," she said, almost gasping for breath. "This is the only exercise I get." Her upper arms, though thin, were ropy with muscle. She had eaten nothing for breakfast. But Penny Shaw, the pig, had appeared later and gobbled up a whole plate of bacon, eggs, grits and biscuits. It was disgusting. Dahlia Lee had come to hate having Penny around. The lovesick fool was nothing but trouble.

"Dahlia Lee," Upchurch said impatiently, "stop. We need to talk. Penny got out somehow last night, didn't she?"

Dahlia Lee didn't answer. She rowed harder. Sweat began to darken her designer leotards.

"Dahlia Lee!" Upchurch's voice was urgent and angry.

Dahlia Lee stopped rowing. She looked up at him through her damp reddish bangs. Although her face was thin, her jaw gave it unexpected strength. "Don't ask me," she said tightly. "I'm not in charge of her. If I had my way she wouldn't be here at all." She put her hand to her chest. "Oh, my," she muttered. "My heart—it's beating so fast it's choking me."

"Was she out or wasn't she?" Upchurch demanded. Dahlia Lee was a hypochondriac. All her life she had used poor health as an excuse to escape responsibility. "Answer me, or I'll take the matter up with your aunts. They're due to arrive within the hour."

Dahlia Lee shrugged. She stood up. She usually behaved much better when her aunts, especially her Aunt Paris, were about. She was an extraordinarily immature woman for her age, passive and needing someone to dominate her. Upchurch, she had learned long ago, was not strong enough to do it. She liked teasing him.

"All right," she admitted blithely. "Penny got out. She wanted to see him. That Grady man. Why, I don't know. If a man had treated me like that—"

Upchurch swore. "He didn't see her? Tell me, please, that he didn't see her." He dreaded the Talmidge sisters' learning of this gaffe committed in their absence. Especially Paris. Her wrath, feeble as she was, was still formidable. He needed to talk to Terry Perry. Yes, that was it, he'd talk to Perry. Perry always managed to remain cool.

"He didn't see her," Dahlia Lee said, moving to the ballet bar. "Nobody saw her. She went through the woods. I wouldn't go through the woods. Chiggers and ticks—ugh."

She stretched out her leg, raised one arm above her head. She touched her head gingerly to her knee. Her lean muscles rippled. "I think I'm actually a little better."

Upchurch moved to her side. He was a tall man, still handsome, but Dahlia Lee was almost as tall. "She mustn't get out anymore," he said firmly. "For any reason. I thought that was clear."

"Umm," Dahlia Lee replied vaguely. "It's asking a lot of poor Penny—just to sit around while that man's in town, practically licking Valery Essex's face. Who knows what

Penny might do if that keeps up? I, personally, don't want any more trouble. Neither do my aunts. But then, I'm not in charge here, as you well know, any more than you are."

She smiled at him, her gaunt face trying to be girlish under its crop of curls.

He knew. He felt sick inside, sick unto death. Dahlia Lee was right. She was not in charge. And he hated and feared the woman who was.

The woman had appeared right after the accident that had shaken the whole household to its foundations.

She had come among them once before, years before, nearly bringing disaster then. Penny Shaw, of all people, had saved them. Now Penny was next to useless. Circumstances had once more given this woman control over all of them. If she had her way, Nikolas Grady and Valery Essex would be dead tonight.

"Take it easy," Nikolas said. "We're not working against any deadline. We've got lots of time."

Valery sighed in frustration. They had driven Tony to Willadene's. Willadene had invited Tony to stay the afternoon and then sleep over with her nephews. Valery said he could spend the day, but not the night. She wasn't used to having Tony gone. She would miss him too much.

She and Nikolas returned to the house. They had spent most of the morning sifting through all the old information again and again.

Valery told him her theory that Chrissy was fiction, her letters part of a frame whose source she couldn't fathom.

Nikolas agreed the letters were so suspicious they stank. They had appeared too suddenly, and their contents were too conveniently damning. He planned to go back to MacGregor as soon as possible to question the postmistress about the person who'd rented the box. If not today, tomorrow or the next.

To Valery's list of people saying untrue things, he added the name of the bartender, Freddy Perry. He didn't like the discrepancy between Freddy's version of events and Valery's. Valery said Dahlia Lee had never loved Charles, and she said as far as she knew, rumors of Dahlia Lee's later romantic indiscretions were just that—rumors. She had never believed them. The only thing she could confirm was that Dahlia Lee had taken up with strange people from time to time. As for the rest, it was only talk.

Nikolas didn't like it. Maybe the bartender just passed on cheap gossip. But if he'd lied, why?

Besides that, it added another person named Perry to the scenario. He enumerated them: Freddy, Osgood, Terry. Plus, half the people on Valery's list were somehow related to the Perrys according to Charmian's slapdash notation. There were just too damn many Perrys in the picture for coincidence.

Valery was trying to remember and chart the complex relations among the various Perrys when she gave up in despair. She put her elbow on the table and covered her eyes with her hand.

That's when Nikolas had tried to comfort her by telling her they had plenty of time.

"Two months until the trial," she muttered, shaking her head. "I've been staring at all this for six weeks and gotten nowhere. Nikolas, I think all these Perrys are related, but I don't know."

He watched her, concerned. But he couldn't tell her to take it easy. She had to push on. They both did. "And the Perrys are related to the Talmidges?"

She shook her head, her eyes still covered. "Yes, but way back. Something like four or five generations. But even I'm related to Talmidges that far back. So's Tony."

She heard the rustle of mail falling through the slot in the door. The postman was late today. She rose and went to gather up the spill of letters and cards.

She picked them up, then paused. There, on top, was another threatening card from the library. If she did not return the overdue book of poetry immediately, the matter would be put in the hands of the police. Action would be taken. No quarter would be given.

Ha, thought Valery bitterly. They'd come to put her away for murder and she could say, "Too late, I'm already serving time—for an overdue book."

She went back to the table; shuffling through the unpleasant number of envelopes containing bills. Suddenly her back stiffened. A chill sped through her bones.

Still standing, she dropped the rest of the mail on the table and kept one envelope. It looked eerily familiar. It was a twin to the one that had arrived before, demanding rent for Charles's post-office box. Except this was from a different town.

"Nikolas," she breathed, suddenly frightened, "there's another one." She didn't seem able to move.

Nikolas shoved back his chair and came to her. His muscular arm brushed hers, and she, still cold, was grateful for the warmth of his nearness. He took the envelope and opened it carefully.

It was a notice that rent was due on a post-office box reserved for Charles Lonnie Essex in Corday, Arkansas.

"Where's Corday?" he asked between his teeth.

"About a half an hour away." The sensation of cold wouldn't leave. She started to tremble.

"Hey," he said, concerned. He put his hands on her upper arms. He looked down into her eyes. "Hey, it's all right. I'm not going to let anything happen to you. Understand?"

"What if it's more of those horrible letters?" she asked, alarmed. She was not sure she could face more. She remembered her dream about the letters multiplying, becoming so many that she couldn't hide them, and finally she and Tony were buried alive beneath them.

"What if it's not?" he demanded, drawing her closer to his sheltering height. "What if it's something completely different?"

"What if it's something worse?" she questioned. Perhaps Charles had post-office boxes all over the state, each full of evidence that made her look more guilty.

"Let's see what it is before we worry," he said, running his hands up and down her arms. His tone was comforting.

In his own mind, however, he was deeply disturbed. He was certain that the second box would contain exactly what the first had: letters designed to put Valery in prison for the rest of her life.

He was wrong. The box in the drowsy little town of Corday contained more junk mail and one letter, written in an obviously masculine hand.

This time Nikolas was less hurried, more careful. He quizzed the aging postmaster of Corday. Yes, the old man remembered Charles clearly. Came in to rent the box slightly over two months ago. A big fellow, the postmaster said, but not as big as Nikolas—stockier. Blondish fellow. Had some sort of silver airplane pin on his leather jacket.

Nikolas thanked him and thought this might be a different breed of cat. He took the mail back outside and handed it through the window of the car to Valery. He got in beside her.

For the second time that morning, Valery looked stricken as she stared at an envelope. She felt as if she'd had the wind knocked from her. "This is Charles's writing," she said, her eyes meeting Nikolas's. "For some reason, he sent a letter to himself."

"Let's get out of here. Open it while we're on the road. I've a funny feeling."

"What do you mean?" she asked, alarmed.

"I don't know," he said, the car screeching away from the curb. "I had it last night, too. As if someone was watching."

"Watching?" Valery demanded, even more alarmed.

"It's just a feeling. That's all."

In a moment, the town limits of Corday lay behind them. As the Lynx sped down the highway, Valery opened the letter, her fingers trembling.

Nikolas glanced in the rearview mirror. Far behind them a white Chevrolet pickup lumbered. He swore to himself. He was almost certain such a truck had been behind them on the way into Corday. Foolishly he'd paid no attention. His mind had been focused on reassuring Valery. On the other hand, every other vehicle in Arkansas seemed to be a white Chevrolet pickup. Perhaps it meant nothing. He vowed to pay closer attention.

"What is it?" he asked. Valery had opened the envelope.

Her heart began a runaway racketing rhythm. "Nikolas," she said, feeling slightly faint, "the book. The library book."

Blood seemed to be trying to rush to her head or from it, she couldn't be sure. Her brain reeled, slightly numbed. In her hand she held the library-card pocket torn from the inside of a book. It was stamped Constant Public Library and typed neatly beneath was the book's title, *Best-Loved Poems of the English and American People.*

This was the book that the library kept insisting Tony

had checked out and that Tony swore he had not. Charles must have checked it out on Tony's card, she thought, things beginning to fall into place at long last. In Constant's small library, one member of a family could charge a book on another's card. It was done all the time.

Charles had checked out this book, never returned it, torn out its card pocket and mailed it to himself. Why?

Her eyes met Nikolas's black gaze.

"Nikolas, what do you think this means?"

She held the card out to him. He took it. He examined it. Then he kissed it.

"I think," he said, "it means you finally got lucky, baby." He handed it back to her.

Lucky, she thought in wonder. Was he right? Was there at last, after all this time, a break in the darkness, some hint of an answer?

Where was the book? And what did it contain that was important enough for Charles to reach back like this, from the grave itself?

Nikolas glanced in the rearview mirror. He had turned off the main highway, taken a side road. Far behind, the white pickup appeared again, nearly obscured by a cloud of dust.

They were being followed.

Chapter Eight

When Nikolas reached the outskirts of Constant, the white pickup disappeared down a dirt side road. He said nothing about it to Valery. She had, he figured grimly, enough to worry about.

But his instincts, always sharp, nagged him again when they pulled up in her driveway. Her house was so damned isolated, he thought. His, too. Both stood at the farthest reach of a dead-end street, with woods behind and, across the street, a stretch of the pine forest that edged the town. He should buy her a dog, he thought. A damned big one, a Doberman or German shepherd.

"Where could he have put that book?" Valery fretted, getting out of the car. "What if the police have it?"

He put his arm around her protectively. "If the police had it, they'd notify the library. You wouldn't be getting notices."

"I guess." She shook her head in confusion. She was glad for the reassuring strength of his arm around her shoulders.

"Hey," he said, giving her a comforting squeeze as they ascended the porch stairs. "Don't worry. I'm here. Together we'll find the answer."

She fumbled in her purse for her keys. There was hope, she thought. She was no longer alone. Things actually had started happening since Nikolas appeared on the scene.

As she thrust the key into the lock, the door swung open. It was already unlocked.

Nikolas's grip on her shoulder automatically tightened.

Anxiety clenched her stomach like a cold fist.

"This was locked," she said. "I know it." She distinctly remembered double-checking before she left. She stepped back, closing the screen door again.

"Stand back," Nikolas ordered, thrusting her toward the stairs. He pressed his car keys into her hand. "Here. Get in the driver's seat. Be ready to take off."

The oak door had creaked halfway open. Nikolas snatched the screen door open again and kicked the wooden door open the rest of the way. It crashed loudly against the foyer wall.

He had no gun with him, but hoped he was making enough noise to scare off anyone who happened to be inside, preferably through the back door.

He stepped inside, every nerve alert. Valery, unable to move, watched him. He looked invincible enough, but who knew what might be inside? He disappeared around the corner of the foyer. She heard the rough intake of his breath, then his swearing.

She edged backward, trying to follow his orders to go to the car. But she couldn't. She waited, her heart beating erratically, for him to reappear. No sound came from within the house. From her vantage point, she could see nothing except the entryway.

Again she tried to move, to obey Nikolas. Paralyzed, she stayed where she was. She felt as if she were caught between two magnetic forces of equal power. The frightened urge to flee made her knees prickle. At the same time she could not move away, because Nikolas might need her.

No sound came from within. "Nikolas?" she called tentatively. There was no answer. A redbird cried out from a sweet gum tree. Somewhere in the far distance, a dog barked.

"Nikolas?" She began to think she could hear her heart beating. Thud, she distinctly heard it say. Thud, thud, thud. At last, she took a step toward the door. A porch board creaked beneath her hesitant foot.

A shape loomed in the foyer. She gasped. Nikolas had suddenly reappeared. No sound had announced him. He was simply there, silent, his expression foreboding.

"Oh," she uttered, her heart ricocheting into her throat.

He opened the screen door. His face was grim. "Come in. I warn you—it isn't nice."

She stepped inside. Again he wrapped a comforting arm around her. "What—" she began, but cut herself short. The living room was in shambles. She gazed at it with incomprehension.

"Somebody decided to get ugly. They succeeded. Don't shake, Valery. They're gone."

She barely heard him. The television set was lying on its side, the screen kicked in. Her father's oak rocker was overturned, several rungs splintered. The picture that had hung above the mantel, an antique print that had been in the family for years, had been smashed against the wall over the sofa. The frame was twisted, the print itself ripped in two. Glass littered the sofa cushions and twinkled brightly.

In the dining room, the china cabinet had been tipped over, its glass doors kicked in. Valery's mother's best dishes lay in ruin, shattered on the carpet. The curtains in that room had been hauled down, the rods twisted.

In the corner, stood her father's desk, most of its drawers pulled out. The contents were strewn about the room, mingled with the broken china.

Numbly Valery slipped out of Nikolas's embracing arm and knelt. The folder in which she'd put the copies of Charles's flight logs had been hurled beneath the table, its papers spilling out. She opened the folder, riffling through it. Nothing was missing.

"Is it all there? The letters, too?"

She nodded. Clutching the folder to her chest, she stepped to the desk. Only one drawer remained shut, the one with the lock. Its key still lay on the blotter. She picked it up and opened the drawer. The four five-hundred-dollar bills still lay inside, crisp and green.

"They didn't take anything," she murmured, still stunned. "That's something." Carefully she locked the drawer again. She put the key back on the blotter, as if glad one thing still had its rightful place.

"They didn't take anything. That's worse, Valery." Nikolas stood behind her. He grasped her by the shoulders. She half turned, staring up at him. His face was dark, brooding.

"This wasn't robbery," he said. "This is something else. Come on. Stay calm. I'm going to show you something. In the kitchen."

She stiffened, clutching the folder to her more tightly. "Oh, no. Not the kitchen, too."

"Not much. But enough. Come on." His touch was gentle but inexorable. He turned her around, then led her into the kitchen. Broken china crunched beneath their shoes.

On the kitchen tiles, an empty catsup bottle lay broken. Down one white wall, written in dripping red, as if in blood, was a message:

YOU'RE GOING TO BURN

An obscene word was scrawled beneath. She gasped. Tears bit her eyes. Nikolas took her in his arms. "That's all, love," he said. "That's the worst of it."

His hand on the back of her neck, he pressed her face

against his shirt so that she wouldn't have to look at the scrawled scarlet words. "They didn't touch anything else," he said soothingly.

Valery wound her arms around the hard column of his waist. She needed his strength, his dependability. She willed herself not to cry. "Tony can't see this," she said between her teeth.

"He won't. Call up Willadene. Tell her he can spend the night, after all. We can get most of this cleaned up."

He held her close, one hand buried in the dark silken waves of her hair. But he eyed the words on the wall apprehensively. He thought again of the white pickup that had followed them to Corday and back.

"In fact," he said, trying to sound casual, "maybe you should get Tony out of town for a while. Is there anywhere you could send him?"

She drew back, staring up at him. Fear warred with puzzlement in her eyes. "No, nowhere. Except—" she paused, feeling suddenly short of breath "—except there's a camp in the next county. Maybe I could send him there. . . ."

"Then do it. Make arrangements." He made her lay her face against his chest again. He stroked her hair.

"I can't believe it," she muttered, her eyes closed. She bit her lip. Whoever had done this had an unerring instinct for destroying what she loved most: her father's chair, her mother's china, the framed print she could remember from earliest childhood. And, of course, the television, which would hurt Tony and therefore hurt Valery.

"We're not even safe anymore," she said against Nikolas's chest. "First the car. The tires and the windshield. Now this—in broad daylight. My child's no longer safe in his own home. I can't believe it."

He pulled her closer still and kissed the top of her head.

"Shh. Get hold of yourself. Then call Willadene. We'll get through this together."

She felt the steady beat of his heart beneath her cheek. He was tall and warm, his chest hard as a protecting wall. "Thank heaven for you."

He said nothing. He stared at the crudely lettered words in dripping red. All his instincts were on full alert again. Something was not merely wrong. It was extremely wrong.

This incident wasn't an acceleration of violence against her. It was its first real appearance. But she didn't know that and he couldn't tell her. He himself had cut her tires, smashed her windshield. He had engineered her terror so that she would end up in his arms, seeking shelter.

Now she was there, and he wasn't sure that he could defend her. They had been followed to Corday and back. Her house had been trashed in the relatively short time they'd been gone. Somebody knew their movements.

And somebody had been crazy enough—or confident enough—to walk into the house in the middle of the day. Somebody who hadn't bothered to take money or even look for it. Somebody who had let himself into the house as expertly as a professional. Professional—like the police themselves. Was she right to fear the police as deeply as she did?

The vandalism seemed to have only one purpose: to scare the living daylights out of her.

Why?

He didn't trust the police anymore, and he didn't trust all these lawyers; too many of them were Perrys. He hadn't liked the looks of the Talmidge company lawyer, the fiery-haired Terry Perry. He hadn't liked the lordly way he'd sat in the Rose Café at Amanda Talmidge's elbow, as if he were adviser to the crown. He hadn't liked the way the guy had kept watching them, either.

Valery shuddered again. He kissed the top of her head again, trying to comfort her. He was going to start carrying his gun.

He identified himself when the phone rang, but the woman on the other end didn't. Her voice sounded querulous with nerves. "I want to speak to Dahlia Lee."

"She isn't in. We don't know when to expect her." The man's usually hearty voice quavered slightly with fatigue and apprehension.

He closed his eyes and sighed, massaging the bridge of his nose. Paris and Amanda had returned from Nantucket wearier than when they'd left. Nantucket hadn't been soothing, after all. Cold rain had poured down in buckets, both had gotten seasick on the returning ferry, and neither Paris nor Amanda seemed fit enough to cope with the mounting chaos that filled the house. Who did?

He wondered bleakly how much strength Paris had left. For years he had depended on Paris's indomitability. Everyone had. Now that she was weakening, what would become of them? He had to stand in her place. He was fighting as hard as he could, but he suddenly feared that he, too, was too weak. The woman upstairs, the one who wanted to kill Grady and Valery Essex, was like a vampire, draining everyone's strength as she herself grew stronger.

The voice on the other end of the phone brought him back to himself with a jolt. "This is Willadene Davis."

His eyes snapped open. Adrenaline flooded his fatigued system.

"Yes?"

"Dahlia Lee told me to keep the boy as much as possible this week. I wanted her to know I have him for the night."

The man was silent a moment, his mind plunging sickly.

Willadene couldn't know, but it wasn't Dahlia Lee she had talked to. She had talked to the vampire, the woman determined to kill. The other woman found it child's play to imitate Dahlia Lee's reedy voice. It was a simple voice to imitate: breathy and childish with an exaggerated Southern accent.

If the woman was zeroing in, keeping track of Tony Essex's whereabouts, she was truly determined to impose her will, to speed events up to an insane velocity.

"Thank you, Willadene," he said tightly. "I appreciate the information. I'll relay it to Dahlia Lee. There's no need for you to contact us again. I'll be in touch with you if we need to communicate."

Tension and confusion marked Willadene's voice. "Well, she *asked* me. I don't even know why. She says I'm in danger. That everything is. What's going on? I'd like some answers."

He itched to get rid of her, ached to get rid of her. She needed to know nothing more. "That's all, Willadene. Don't call again."

"But," Willadene protested nervously, "Dahlia Lee said it's an emergency, that I could be in danger, that I had to help her—"

"Willadene," the man rapped, "do as I say. Hang up. If we want to communicate with you, we'll call. Understand?"

"No. I don't." Anger had crept into Willadene's tone. "I'm frightened. She said she would be sending someone. . . ."

The man paled. He knew who that someone was. "Thank you for calling. Goodbye." He hung up the phone. His hand was sweating, and he wiped it nervously on his expensively clad thigh.

Good Lord, he thought in panic, what was she doing,

that vampire, getting Willadene caught up in all this more intricately, more dangerously than they'd planned? The witch really was pushing it, wanting to kill Grady and Valery Essex now, not waiting until it could be done safely. Didn't she realize she was endangering Dahlia Lee, endangering all of them?

He went to the bar, opened the cabinet and poured himself a stiff shot of brandy. He had been trapped in this nightmare for months. For a time, everything seemed so hellish he had truly convinced himself that murder was the only way out. But a carefully planned murder, murder that would stop the torment that held them all prisoner, not increase it.

He drained the brandy from his glass, then stood for a moment trembling beside the bar. He was certain of two things. One was that he had to slow the woman down somehow, stall her. The other was that she must not know that Willadene Davis had little Tony Essex. The knowledge would surely galvanize her to move even more swiftly, more recklessly.

But upstairs, the woman already knew about Tony Essex. She sat on her bed, smiling at the extension phone. She had replaced the receiver carefully, so that the man didn't know she had lifted it. She had heard everything.

She rose and looked in the mirror. Her confident expression was startlingly reminiscent of Paris Talmidge when Paris had been young and strong. An ironic coincidence, for physically she didn't resemble Paris in the least.

She smiled with still-greater satisfaction. Paris had never liked her, back when Dahlia Lee had brought her home so many years ago. But it didn't matter. Paris was no longer the strong one. She was.

"Everything's fine," Nikolas assured Valery. "Tony's safe

at Willadene's. Tomorrow I'll drive him to camp. He never has to see this mess."

He had found a can of paint in the garage, and after scrubbing the words from the kitchen wall, he was covering the remaining smear with a fresh coat of white.

Valery shook her head hopelessly. They had cleaned up most of the damage more easily than she had thought they could. The television was old, and she would somehow find the money to replace it.

She thought the chair could be repaired, although the picture was ruined forever. Her mother's china was almost a total loss and could never be replaced. Yet what bothered Valery most deeply was a sense of having been violated, invaded and despoiled.

And, although she knew it was for the best, she dreaded sending Tony away. With the trial only two months off, she wanted to savor every moment with him. The thought of losing him, truly losing him, to Thelma Bellarion pierced through her as painfully as a sword.

Nikolas saw the worry on her face. He thrust the old paintbrush into a jar of turpentine. He came to her, took her in his arms. "Hey," he said. "Maybe things are breaking at last. This incident may give us a lead. We may not see it today, but maybe tomorrow or the day after. Wasn't there another valiant Southern lady who always said, 'Tomorrow is another day'?"

She slid one arm around his waist. She looked up fondly into his face. He had a fleck of white paint on his upper lip. She raised her forefinger and wiped it away. He captured her hand and held it. "Say it," he ordered, his dark eyes drinking her in. "Say, 'Tomorrow is another day.' "

She smiled wanly, shook her head. "Nikolas, sometimes I feel tomorrow may not come. Sometimes I feel like my whole life's become a nightmare in the head of a maniac. Nothing makes sense and nothing's predictable. I might suddenly just disappear—not even exist anymore."

He put his hands on either side of her face. He had never seen her so dejected. Valery was strong and her purpose seldom wavered. To see her so shaken made something shrivel up within him. "The only way you'll disappear is over my dead body."

She shuddered slightly. "Don't say that."

"All right," he murmured, lowering his face to hers. "I won't say anything. Actions speak louder."

His lips met hers and his hands moved to her shoulders, then slid down to her waist and pulled her body closer, so it met more intimately with his.

Valery closed her eyes and gratefully gave herself up to the drugging warmth of his kiss. Beneath her fingers the muscles of his back moved in subtle and intricate play. Her mouth fit against his as if she had been created for him. She felt as if she were awakening after a long and uneasy sleep, that Nikolas was bringing her back to life, tingling and heated.

The phone shrilled and they both started slightly. She stepped back from him, embarrassed at how quickly and naturally she had given herself to his embrace.

Nikolas frowned and raked a hand through his dark hair. "There's a special hot spot in hell for Alexander Graham Bell. I know it." In truth, he was half-grateful for the interruption. He had been in danger of losing control again, and he should be thinking. Thinking hard.

Valery answered the phone, turning toward the window so that Nikolas wouldn't see her flushed face. "Yes?"

"Valery? This is Osgood Perry. Your attorney. Remember me?"

Osgood sounded more priggish and irritable than usual. "Of course, Osgood," she said. She cast Nikolas a significant look.

"I wondered," he said acidly. "I hear you're busy carrying on with some man who just moved to town. Spending every waking minute with him—when he isn't off drinking. Well, if you've got time, perhaps you'd be interested in hearing of a new development in your case."

She felt the color drain from her face. From Osgood's tone, she knew his news wasn't good. "Spare me the sermon," she said. "What's happening?" Her throat tightened in apprehension.

"Well," Osgood sniped, "Sheridan Milhouse was cleaning out some old lockers this morning. At the hangar at the Talmidge Corporation. Lockers he didn't think anyone used. But somebody had. Charles."

The anxiety closed tighter around her throat, threatening to cut off her breath. "Charles? Explain, Osgood."

"Charles was using a locker to hide letters. Love letters. Almost a dozen of them. You told me he didn't have another woman. Valery, you had to know. The letters prove you did know. Why did you lie to me?"

"I didn't lie to you," she said, feeling both hot and cold all over. Nikolas, reading the alarm on her face, moved behind her and put his hands on her shoulders. He massaged the back of her neck.

"I don't know who this woman is," Osgood said pettishly, "but she certainly writes an incriminating letter. Incriminating for you. Are you trying to tell me that you didn't know there was another woman? In New Jersey?"

Valery found it difficult to speak. "No. No." She hadn't known, not until yesterday, and she still didn't believe it. She fought to think clearly. She didn't want Osgood to know about the letters in her possession. Not yet. It would look too incriminating. "What's her name? Who is she? Where is she?"

"I told you, New Jersey. There were no envelopes, so no postmarks, but she mentioned Newark more than once. The only name she gives is Chrissy. I'm going to challenge the admissibility of these things as evidence, but if the prosecution finds out her real name, miss, your goose is cooked. According to these letters, you knew about her, you knew about the whole affair, and you threatened Charles. Valery, I don't take it kindly when my clients lie to me. What else haven't you told me?"

"Nothing," she answered, then bit the inside of her cheek. Osgood had convicted her already. She didn't dare tell him about the post-office box and the two other letters and the money. "Osgood, how do you know those letters weren't planted? How can you be sure they're genuine? That somebody didn't fake them?"

"I'd like to know if *you're* genuine," Osgood said acidly. "Perhaps when you decide to tell the truth—and you've had enough fun with your new lover boy—you'll condescend to talk this over honestly. You'd better think about pleading guilty and hoping for a lighter sentence. That's all *I* have to say. Good day."

He hung up. Numbly she set the receiver back in its cradle.

"What is it?" Nikolas asked, turning her so that she faced him.

She told him, her face bloodless and her voice uneven. "Nikolas, I'm frightened," she said when she had finished. "If my own attorney reacts to those letters this way, what will a court do?"

He, too, was frightened for her. Some sort of net seemed

to be closing around her. He gripped her firmly by her upper arms, then bent his head so that his black eyes were level with her hazel ones. "Tell me again, everything he said. Every word."

Haltingly she did so. "The worst thing is that I did lie to him," she admitted unhappily. "I did know about the letters. And about more—the money. You were right, Nikolas. I should have given them to somebody. To Osgood or even the police."

His grasp tightened, biting into her flesh. "Valery, listen to me. Something's wrong here. Somebody's not only trying to frame you, they're trying to scare you—as badly as possible."

"If they're trying to scare me," she said, lifting her chin, "they're doing a wonderful job. I've withheld evidence. Now still more evidence turns up and it points straight at me. In the meantime, somebody's walked in my front door and wrecked my house. I have to send my son away from home for his own safety. What sane person wouldn't want to run?"

"Any sane person," he said intently. "That's what they're counting on."

"Who?" she demanded. "Who's counting on it? If somebody's writing these letters and planting them, who? And why? And why did they wreck my house?"

"I don't know," he returned, his mouth crooking angrily. "I've got some questions of my own. Why, after all this time, do all these letters suddenly show up? How does somebody know that you left your house in the middle of the day, and how do they get in?"

"I don't know," she muttered in frustration. "I just don't know." She tried to pull away from him because he was hurting her.

"They trashed the house, but they didn't hurt the letters," he continued, his jaw set. "They left the money—they almost made a point of leaving the money—and the money could incriminate you. It could also allow you to run. They kicked in your TV and smashed your china, but they didn't touch your phone—almost as if they wanted to make sure you heard from Osgood today. So you'd know you were in deeper trouble than ever."

She went suddenly still. "What are you saying?"

His lip twisted even further in disgust. "I'm saying that I think somebody's trying to make you run, Valery. Somebody wants you to bolt."

She stared up at him numbly. "Because if I run, then everyone will think I'm guilty. I'll go to prison. And Thelma Bellarion will take Tony."

"Right," he agreed grimly. "So whatever you do, you don't panic. And I've got another question or two. How did Osgood Perry know you've been spending so much time with me? Except when I was 'drinking'—when I went to that bar last night. How did he know that?"

She shrugged. "It's a small town. People gossip."

"They can't gossip about what they can't see," Nikolas argued. "People saw us together yesterday morning in the Rose Café. But we're isolated out here. Nobody could have seen us last night—or this morning, or now—unless we're being watched. And I think we are. We were followed this morning to Corday."

Valery's lips parted in disbelief. "Watched? Followed? Nikolas, what—"

"Valery, at first I thought someone was trying to frame you. Now I think it's more than one person. It could involve the police. Whoever came in that front door this morning knew how to get past a lock. And wasn't afraid to do it in broad daylight. And could keep track of where you were. That sounds like police to me."

"The police? But that's impossible," she protested, overwhelmed by the enormity of it.

"Think. There're also a lot of Perrys who keep turning up in this. Terry, Osgood, Freddy. The two Milhouses. Half the Perry family are lawyers. Lawyers and the police work together—not always, but sometimes. Is there any other connection between the Perrys and the cops? Think hard."

Her mouth was dry. She licked her lips. She tried hard to remember every thread of family relationship, the sort of knowledge that Charmian had mastered so completely. "I think," she said falteringly at last, "that Cameron Carter, the chief of detectives, is a Perry. That maybe he and Terry are some kind of cousins. I think."

"And the chief of police," Nikolas insisted. "What about him?"

She shrugged in exasperation. "I don't know. Charmian says he's related to the Talmidges some way, so he could be related to the Perrys, too."

"I want you to ask her," he said. "Now listen. I'm going to my house to get a few things. I'm not leaving you alone anymore. They've tried to scare you out of here once, and they may try again. They'll have to contend with me next time."

"Nikolas, no." She put her hand on his chest to stop him. "You can't. If we're being watched, people will know you're here. I can't afford it. My reputation . . . I have to think of Tony."

"Dammit," he returned. "I'll sleep on the porch. I'll sleep on the rocks in the garden. Move your aunt in as a chaperone. I don't care. But I'm not leaving you alone, Valery."

Self-consciously she looked at her hand resting on his chest. "Determined to serve and protect," she said softly. "Can't stop being a policeman, can you?"

Good Lord, he thought, suppressing the desire to grind his teeth. She thought he was downright noble. How had he ever gotten himself into such an inescapable morass of lies and deception?

But he smiled and nodded. "To serve and protect," he agreed, tilting her chin up so her eyes had to meet his. He kissed her as zealously as if he had been an honest man.

Then he went to his own house. Primarily he wanted two things. The first was his gun. The second was to call Thelma Bellarion. He had to string her on just a little while longer. One more woman to keep on deceiving.

He shook his head. So many years, so many women, so many lies. His luck should have run out long ago. It had faltered with Fields and Penny Shaw, but somehow it was holding. It had to last him a little longer. Just a little. A week, he thought. If he could just have a week. He found, for the first time in years, that he was praying.

Chapter Nine

"No further, Mrs. Bellarion. I can deliver you enough circumstantial evidence to convict Valery Essex. But first you come across. Where's Penny Shaw?"

The silence on the other end of the phone was ominous. At last Mrs. Bellarion spoke. Her whiskey voice was raspier than usual. "Don't bully me, young man. Don't even try. I've already heard there's new evidence. Letters. The prosecutor's office has letters that practically prove Valery did it. I doubt if you have anything comparable."

"Wrong," Nikolas snapped. "I have something just as good. Better. But you don't hear it until I hear about Penny. And how do you know about those letters of the prosecutor's? He only got them this morning."

"I have powerful friends."

"Which means your daughter-in-law has powerful enemies. Do your friends include the Perry family? The police?"

"I have never been friends with the Perry family," she said icily. "The Perry family is nothing but a great pack of shyster lawyers trying to hang on to a dissipated fortune. I do not associate with them. And I do not associate with *police*." She said the word police as if it signified some particularly disgusting form of vermin.

"But you associated with an overweight, neurotic secretary naive enough to fall for the kind of line I dish out? You have a strange way of choosing friends, Mrs. Bellarion."

"I didn't choose her," Mrs. Bellarion retorted frostily.

"She's family. One doesn't choose family. It is thrust upon one. And she wasn't simply a secretary. She was an executive secretary. A very adequate one, until you came along."

"Where is she? It's time you put up or shut up, Mrs. B. I've got information you want. You get it when I get what I want. It's zero hour. Tell me where Penny is or I walk."

He was bluffing, but he was doing an excellent job of it, and he knew it. He knew of nothing that would incriminate Valery except the letters she had kept, and they were suspect themselves. He knew he could convince Mrs. Bellarion he had more.

The silence loomed between them again. She said nothing.

"Mrs. Bellarion?"

"Go back to Dallas," she said at last, disgust in her voice. "You're fired."

He blinked. The words truly astonished him. "Mrs. B.," he said slowly, "you don't understand. The prosecutor's letters may not be admissible evidence. What I have is. It can convict Valery Essex. I guarantee it. In return, I demand to know—"

She cut him off. "No. You're the one who doesn't understand. You're fired. Get out of town. Go back to Dallas. Leave her alone."

"Mrs. Bellarion," Nikolas growled, "we had a bargain. I've kept my end. If you want my information—"

"If I *need* your information," Mrs. Bellarion said contemptuously, "I'll have you subpoenaed, you presumptuous fool. I'll have you testify under oath—and have you convicted of perjury if you lie. That's what *I'll* have, Mr. Grady."

Nikolas swore inwardly. Thelma Bellarion had suddenly decided to play hardball, and she was aiming the missile straight at his skull.

"If you don't tell me where Penny Shaw is, Mrs. Bellarion, I'll put the FBI on to you. I should have done it long ago. I'm not the only person who wants to know where she is."

"She's dead." Mrs. Bellarion practically spat the words out. "Forget her, Mr. Grady. It's too late. Go home to Dallas."

Nikolas didn't believe the old woman. He refused to believe her. "If she's dead, where's the body? Where's the death certificate? These are modern times. When you die, you don't evaporate. You leave behind a mountain of red tape. You damn well leave proof you're dead."

"She died at sea," Mrs. Bellarion said with cruel satisfaction. "Her body was never found."

"Listen—" Nikolas sneered, ready to tear into her. But she'd hung up on him. Furiously he dialed her number again. He listened to the repeated unanswered ring. The old gorgon had unplugged her phone. He slammed down the receiver.

Who did the old bat think she was fooling? Dead at sea? What kind of fairy tale was that? What was the old gargoyle trying to pull?

He knew she was related to Penny Shaw, if only distantly. He knew she had been in touch with Penny or someone close to her. Mrs. Bellarion had known too much about his relationship with the secretary; she even had his notes and cards. Penny *had* been alive, of this he was certain—at least long enough to tell somebody how Nikolas had romanced her to get information about Fields.

He had a gut feeling that Penny was still alive somewhere. What was Mrs. Bellarion up to? Why was she suddenly pulling him off Valery's case? Mrs. Bellarion was nobody's fool. She had to know that the letters might not be admissible evidence if nobody could prove the identity—or even the existence—of Chrissy.

Mrs. Bellarion had been eager enough at first for him to nail Valery. Now she'd fired him, told him to get out of town. Why? Did she, too, now want Valery to break and run?

The old woman's about-face could only mean that she knew about the letters in the box in MacGregor; that Valery had found them and that Nikolas had seen them. He could be pulled into court to testify against Valery.

Now Mrs. Bellarion was in a position to blow the whistle on him if he didn't get out of town in the next few days. Things were getting hinkier all the time. He sensed time was running out fast. Too fast.

Troubled, he checked his gun again. He wore it in the leg holster, the arrangement he liked least. When there was trouble, he liked the shoulder holster, the reassuring heft of the automatic against his ribs.

The gun insured he could take care of anybody who menaced Valery. But it was, he observed hollowly, of no use in helping Penny Shaw. Mrs. Bellarion's militant retreat closed off the only path he had to Penny. He was going to have to trust forces greater than himself to keep Penny from harm.

He was, he discovered, praying again. He wasn't actually using words, but he was praying because, as far as Penny Shaw was concerned, it was the only power he had left. It scared him. He checked the gun one last time.

Valery brought the receiver down on the cradle harder than she should have. She had called Charmian at the telephone company where she worked to ask her about the relationship between the Perrys and Dennis Finch, the chief of police.

"Dennis Finch is second cousin to Terry Perry and Cameron Carter," Charmian had snapped. "Didn't I just tell you all this last night?"

"It's hard to keep track of," Valery answered dryly. She wasn't sure she could name her own second cousins, even if someone held a gun to her head and demanded it.

"I hear you're still running around with that Grady man," Charmian said with distaste. "I intend to come over tonight and keep my eye on you. I will not have you carrying on with this man when Thelma Bellarion is stalking you and your child. If you won't think of how your actions might hurt Tony, then I will."

"Charmian, don't you dare. I'm not a child."

"You're acting like one. And I don't trust this 'policeman' of yours one iota. I'm going to do a little sleuthing on my own. Even if it costs me my job. Never let it be said that I stood idly by while my own niece went to hell in a handbasket."

Valery tried to argue, forgetting that Charmian, incensed, was no more reasonable than a rock. Charmian had slammed the receiver down in her ear. Valery's only satisfaction was slamming her own down just as childishly. She was in no mood for one of Charmian's fits.

She was so rattled that when she began to gather up the papers Nikolas had spread to catch paint spills, she knocked over the jar of turpentine in which he had been rinsing the brush. Turpentine as white as milk cascaded across the linoleum.

Valery swore, trying vainly to wipe the stuff up with the sodden newspaper. She and Nikolas had used all the paper towels cleaning the wall. By the time she found a rag, the pigment was sinking into the porous old linoleum tiles, staining them almost as effectively as paint straight from the can.

Valery swore again. Then she laughed ruefully. *My tires have been slashed,* she thought, *my windshield's smashed, my house trashed, I'm on trial for my life, and Thelma Bellarion's after my son. Am I going to lose my grip because of white gunk on the linoleum?*

She tried to pour more turpentine from the original container onto the rag. It was empty. Of course, she thought. The turpentine was gone. She strode out to the garage. There was no more paint remover of any kind among the meager paint supplies.

She did what she never would have done when Charles was alive. She invaded his sacred work space, the bench where he made his model planes and tinkered with small engines. The territory had always been strictly off-limits. Even Tony at his most daring and mischievous had never violated its sanctity.

She rummaged through a cupboard full of airplane paints, oil paints, linseed oil, tiny decals, alcohol and artist's brushes. At last she found a small bottle of turpentine, half-full.

"Forgive me, Charles," she said, reaching for the bottle. Her hand stopped midway to the shelf. She looked at the workbench, the cabinets above it, the unfinished models gathering dust on the shelves.

The inner sanctum, Valery thought, the back of her skull tingling oddly. After Charles's death she had looked here, but found nothing except her own guilt for having disturbed his special retreat. But back then, she had been stunned by shock. And she hadn't known what to look for.

The book, she thought. The realization hit with such force that the edges of her vision seemed to darken. If the library book had been important to him and he hadn't left it at work where the police would have found it, then this was where he would have put it. His workshop.

Almost blindly she began sweeping things from the shelves. A model airplane crashed to the cement floor and fell apart. A toolbox spun to the edge of the workbench, teetered, then hit the floor with a rattling clang.

She pulled boxes of unassembled models from the cabinet shelves. They fell to the workbench and some flew open, scattering plastic parts.

"What in the name of all that's holy are you doing?"

She spun around, looking as guilty as if Charles's ghost had come back to chide her for the desecration. Nikolas stood in the door between the kitchen and garage. He cocked a dark brow. "Valery?"

She supposed she did look a bit insane. "The book," she said breathlessly. "Nikolas, I think if it's anywhere, it's here. Charles didn't let anybody near this bench. It simply wasn't allowed." But the shelves, almost empty now, stared bleakly back at her.

A new inspiration seized her. She fell to her knees and tried to open the toolbox. It was padlocked. She fumbled frantically through the mess on the floor until her fingers closed around a key that seemed the right size.

She held her breath and with shaking fingers inserted the key. It fit. The box yawned open. In its upper tray, jumbled by the fall, were tools and nothing else. She lifted the tray and took a deep breath. The lower part of the box was filled with books, coverless airplane manuals.

Nikolas knelt beside her. "Take it easy, baby," he counseled. She was flushed and looked a little wild. She began rummaging through the manuals. On the very bottom of the box she found what she wanted.

It was another book, its back and front covers stripped away. Its first page was a flyleaf, blank. Carefully she turned it so she could see the title page. She gave a gasp of gratitude combined with disbelief. *Best-Loved Poems of the English and American People*, the page announced.

She had found it.

"This is it," she murmured, her voice shaking. She opened the book. It seemed precisely what the title page said, a book of poems and nothing more. Well-worn, and now mutilated, but containing nothing exceptional.

"Damn!" Valery said in exasperation. "What does it mean? Charles wasn't a poetry lover. Why did he have this thing?"

"Let's see," Nikolas said. He stood, drawing her to her feet. "Come on. We'll look it over together. But in the meantime, you'd better eat. You haven't had anything since breakfast. No wonder you've got the shakes."

"I'm not hungry."

"I am. Come on, Valery. This is no time to starve your brain cells."

Taking her hand, he led her back into the house, then forced her to sit at the kitchen table. She no longer thought of the paint-and-turpentine stain drying on the floor. She opened the book and immediately began to pore over it.

He put his hand on the back of her neck. "Good work, Valery," he said softly. "We could have looked days for the thing."

She made no reply. He sighed roughly and went to the refrigerator, hoping she had eggs on hand. He could cook precisely three things: fried eggs, scrambled eggs, and boiled eggs. He hoped she liked eggs.

He puttered around, dirtying too many dishes, worrying about Valery and replaying his disturbing conversation with Mrs. Bellarion.

He set down two plates of overdone eggs and underdone

toast. "Eat," he ordered. He took a forkful of eggs. They tasted like hot rubber.

Valery, frustrated from skimming through the poems, turned her attention back to the book itself. The front and back covers were gone, but the cloth spine remained, though Charles had blacked out the title.

She thrust a finger between the limp spine and the gathered pages She touched something.

"Eat," Nikolas commanded again. He peppered his eggs liberally so he wouldn't have to taste them. He worried some more about Thelma Bellarion. Something she said nagged at his subconscious. What? Too much information was coming at him too fast. He needed time to process it. He also needed a good night's sleep. But again he had the feeling that there was no time.

"Nikolas," Valery said, her hazel eyes widening, "there's something in here. Something hidden."

She scissored two long fingers behind the book's spine and managed to retrieve the hidden object. At last she withdrew a small, folded piece of cardboard. An empty matchbook cover, crimped so that it could be slid between the book's spine and its pages.

She unfolded it. It bore the name of an economy chain of motels, but no address, city or phone. "Scotchtreat Inn" was all it said. There were hundreds of the cut-rate inns scattered across the country. Charles might have picked it up anywhere.

Including Newark, she thought, suddenly hopeful.

She opened it. There was writing inside. She closed her eyes, then looked again. She wasn't dreaming. It was Charles's writing.

She read it anxiously. A list of words that made no sense. A list of numbers that made no sense, either. But somehow, some way, they meant something, and it was important. Or why would Charles have gone to such trouble?

Nikolas saw the wonder and puzzlement in her expression. Wordlessly he pushed away from the table and moved around to stand by her side. He stared down at the words and numbers. They were written in black ink with elaborate care, so that every tiny marking was clear and distinct.

The words were a crazy salad, with little in common except the initial letter: Toby, Tony, Tontine, Totten, Toluca, Towaco, Tea, Tequila.

The numbers were even more confounding. They were written beneath the list of words, in a precise column:

```
5-2-3
1-1-5
9-5-1
12-6-2-3-4-5-6
12-6-1
0-1-2
5-8-3-4
6-3-3
5-1-1
4-4-1
6-5-6
13-7-1-3-4
13-1-3-4
```

Nikolas frowned. Valery had found something, all right. But what? The last thing he needed was another riddle.

"Does it mean anything to you?" he asked, his brows knitted.

She stared at the words and numbers. "Nothing," she answered. Then she turned in her chair and glanced up at him with half a smile. "Nothing yet. We'll just have to work on it."

His heart had done a slow, elaborate dive when she smiled like that. He could stand around forever looking at that smile. He wondered again just how much safe time he had left with her before Mrs. Bellarion blew him out of the water.

Food forgotten, he picked up his chair and set it beside hers. "Get some pencils and paper," he said. "Let's crack this thing."

She nodded. She rose and went into the dining room to the desk. "By the way," she called to him. "You were right. I called Charmian. She said that the chief of police is a Perry. That all of these people are second cousins—or second cousins once removed."

Nikolas rubbed his jaw reflectively. He'd been hoping for better. A conspiracy of second cousins didn't make much sense. He didn't even know any of his own second cousins, for God's sake. For all he knew they might still be in Greece and Ireland.

Second cousins, he thought in disgust, then allowed himself to swear.

"What?" Valery asked from the dining room.

"Nothing," he answered, frowning and rubbing his jaw again. "Is Thelma Bellarion a friend of the Perry family? Especially any in the police department?"

Valery returned to the kitchen, carrying pencils and writing tablets. "Thelma Bellarion hates the Perrys," she told him. "At least, Charles said she did. Back when they all were young, Terry Perry's father represented Charles's father when Thelma divorced him. They dragged her name through the mud so badly that she didn't get a dime of alimony. She vowed never to speak to any Perry again."

Another blind alley, Nikolas thought grimly. "What about the police?"

She sat down beside him again. "Thelma only likes rich people. She once insulted a dentist for getting too friendly with her at a dinner party. Actually he was quite wealthy. But not wealthy enough for Thelma. Police? I doubt it."

Thwarted again, he rumpled his dark hair. "How about if she could use them to get to you? Would she? Or does she have other powerful friends in this town?"

Valery looked grave. She thought for a moment. "She really hated the Perrys. She hates me, too, of course. I don't even know why, really. She and Charles never got along that well before I entered the picture. But as for making up with the Perrys—I doubt it. Her best friends were the Talmidge sisters. But they had a falling out, too. I don't know if they ever made it up. She liked John Upchurch. He's almost wealthy enough to be in her league, and he's terribly charming."

Nikolas cracked his knuckles in irritation. Every lead he thought he found took him into a stone wall. Valery's case seemed murkier by the hour. It could take him weeks to check out all these old alliances and enmities. And he was no longer sure he had weeks. For now he'd concentrate on the one solid clue they had.

He copied down the words and numbers. "Which do you want to work on?" he asked without enthusiasm. This gibberish could take days to decode.

"Words," Valery said. "I'm not good with numbers."

"Words it is," he said grimly. "Great. What the devil are these numbers? Charles was a pilot. They're not flight coordinates or something, are they?"

Valery studied them and shook her head. She didn't know much about flying, but she knew that much. "No. I have no idea what they are."

Nikolas stared at the numbers. His head began to ache.

He hoped the numbers weren't combinations to a whole string of post-office boxes or lockers scattered across the country. If they were, it might take months to track them down. He tried adding them and subtracting them and assigning them letters of the alphabet. Nothing worked.

Valery frowned over the list of words. They seemed to float before her eyes, taunting her: Toby, Tony, Tontine, Totten, Toluca, Towaco, Tea, Tequila. They made no sense. Tony was her own son, but who was Toby? Tea and Tequila were drinks, but what was their significance? Tontine—that was an elaborate insurance scheme developed in seventeenth century France. Nobody, as far as Valery knew, used such an unwieldy system in this day and age.

But what in heaven's name was Totten? It wasn't in her dictionary. Toluca was a city in Mexico, but what was Towaco? That wasn't in the dictionary, either.

Checkmated and grouchy, Nikolas asked Valery if she had any beer. She rose, rubbing the back of her neck. She was having no luck with the words at all. If they were some kind of code, the key eluded her. She was no cryptographer. Her only advantage was a refusal to quit. She'd stay up staring at the blasted words all night long if that was what it took. She found two bottles of beer far back in the refrigerator. She opened one and took it to Nikolas. She set it down on the table self-consciously. Charles had bought the beer, months ago. He had never lived to drink it. Now she was serving it to another man, a man trying to clear her of Charles's murder, a man with whom she thought she was falling in love.

Nikolas saw the pensive look cross her face. He caught her hand. "What's the matter?"

"Nothing," she said, not wanting to tell him the fleeting thought. "I'm not having any luck with these words."

He kept hold of her hand. Pressing it against his cheek, he stared down at the lists again. "I'm not having any luck, either. Maybe we need to break the word code before we can understand the numbers. The words are written first."

"Can you see any pattern?" she asked. The feel of his rough cheek against her hand was somehow comforting. She put a hand on his shoulder and rubbed his taut muscles.

"Only wild guesses. Charles and two guys named Tony and Toby were involved in some scheme like a tontine. If the others died, the survivor got the money. They were smuggling tea—an old slang term for marijuana—up from Mexico. How's that for a scenario?"

She shook her head. "No good. Charles was wildly allergic to marijuana. Somebody tried to smuggle some on his plane once and he broke out in hives. He couldn't be around any sort of hemp. Even rope made him itch. Sorry."

"So much for tea from Toluca," Nikolas grumbled. He kissed her hand, then released it and bent, frowning at the numbers.

Valery sat and eyed the mysterious words with weary distaste. "What the heck is Totten? And Towaco? Or who are they?"

"Maybe they're not a who or a what," Nikolas suggested idly. "Maybe they're a where. Or a which. Or a why. You've got me." He didn't look up from the numbers.

Valery sat up straighter. She stared at him. "Nikolas, why didn't you say that an hour ago?"

"Say what?" he mumbled, scratching out another wrong answer. He didn't seem to realize he'd said anything of significance.

She rose and fetched her father's old oversize atlas. She sat down again, opened the book and studied the index. She suddenly began scrawling names on her notepad.

Nikolas sipped his beer. He furrowed his brow as he glanced at her. Her face shone with a strange light.

"Bingo," she said, then rapidly started turning the pages of the atlas.

"Bingo? You found something?"

"I think so. Really."

He rose and stood behind her, his hand on her shoulder. She loved the feel of his hand, its hardness and strength.

"There're two Tolucas," she said. "One in Mexico, one in Illinois. There are three Tottenhams, none of them in the States, but no Totten. But, Nikolas, there is a Towaco, and it's right where I hoped it'd be." She turned a final page and revealed a map. "New Jersey," she said with satisfaction. "Right here. Towaco."

His hand tightened on his shoulder. "It's practically next to Newark."

"Right. About twenty miles. It's small, but it's there. The most beautiful dot on a map I've ever seen."

Her happiness crested quickly, followed by an equally strong wave of confusion. "But what does it mean?" she asked, her euphoria vanishing.

He drew her to her feet and took her in his arms. He began to dance her around the table in an elaborate parody of a waltz. "Who knows what it means? Savor the victory for a minute. We've got this far, haven't we? What a team. We can dance, too. Eat your hearts out, Fred and Ginger."

Valery laughed. She suddenly felt almost lighthearted. Smiling up at him, she let him guide her around the kitchen table. He stopped long enough to bend her backward in an old-fashioned dip. Then he drew her erect again. He stopped dancing and stared into her eyes. They smiled at each other.

Then suddenly, Charmian was standing in the kitchen

doorway. "Well!" she exclaimed. She put her hands on her hips and glared. She looked as formidable as it was possible for a maiden aunt to look.

Valery froze. So did Nikolas, his arms still around her.

"Oh," Valery murmured in dismay. She tried to extricate herself from Nikolas, but he held her fast.

Charmian glowered at everything in general, then at Nikolas in particular. He met her stare coolly. "Do you know how to knock?" he asked pleasantly.

"Knock, indeed," Charmian answered scornfully, tossing her white curls. Her eyes flashed and she put her hand to her beads, rattling them angrily. "Don't get fresh with me, young man. What's the meaning of this? Dancing in the kitchen with a strange man, Valery? Beer? Where's Tony? What happened to the television? To the picture over the mantel? The china? Or have you broken everything in your . . . your revels?"

Nikolas withdrew his arm from around Valery, but took her hand. "Your niece has had a hard day, Miss Donovan," he said evenly. "I've been trying to help her. We just had a little luck and were celebrating."

"So I see." Charmian squinted malevolently at the beer, then at Nikolas. "A hard day. A little luck. Would you care to explain?"

"I'm not twelve years old, Charmian," Valery returned. She didn't wish to hurt or anger her aunt, but the woman's attitude was intolerable. "What he said is true. Besides, this is my house, and Nikolas is . . . my guest. And my friend."

Charmian rattled her beads again and turned her glare to Valery. "With friends like this, you don't need enemies, as the saying goes. Could you kindly remember your reputation, miss? Could you kindly remember that you're about to be on trial? Where's Tony? What's happened to this house?

What's that white stain on the floor? Why do you have a book of maps in here? What are all those papers?"

"Tony's with Willadene Davis," Valery replied, her hand still in Nikolas's. "Her nephews are visiting, and she invited him to stay over."

"Willadene Davis?" Charmian practically squawked. "Valery, I told you not to trust that woman! You were asking about Perrys. Well, Willadene Davis is a Perry on her great grandmother's side. Now what—"

"What does that make Miss Davis to the other Perrys?" Nikolas demanded, cutting her off. "Terry, for instance? Or Cameron Carter?"

The question briefly halted Charmian's assault. For a few seconds she concentrated on the whir of her mental computer. "She's third cousin to both, I believe. But that's not the issue. The issue is what's happened, what are you doing, and why, Valery, is this man here?"

Valery gave a sigh of sorely tried patience. Charmian was impossible. What difference did it make if Willadene Davis was somebody's third cousin? How far back did you have to go to be somebody's third cousin? To Adam and Eve?

"Look," she said bluntly. "Someone vandalized the house this afternoon. I didn't think Tony should see it, and neither did Nikolas. Someone's been watching this house, and Nikolas thinks, well . . ."

"I intend to stay as close as possible to see that she isn't hurt," Nikolas finished.

Charmian's wide blue eyes grew wider and more alarmed. "Vandalized? Again? Great Scott, the car isn't even repaired! Does this fiend have no mercy? Valery, you and Tony will stay with me. I insist on it. If anyone comes sniffing around *my* house, I'll take father's shotgun and ventilate him. Go pack."

"I'm not going anywhere, Charmian," Valery said firmly. "This is my home, I won't be driven out of it, and I have work to do."

"Work? What work?" Charmian stalked to the kitchen table and picked up the paper Valery had been scribbling on. "What's this? Toluca, Towaco, Tontine, Totten? What is this nonsense? What is Towaco? I've never heard of Towaco."

"It's a town," Valery said between her teeth. She took the list from her aunt's hand and set it back on the table. "A better question is what's Totten? Do you know? If you're here, you might as well work, too."

"Know? Know?" Charmian bristled. "Of course, I know. I am an aficionado of the crossword. A totten is a very helpful word, with all those *t*'s in it. It's a sort of bank account. It's set up by one person in his own name but in trust for somebody else. So if he dies, the money goes to the beneficiary."

If he dies, thought Valery. She stared at the list again. She thought so hard she tuned Charmian out almost completely. A totten was a bank account, a kind of trust. In case somebody died. As Charles had.

Charmian's words began to penetrate her thoughts again. "Those Talmidges are against you," Charmian was saying fervently. "Those Talmidges are in league with Thelma Bellarion, Valery. They want you convicted and they want Thelma to have Tony, and I can prove it."

Valery looked up from the list, frowning in puzzlement. Charmian dug into her gigantic satchel of a purse. She pulled out a crumpled computer printout, the pages still attached to one another.

"Here," she said, thrusting them at Valery. "It's there in black and white. If anyone finds out I have this, it's my job.

Thirty years of loyalty to the telephone company—poof! Gone. But I've known from the first the Talmidges are involved in this, and here's proof, by the great horned spoon."

"What is this?" Valery asked, bewildered. The flimsy pages were attached and spilled clear to the floor, like a long piece of paper toweling.

"Records of the Talmidge's telephone calls since March. Since Charles died. Look and you'll see. Calls to Thelma Bellarion in Mississippi. That's her number, all right. I checked. Right up to this week. Right up to today. Thirteen calls in all. All since Charles died."

Valery heard Nikolas suck in his breath.

She stared at the columns of dates and times and telephone numbers. Charmian had circled all calls to Mrs. Bellarion with red scrawls. "This may mean nothing," Valery said at last. "She and the Talmidge sisters used to be friends. Why shouldn't they call her after Charles's death? I don't like Thelma Bellarion, but Charles was her only child, and this has been a tragedy for her. Why shouldn't they call?"

"She and the Talmidge sisters were estranged for years," Charmian snapped. "Did they call her before this happened? No. They're tied up with Charles's death somehow, and they're using Thelma Bellarion to help throw the blame onto you."

She rummaged in her huge purse again and drew out a sheet of papers even fatter than the first. "Look," she commanded. "Calls from the Talmidge house for a year before Charles died. I took these off the microfiche records. Is there even one call to Thelma Bellarion? No, not one. Until they could use her hatred for you to help them cover up that they killed Charles."

She shook the papers at Valery, but it was Nikolas who took them. He glanced down at them, his face serious, then looked back at Charmian. The woman was a wild card, he realized. Her imagination could range out of control ninety percent of the time, and then for the last ten, suddenly zoom in and see what everyone else had missed.

"Why would these people want to kill Charles?" Valery demanded. "And why blame me? And use Thelma Bellarion to help frame me? Why bother? And please, Charmian, not another *Miami Vice* fantasy."

"I don't know why they'd kill him," Charmian admitted, frustrated. "But those records show something funny going on. There was a flurry of calls to Dallas about the time of Dahlia Lee's accident. When the Count was killed. Day and night for two days. As if something was terribly wrong. But not one single call to Colorado—where the accident was supposed to have happened."

Valery felt Nikolas slipping his arm around her waist again, but she kept her gaze trained on Charmian. The woman was right. The pattern of calls was strange.

Charmian plunged on. "And then as soon as Dahlia Lee came home, the calls to Newark started. To New Jersey. Some were to the company they were supposed to be interested in buying. But some were simply to a residence. A Mr. Henry Barbuti. I checked. Then shortly after Charles died, the calls to New Jersey stopped. And the calls to Thelma Bellarion began. Something, I tell you, is going on."

Valery started to protest. It was enough to distrust the Perrys and the police and fear Thelma Bellarion. To draw the Talmidges into the picture, as well, seemed outrageous, paranoid and melodramatic. What Charmian said was troubling, deeply troubling. Still, Valery's first impulse was fear that the older woman was putting herself in jeopardy.

"Charmian, you should be careful. You'll get yourself fired . . ." she began, but Nikolas squeezed her waist. The look he gave her silenced her.

He challenged Charmian. "Why," he said levelly, "after all these years, would Thelma Bellarion and the Talmidges reunite to incriminate Valery?"

Charmian tossed her head. She rattled her beads nervously. "I intend to check *you* out next," she warned Nikolas, her chin rebelliously high. "I don't trust you. You appear so suddenly, looking so kind and acting so considerate, and at the same time flaunting your sexuality—"

"Charmian!" Valery gasped.

"Valery, wake up!" Charmian commanded. "How can you stand there, with that man's arm around you? Am I the only one in this family who knows how dangerous sex is? First my brother, then Charles, now you. Am I the only one to note this fact?"

Valery flinched, and let Nikolas draw her closer. "What do you mean, sex was dangerous to Charles?" she asked. "What do you know about it? Do you have records of that, too? Phone calls to another woman?"

"No," Charmian flung back. "I intend to check that out, too. But everyone knows there was another woman. I've heard about it, Valery—those letters from Charles's mistress. It's all over town. That dreadful Sheridan Milhouse turned them over to the prosecutor's office."

Charmian tossed Nikolas a brief unfriendly glance. "Not that it's any of your business," she said pointedly, then turned her attention back to Valery. "That snaky Osgood Perry's told you about those letters, Valery. I can tell from the look on your face. Well, those letters are one more point for the Talmidges, say I. They'll just use this woman to make *you* look more guilty."

166

Humiliation flooded Valery. So her name was on everyone's lips again, and once more the rumors were shameful and evil. Nikolas held her fast, refusing to let Charmian intimidate either of them.

He realized the older woman had said too much in her excitement, and he intended to find out more. "What do you mean?" he asked. "Sex was dangerous to your brother? To Valery's father?" His voice was quiet, even respectful, but it had a steely edge Valery had never heard before.

Charmian heard it, too. She looked Nikolas over from head to toe. Then she looked at Valery, standing in the crook of his arm as if she belonged there.

There was a pause, long and tense. She took a deep and disdainful breath. "My brother could have had any woman he wanted," Charmian said at last. "As difficult as he was, he was a beautiful man when he was young. Beautiful. Thelma Bellarion loved him, back when she was still Thelma Essex, a young divorcee with a child And so did Amanda Talmidge. Desperately."

Valery's lips parted in disbelief. "Thelma? Amanda Talmidge? In love with my father?"

Charmian bit her lip. Her eyes raked Nikolas again, then Valery. "Didn't you have eyes in your head, Valery?" she demanded. "He was the handsomest man in three counties once. When he came back from graduate school and started teaching, he could have had any of them. That's when Thelma had her falling out with Amanda and Paris—and your father was why. Both Thelma and Amanda wanted Arthur. But he married your mother. Because he had to."

Valery's body stiffened. "No." She breathed the word softly, as if it were a prayer. What Charmian was saying couldn't be true. It was another of her bizarre fantasies. It couldn't possibly be true.

Nikolas's arm tightened around her. "It's true," Charmian said relentlessly. "If Thelma had had her way, you'd have never been born. She would have been his wife and Charles would have been his stepson."

Valery's mind stalled, stopped, then began to spin frantically. Perhaps what Charmian said was true; it would explain why Thelma hated her so bitterly.

Things began to make a perverse sense. Valery knew she had been born a bit early in her parents' marriage. She knew, too, that her parents' union had not been a particularly happy one, but she had never known why.

Now she understood. It was because of her. Arthur Donovan had done the honorable thing, without complaint, but without joy. He grimly met his responsibilities. No wonder he had insisted that Valery keep her marriage vows once she made them.

"Charmian," she asked, dazed, "why are you telling me this now?"

Charmian cast a resentful look at Nikolas. "So you won't make the same mistake your father did. An attractive person, a moment of weakness—suddenly your whole life is changed. And for another reason. If Mr. Grady is working for Thelma Bellarion—and those Talmidges—he should know precisely what kind of vendetta he's involved in. Valery is guilty of nothing, Mr. Grady. Except being Arthur's daughter and Charles's wife."

Damn, thought Nikolas. Charmian was closing in again, and he had to shake her off his trail. "I'm not working for Mrs. Bellarion," he said so convincingly that anyone except Charmian might have believed him. "Or the Talmidges," he added for good measure. "And I know Valery's not guilty."

"Precisely the thing you'd say if you *were* working for them," Charmian countered icily. "Can't you see why

Thelma hates Valery? In a sense, Valery stole the man she loved—Arthur. He might have married Thelma if Claire hadn't become pregnant with Valery. Thelma was the most vivacious and clever woman in Constant, and Amanda was one of the richest—but it was Claire who got him. The little nobody from the wrong side of the tracks."

"The little nobody gave him a daughter in a million, Miss Donovan," Nikolas retorted. "You can't deny that."

Charmian's shoulders sagged slightly. "I don't deny it, but can't you see? Thelma's always resented Valery. Then her own son, Charles, was being groomed by the Talmidges for Dahlia Lee. They probably all would have reconciled. Then off he ran with Valery, of all people. Thelma's fondest dreams destroyed twice—by the same girl. Amanda's, as well."

Valery listened, stunned, none of the words quite registering.

"The Talmidges may pretend to be friendly, Valery, but they bear you no love," Charmian said earnestly. "Because you came along, Arthur didn't marry Amanda, either. And Dahlia Lee never had a chance at Charles. The Talmidges wanted him for Dahlia Lee, but he fell in love with you the moment he laid eyes on you. And by then Arthur had already added insult to injury by attacking the Talmidge Corporation. Do you think any of those women bear this family any love, Valery? Think again."

Valery, still numbed, could make no reply. Nikolas made her sit down at the kitchen table. He put the kettle on to make her a cup of coffee. He turned to face Charmian, skepticism etched on his face, his mouth curved sardonically.

"You've figured out things very neatly, Miss Donovan."

"I'm not a fool, Mr. Grady. And I know how long bad blood can fester."

"Of all those women," Nikolas asked, looking Charmian in the eye, "which did Arthur Donovan really love?"

Charmian tossed her head and stared at him from beneath her white curly bangs. "He loved none of them. None. The only thing my brother loved was the truth. And, in his way, Valery, although he may not have always shown it. I love Valery, too. And to prove it, I will fight to the death to protect her."

Nikolas didn't doubt it. The kettle began to shrill and Charmian elbowed him out of the way and made Valery's cup of coffee herself. "I intend," she said, looking up at him belligerently, "to protect her from you. I don't trust you, Mr. Grady. I haven't from the start."

She set the cup smartly on a saucer and the saucer smartly on the table in front of Valery, who still looked stunned.

Nikolas sat down beside Valery, as if to emphasize his alliance with her. Once more his gaze met Charmian's and didn't waver. "I'm a friend, Miss Donovan, believe me."

Valery, trying to regain her emotional balance, put her hand on Nikolas's bare arm. As the storms around her increased, Nikolas alone remained solid, her rock in a sea of uncertainties.

"It's true," she said, trying to convince the older woman. "We can trust him, Charmian. We can."

Valery's eyes were those of a woman determined to believe. Charmian's were cold with proud indignation. "Don't trust him," she said shortly. "He's come here to destroy you."

"No, he hasn't," Valery said, shaking her head emphatically. "He's helping. Besides you and Tony, he's the only person on my side. The only one. I won't let you speak against him. I can't let you." She put her hand in his.

He took it. He could almost feel the trust radiating from her body. She squeezed his fingers, a signal of her faith in him. He squeezed back. He gave her an encouraging look.

But the knowledge lay like a poisoned stone within him. Charmian was right. He had come to Constant for no other purpose than to destroy Valery. Her touch burned into him like a brand.

Chapter Ten

He sat, hand in hand with Valery, his gaze coolly meeting Charmian's. He knew precisely what he was: a would-be hero and a certain hypocrite, a man who was both an enemy and a lover, a man whose time was running out.

He also knew the best defense was a good offense. "You're an intelligent woman, Miss Donovan," he drawled. "I'm surprised you're not bright enough to check out the phone calls in the executive offices of the Talmidge Corporation—not just the Talmidges' home calls. And I'm equally surprised you haven't checked out the calls from Charles's office. If he called another woman, he'd probably do it from there."

Valery gave him a glance of gratitude. He was the only one left who was thinking clearly. But at least someone was, she thought with relief.

Charmian looked taken aback. "I haven't had time," she snapped. "Do you think this was easy? If I'm caught, I'll be strung up by my thumbs."

"Which, of course, you wouldn't mind," Nikolas said easily, "if it'd help Valery. So you claim. Or do you just want to learn enough to prove how right you are? You're willing to go that far and no farther?"

Charmian took a step forward. She crossed her arms angrily. "What are you implying, you rascal, you gigolo?"

Valery blinked hard, fearing another clash. But she had faith in Nikolas's ability to use his reason.

Nikolas gave her hand another squeeze, released it and

stood again. He leaned against the doorjamb, almost lounged. "I'm implying," he said to Charmian, "that you'd make a good detective—if you had more nerve, more patience and more imagination."

Charmian almost sputtered. Valery looked up at him in astonishment. Nobody had ever accused Charmian of deficient imagination.

Nikolas continued smoothly, "I don't know why you're accusing me, Miss Donovan. If the Talmidges and Mrs. Bellarion are the enemy, go after them. In your eyes, I'm only a minion, a paid soldier, the hired help. Why take the pawn when you could corner the king? Why go only as far as you did, then stop?"

Touché, Valery thought in admiration. But she hoped he wasn't setting her aunt off on mad new courses.

Charmian looked at him in resentful amazement. Her anger had not abated, but it had been eclipsed by surprise. "Are you saying—"

"I'm saying that you're brave enough to take chances. Big ones. You've discovered things. Interesting things. But you quit too soon. If there's another woman, couldn't the phone records from Charles's office trace her? If there are no calls to Dahlia Lee in Colorado on the Talmidges' home phone how about on their business phone? If there was a flurry of calls to Dallas, was it personal? Or did it have to do with the corporation? Couldn't you tell if John Upchurch was involved in all this? Or Terry Perry?"

Valery looked between Nikolas and Charmian. Nikolas was doing the impossible: backing the older woman down, putting her on the defensive. But he was also suggesting that Charmian get more deeply involved in stealing information.

She rose and went to him. She wanted to caution him

against setting Charmian into even more furious motion. She put her hand on his arm. "Nikolas—"

"You're suggesting I get into those records and steal even more information?" Charmian asked in disbelief. "I thought you were a policeman What sort of policeman goes around encouraging people to steal?"

Valery had both hands on his arm now. He gave her the slightest of smiles, but went on talking, not missing a beat. "I'm not an officer anymore, Miss Donovan. I'm just a citizen like you, who wants Valery cleared. If you'll break laws in search of secrets about me that don't exist, why not break them to find secrets about people you're sure are guilty of murder? The people running the Talmidge Corporation? Or aren't you fueled by real curiosity—or loyalty—or love?"

"Nikolas!" Valery warned severely.

"I—you—don't be ridiculous," Charmian retorted, flustered. "You're trying to throw me off your trail, you fox, you scoundrel. You're trying to . . ." She searched frantically for a word and found it at last. "You're trying to obfuscate."

Nikolas shrugged a wide shoulder, put his arm around Valery. He cast a slightly mocking glance at Charmian. "I never do things I can't pronounce. If you want to check me out, fine. Do it first thing. I invite you to. I ask you to. I beg you to. Just don't get caught before you get to look for *real* information."

Valery shook her head in disbelief. She stared first at her aunt, then at Nikolas. "Nikolas," she said, "I can't believe you're encouraging her to do this. To break the law."

"Why not? The law's trying to break you. Fight back."

"No," Valery stated firmly. "I don't want Charmian poking around in those records anymore. She and I'll end up in adjoining cells—"

"I'm an adult," Charmian said with a superior sniff. "I'll

be the one to decide what chances I take."

"No," Valery protested. "This is crazy. I'm in enough trouble without—"

"If you do it," Nikolas interrupted, looking earnest and righteous, "check me out first. I insist. When you get into those records tomorrow, I want mine to be the first you get into. I deserve to be cleared."

"You'll take your turn," Charmian returned sharply. "And I don't have to wait until morning. I haven't worked at the phone company for thirty years without knowing a few ins and outs—figuratively *and* literally. I'm a supervisor. I'll just go in and say I'm rechecking the computers."

"Miss Donovan," Nikolas warned, "whatever you do, don't go right back there after you've just walked out with a year's worth of classified information."

"He's right—" Valery began, but Charmian cut her off.

"Valery, please! Don't tell me what to do. I'm the only one around here who's accomplished a thing, and the only one who's likely to. Your job, young lady, is to pack, get Tony and come to my house where the two of you will stay. Here's a key." She rummaged in her purse and smacked her spare key on the table. "And don't wait up for me. I may be very late indeed."

She started to wheel away, then turned to face Nikolas again. "And I don't," she said pointedly, "wish to see you there. If your interest in Valery is sincere, you can wait until after the trial, like a proper gentleman. You can prove your sincerity by staying out of our way."

She turner her back on both of them, and strode off. The front door creaked open, then slammed shut as she left.

Nikolas looked down at Valery and gave her a slightly crooked smile. "I feel like I just survived a hurricane. Is she always like that?"

Valery shook her head, feeling half grave, half giddy. "Actually, no. Never that bad. But she's so worried about Tony and me it's made her awfully aggressive. I'm afraid she'll get caught. She'll get herself fired. You shouldn't have encouraged her, Nikolas. I'm worried for her."

"Don't underestimate her."

"I hope she does check you out before she does anything else," Valery said loyally. "So she'll stop all these accusations."

"I do, too."

He was lying. He hoped he'd deflected Charmian and believed that he had. At least for now. He had convinced her that he was only a small fish, but there were big ones out in the deeper waters, waiting to be hooked by her superior wiles. Checking out the Talmidge Corporation calls ought to keep her occupied for weeks.

Yet, once more, he had the strange sensation that time was running out. He put both arms around Valery. He liked the feel of her against him, and had an uneasy, desperate urge to enjoy it while he could.

"Are you all right?" he asked, tipping her face up to his.

She nodded. She gave him a weak smile. "I'm still in shock. Thelma Bellarion in love with my father? But it suddenly makes a lot more sense—why she never liked me. And why she wants Tony. Not only does it hurt me, she gets a part of Charles back. And my father, too. She may never have had his child, but she thinks she'll get his grandchild."

"Valery," he said, concerned at the worry he saw in her face, "I'm going to do everything in my power to see that she doesn't get him."

"I know." She stood on her toes and kissed his cheek. "Let's get back to work."

Nikolas looked at her. He could feel a nerve twitching in

his temple. She'd done it again. Been knocked down and gotten right back up. He wanted to take her upstairs and kiss her until every bruise and hurt was forgotten. He wanted to make love to her until the rest of the world disappeared. But that wasn't possible. The world would come back, and there were only the two of them and an eccentric elderly lady to fight it. He'd had better odds in his time.

He looked down into her determined face. There was a job to be done. And she wasn't going to quit. They'd have to kill her before she quit.

He nodded. "Let's get to work."

"Look, children," Willadene Davis said brightly, "we have company." She was frightened. Outside, the light was dying from the summer sky.

The three boys, sunburned and exhausted from swimming all day, lay on the floor in front of the television. They were watching a movie about pods that came from outer space and could grow to look exactly like human beings.

"Hello, boys," said the tall lady whom Willadene had let inside. She wore a black dress and a black hat and black gloves and carried a white box.

"Hello," said one of Willadene's twin nephews. The other only smiled shyly, then yawned.

"Hello," Tony said, shy himself. The lady was very tall, taller even than his mother, and she smelled like roses. But her hat made him uneasy. A little black hat made of feathers, it looked like it was made of actual birds' wings, which meant that the birds had had to die. From it draped black veils that crossed and recrossed the lady's face. He could not see her clearly, although he tried. It made her spooky.

"Don't mind this." She touched the veil with one gloved

hand. She seemed to be looking right at Tony. "I was hurt once. But now I'm strong again. And getting stronger all the time."

Tony turned back toward the television screen, embarrassed. He hadn't meant to stare.

Willadene stood in the door between the kitchen and the living room. She was making nervous twisting movements, with her hands. Dahlia Lee had called and said she was sending this woman over and to do whatever she said. The woman frightened her.

"I heard Willadene had some little boys visiting her," the lady in black cooed, sitting down on the edge of the sofa, "and so I just *had* to come over. I even brought you boys a wonderful, wonderful treat." She opened the box. She looked at Willadene. Willadene twisted her hands again.

"Don't just stand there, Willadene," the lady in black said. "Get some milk."

Willadene stared at her a moment. "Yes," she said at last. "Yes. But maybe . . . maybe they should put on their pajamas first?"

"Certainly." The lady nodded. "That would be fine."

"He doesn't have any pajamas," said the bold twin, pointing to Tony. "He's gotta wear mine."

Tony blushed.

"It doesn't make a bit of difference," the lady said sweetly, and held the box out for them to see. "Change, and then you'll have something very, very special."

She showed them what was in the box. There were cupcakes, the fanciest ones Tony had ever seen. The lady in the veils pointed to the bold twin and then at a cupcake with a yellow daisy on it. "This one's for you, dear."

"And this one—" she indicated one with a green frosting clover "—is for you." She nodded at the quiet twin.

"And this one," she said lovingly, lifting up a cupcake with a beautiful red rose on top, "this one is *especially* for Tony. Yes. *Especially* for handsome little Tony."

It rested, waiting for him, in her black-gloved hand.

The sun had set. The last of the twilight was fading. Nikolas stared at the numbers, and the numbers stared back at Nikolas. Hello, stupid, they said.

He tried juggling them a hundred different ways in hopes of making sense of them. They made no sense. He found it hard to concentrate. Too many loose ends flapped in his brain. His mind felt like a ship whose riggings were undone, one that could only limp, drifting, toward its destination.

He was particularly disturbed that Thelma Bellarion seemed reconciled with the Talmidges. He wondered if she'd talked to them today. He needed to check Charmian's records when he had time. Time.

"Do you think the Talmidge sisters really have a vendetta against you?" he asked, leaning back and glancing at Valery. He liked the way she nibbled on her pencil. It kind of turned him on.

She didn't look up. She only shook her head. "Nothing would surprise me. Maybe the whole town has a vendetta against me. The whole county. The whole state."

"Maybe it does. Personally, my money says that it could be Terry Perry at the bottom of this. He's high up in the corporation. He's got links to it all—the Talmidges, the lawyers, the police."

"Charmian's never trusted Terry Perry," Valery admitted "My father clashed with him more than once. He's a scrapper, Terry is."

"So are you. Would you consider a break? Maybe thirty seconds? Just look at me maybe? For even five seconds?"

She smiled at him and let her pencil drop. She leaned back in her chair and began to massage her aching shoulders. Her smile faded.

"It's still hard to believe. My father and Thelma Bellarion. *And* Amanda Talmidge."

"I wonder how he missed Paris," he gibed gently. He reached over and helped rub her neck.

"Paris always wanted Amanda to be happy," she said ruefully. "Paris would do anything for Amanda. She'd never compete with her. But I suppose she resented him for hurting Amanda."

"That—and he cost them a lot of money. He went on to become the corporation's gadfly. Not the most chivalrous move."

Valery gave him a wry look. Once more she took his hand in hers. "My father," she said, shaking her head and studying Nikolas's lean fingers. "I always thought he was frosty and aloof. Little did I know."

Nikolas fought back the urge to rise, draw her to her feet and take her into his arms. The slightest physical contact with her made him hunger for more, much more. He frowned, trying to wrestle the impulse back.

As if she understood, Valery released his hand. It had felt too good. She put her elbows on the table and her chin in her hands. She was struck by how dark and handsome Nikolas was. Someday, if things ever became normal again, she'd like to just sit and look at him, marveling how wonderful he was in every way. Someday.

He sighed, trying to get his mind back on business. "What's this about the Talmidge sisters wanting Charles to marry Dahlia Lee? I thought you said that wasn't true."

She, too, had to wrench herself away from desire and back to duty. She squared her soldiers. "Charles saved

Paris's life, and he was the Talmidges' favorite for a while. Maybe they imagined him as a consort for Dahlia Lee. But she never gave any hint she wanted him. As far as I could tell."

"What do you mean, as far as you could tell?"

She shrugged. "Dahlia Lee wasn't easy to know. One day she'd be one way, the next day another. I never knew that she liked any of the boys in school. The girls, either, for that matter. She was always ranging off on her own and finding some strange friend. Usually older and usually a little odd. And pushy. I remember once she had a guest all summer—a big blond girl from Austria, very loud, very domineering. They'd met at camp, I think. Dahlia Lee was the only one who could stand her."

Valery stared, unseeing, at the papers in front of her. There had been rumors about that, too. In Constant, she thought bitterly, there were rumors about everything. She remembered her father's rule: Believe none of what you hear and only half of what you see.

Pensively she glanced up at Nikolas. Her mouth curved slightly. "Now I'm just like everybody else. Spreading stories."

He couldn't help himself. He reached for her hand again. "You'll never be like everyone else."

He stared into her eyes and her heart slowed almost to a stop, then began to run to catch up.

"Everybody else likes gossip and rumor," he said. "You don't. You don't think it's moral, I can tell. I think you really are your father's daughter, and I bet I know exactly what he used to tell you."

Once more he was making her feel slightly breathless. "You don't," she said softly. "You couldn't."

"I do," he replied, kissing the inside of her wrist. "And

can. He always said, Believe nothing you hear and only half of what you see." He kissed her wrist again, where the pulse point throbbed. He smiled. "Right?"

She sat, slightly dumbstruck, slightly openmouthed. "Right," she admitted in wonder. "You must have been some lawman."

His smile faded. *Yeah,* he thought. *Once. Back in the old days when right was right, and wrong was wrong, and the twain never met.*

He used to think he could be the salvation of a whole platoon, an army, a country. Now he was trying his damnedest just to save this one woman, and he had the jumpy sinking feeling that he was somehow too late.

"Nikolas?" She was puzzled by his expression. It suddenly looked naked, almost hunted. "What's wrong?"

"Nothing," he said brusquely. "Valery, do you know what I want most?"

He took her other hand and held them both, his fingers interlaced with hers. His face was so intent that she swallowed involuntarily. "What?"

"I want you to walk away free from this whole mess," he said, his voice taut. "You and Tony both. And then I want you to come into my arms. And see if that's where you should stay. Both of you—with me. Have I got it?"

The warmth of his hands seemed to run through her veins and straight to her heart.

"Valery, I want you to believe in me," he said earnestly, "no matter what. Can you promise me that?"

"Of course, Nikolas," she breathed, deeply touched. "Why wouldn't I believe in you? After all you've done for me?"

She looked at him with affection, yearning and gratitude. He seemed like the strongest source of safety she and Tony

182

had. The one dependable person in a shifting, deceptive world.

Tony slept. He lay stretched, a small inert shape, on Willadene's sofa. She had placed him there after he had fallen asleep so suddenly on the floor in front of the television.

Now she sat with the veiled woman in the kitchen. The quiet twin had already fallen asleep. He sprawled peacefully in his bed in the guest room. The bolder twin was still awake. Both women could hear him singing softly from his bed:

> "Rabbits have no tails at all,
>   tails at all, tails at all—
> They just have powder puffs."

"Doesn't he ever run down?" the veiled woman demanded.

Willadene poured herself more coffee. Her hand shook. "It takes a while. He's higher strung than the other one."

She tried to raise her cup to her lips and found that she could not. She was trembling too much. At first she had thought this woman was Dahlia Lee herself. But even though Willadene couldn't see the woman's face, she had quickly grasped it was not Dahlia Lee she was dealing with. This woman wasn't nervous and wispy like Dahlia Lee. She radiated power, coiled, cold-blooded and terrifying.

"I should have drugged all three of them," the woman said coldly. She adjusted her veils.

"No!" Willadene made an apologetic gesture, hoping she hadn't spoken too quickly. "It's not necessary," she said, almost pleading. "Really, it's not. The other one will be asleep soon. But I have to know. Where are you taking Tony?"

The woman had been staring toward the guest room. She seemed slightly distracted. "What?" she said, turning back to Willadene.

"Tony," Willadene said, her words coming out in a rush now. "I have to know where you're taking him. I must know. And why."

"As far as you're concerned, I'm not taking him anywhere. As far as you're concerned, this never happened."

"I understand that," Willadene said desperately. "I do. But I have to know he'll be safe."

"He'll be safe. He'll be back here by morning. He'll never know what happened."

"But why . . . ?" Willadene began unhappily. She went silent. She knew she would get no answer.

The woman adjusted one black glove. She listened to the soft singing from the guest room. "Doesn't that brat ever sleep?" she hissed. "I want out of here."

"But—"

"You have a very nice life here, Willadene," the woman said, buttoning and unbuttoning the glove. "A lovely home, a lovely pool, a lovely car. You take a lovely vacation every year. And have a lovely job. Oh, yes, such a lovely job. Such a nice life. I'd do as I was asked, if I were you."

"I don't understand this." Willadene fought back tears of apprehension. "I should know where you're taking him. I have to know he's safe."

"The less you know until later, the better," the woman retorted. "If you don't want to think of yourself, think of your sister. Think of those precious little twin boys in there. They're the closest thing you have to children of your own. You wouldn't want to ruin their futures, would you?"

Willadene said nothing. She was too frightened and confused. She had to believe nothing would happen to Tony.

She had to. But deep inside she was praying that the bold twin, always active, would stay awake all night long, would still be wide-eyed when the sun came up.

The woman in black swore savagely. "Why doesn't he sleep?" she demanded. Even through the woman's veils, Willadene could see the flash of her teeth.

"He'll sleep," she said. "Any minute now he'll drop off."

The woman swore again. She didn't want either twin to see her carrying off Valery's boy. No witnesses. None. Except Willadene, who was really an accomplice now.

She stared greedily at Tony Essex's sleeping form, so young, vulnerable and helpless. He would be hers. As soon as that Willadene's hyperactive brat of a nephew gave up.

From the bedroom, the childish voice quavered on and on:

> "Rabbits have no tails at all,
> tails at all, tails at all—"

Black-gloved fingers drummed with growing impatience.

Valery rubbed her forehead. The house felt odd without Tony and her head swam from staring at the words before her. The one that always dominated the list was Tony's name. It haunted her.

"Nikolas," she said, her hand shading her aching eyes, "I keep having this thought. What if Charles set up one of those accounts—a totten account—with Tony as beneficiary? And if this account is in Toluca, Mexico, or Toluca, Illinois, or Towaco, New Jersey?"

Nikolas, half-blind with numbers, nodded mechanically. "Okay. Fine. Only why, and which of those places, and where did he get the money, right?"

"Right," she answered unhappily. It all fell apart again. "And where does tea fit in? And tequila?"

She stared at the list again. Her eyes burned. "Maybe," she said absently, "it's not every word. Maybe it's just every other word—Tony, Totten, Towaco—then we'd only have tequila left to deal with. We could dump the tea."

"Like the Boston Tea Party, eh?" The joke was so lame, even he couldn't smile. He stretched wearily. Then he paused. "Do you have any tea here?"

"No. Never. Just coffee. Did you want some?"

"No. Did Charles ever go to Mexico?"

"Not that I know of. And not in the company plane. It'd have to show in the log."

"How about Illinois?"

She shook her head. "If he did, it's not in the log, either."

Nikolas leaned back in his chair. "But he went to New Jersey. Near Towaco. Lots of times." His dark gaze was at first thoughtful, then piercing. "Valery, do you have tequila in the house? Did Charles drink it?"

She nodded. "Yes. He liked those things with orange juice sometimes."

"A tequila sunrise. Do you still have it? The bottle?"

"Yes."

"Maybe we should look at it."

She nodded, rose and went to the cupboard. The tequila bottle was far in the back, behind the stores of peanut butter, jelly and pinto beans She pulled it out and set it on the kitchen table, then she sat down again. She looked at it without enthusiasm.

Nikolas picked up the bottle and stared at it. It seemed like a perfectly ordinary bottle of cheap tequila, half-full. The traditional worm lay in the bottom, still and gray.

He studied the label. There was nothing unusual about

it. The longer he looked, the more normal everything looked. He wondered if he was staring at the most ordinary half-filled bottle of tequila in the universe. He set it back down. "You haven't touched this since he died?"

Valery shook her head. "I never understood how anybody would drink anything that had a worm in it."

Nikolas smiled. Booze was booze.

Valery didn't smile. She stared at the bottle.

"Nikolas," she said slowly, "isn't there a poem about a worm? A worm and a rose? A famous one?"

He looked at her, quirking an eyebrow.

She frowned in concentration and thumbed through the book of poems. "Yes. Here." She found the page. Someone had circled the number at the bottom of the page and colored in all the *o*'s with a ballpoint pen. She had noticed it before and thought it the work of a bored doodler.

"I thought you said Charles was no lover of poetry," he said.

"He wasn't," Valery answered, still frowning. "He was terrible with things like poetry. So terrible that he flunked freshman English twice. By the time he passed, he must have known the English book by heart. Listen."

She straightened up and read the poem aloud:

> "O Rose, thou art sick.
> The invisible worm
> That flies in the night
> In the howling storm
>
> Has found out thy bed
> Of crimson joy,
> And his dark secret love
> Does thy life destroy."

Nikolas, too, frowned. He felt as if he were back in high school in Dallas.

"Nikolas, the *worm*. Charles knew I wouldn't touch this bottle unless I had a good reason. And I think he left a reason—in this code."

She rose, went to the sink and started pouring out the tequila. "A worm," she said with distaste.

She'd done it, he thought. She'd figured out that crazy list of words, at least in part. He rose and moved beside her. "Maybe you've got something."

"We'll see," she muttered grimly. She shook the worm out of the bottle. It was, she noted, a worm that had seen better days. And it looked as if someone had tampered with it somehow.

She opened a drawer, took out a knife and shuddered slightly. Then she cut the worm in two.

The knife encountered something hard. "What . . . ?" she started to ask, perplexed, but was silenced by the flash of something sparkling beneath the knife.

It was a jewel.

"Nikolas?" she said tightly. She felt numb all over. She couldn't get her breath.

"Baby," Nikolas said with intense satisfaction, "we're in business." He picked up the gem and held it to the light. It was an emerald, perhaps three carats, and it flashed green fire.

"A jewel?" Valery breathed. "Where would Charles get a jewel?"

"When we know that," Nikolas said, turning the emerald in the light, "we'll know who killed him and why. This is quite a rock. If he had any more, he could have set up quite a trust fund for Tony."

"But why?" She shook her head again, bewildered.

Nikolas set the jewel carefully on the counter. He put his hands on her shoulders and looked into her eyes. "Valery, you cracked it. It's like you said—every other word on the list. There were a pair of names, a pair of places, a pair of drinks, and finally a pair of weird insurance plans. In each case it was the *second* one we were supposed to pay attention to. Charles knew you wouldn't touch the tequila on your own. The jewel was safe there until you got the code and the clues."

"But where would Charles get emeralds?" Her mind spun.

"I don't know where," Nikolas answered tautly. "But I know where he turned them into money—Newark. If I wanted a place to fence hot jewels, Newark would be at the top of the list. Organized crime."

Her eyes widened in horror. "Hot jewels—you mean stolen? Organized crime? Charles was involved in all that?"

"I don't know what he was involved in. We're going to have to check all these things out. First thing tomorrow we call Towaco and find out about this trust fund. I want to know just how much money Charles had socked away. How big this thing is."

Valery swallowed hard. "It must have been big enough for somebody to kill him."

He nodded.

"And then to frame me for it," she added, chilled at the thought. She bit her lip. *Charles,* she thought, *what did you do to yourself? What did you do to all of us? What were you mixed up in? And with whom?*

She started to shiver uncontrollably. Nikolas had set the jewel back on the counter. She looked at it but couldn't touch it. It was like a piece of death twinkling there. It had killed Charles. It could destroy her and Tony.

Nikolas put his arm around her. She leaned against his chest gratefully.

"Charles must have had enough money to start his own flying service," he mused. "And that's a lot of money. He had it safely hidden, so if anything happened, you'd find out where it was. And maybe who he was involved with."

She closed her eyes to shut out the ugliness of reality. She held tightly to Nikolas.

"He must have meant to protect himself by leaving the code," he said, stroking her hair. "But it didn't work. Whoever killed him did it before they knew he had them covered."

He pulled her tighter to him. If the killer didn't know about the clues, Valery might be safe. But if the killer suspected Charles had left behind anything incriminating, she might be in greater danger than he'd thought. He held her close.

"We don't know the whole story yet," she said, her voice choked. "We still don't understand the rest of the code." She burrowed her face against his shirt. Once more he seemed like the only safety left in the world.

"The numbers," he murmured, his lips against her hair. "We have to find out what the numbers mean."

She nodded wordlessly.

He was going to have to let go of her. Either that, or make love to her. He willed himself to loosen his hold on her.

"Look," he said, taking her by the arms and looking down at her. "It's going to be a long night. Why don't you make some coffee? And eat something, will you? You worry me."

She gave him a weak smile. "I couldn't eat."

But his concern, as usual, warmed her. His hands, so

strong and vital against her flesh, gave her the strength she needed to go on.

"Valery," he said between his teeth, "another thing I want to do tomorrow is get you a lawyer. A team of lawyers. Good ones who aren't related to the Perry family. I'll pay for it. Let's get serious about keeping you free."

Tears sprang to her eyes. "Nikolas, you can't do that. Lawyers cost a fortune."

"You're worth a fortune. You're worth a thousand fortunes."

I love you, she thought. *You're the most wonderful man in the universe.*

The phone rang. Nikolas grimaced slightly. "If that's your aunt, wanting you to bail her out, don't."

He released her. She smiled shyly and went to the phone. "Hello?" She hoped it wasn't her midnight caller, checking in early.

"Valery?" The man's voice on the other end of the line was slightly breathless, as if nervous. "This is John Upchurch. I felt—the Talmidge sisters felt—I should talk to you."

She frowned, puzzled. Nikolas stood across the kitchen, his arms folded. He watched her face carefully. He hoped the caller wasn't Charmian, and if it was, he hoped fervently he had thrown her off his trail for the time being.

"Yes?" Valery's own voice was hesitant. Why was John Upchurch calling her? What could he or the Talmidge sisters possibly want?

"Valery," Upchurch said, his tone gaining urgency, "let me be frank. Paris had a call today from Mrs. Bellarion, your mother-in-law. Your former mother-in-law."

"Yes?"

"Paris and Mrs. Bellarion have been in touch from time

to time since . . . since Charles's death. They have, you might say, renewed their friendship."

"Yes? Go on." She clenched the phone more tightly. She looked down at the counter. The emerald lay there, shining brightly.

Upchurch took a deep breath. "The man you were with, the one in the Rose Café, this man who's moved next door to you . . ."

"Yes?" Her heart started to beat faster. The familiar anxiety rose in her chest.

"Valery, he's in Mrs. Bellarion's employ. She told Paris today. The man is a detective. He's been sent to find enough evidence to make sure you're convicted."

"What?" She clenched the receiver so tightly her fingers felt numbed. Disbelief made her half faint. The room seemed to waver before her eyes, and she felt sick to her stomach.

Nikolas worked for Thelma Bellarion? No, she thought. No. Not that. She could bear anything but that.

"His name is Nikolas Grady. He's a private detective from Dallas. He's been sent to find evidence against you. Paris was, of course, concerned over this deception. But her concern turned to alarm when Mrs. Bellarion implied if the man found no evidence against you, he would be paid to create it."

"What?" Valery repeated, stunned. She kept staring at the emerald. If she shifted her gaze only a bit, she would see Nikolas. But she did not dare look at him. She was afraid to. John Upchurch's words had changed Nikolas forever. She no longer knew him. The man with her was a stranger—a deadly one.

The emerald flashed. Numbly she wondered if he had somehow planned this whole thing, planted the jewel somehow. It seemed hardly possible, and yet . . .

"Paris and Amanda discussed this thoroughly," John Upchurch went on. "It's certainly within Mrs. Bellarion's rights to hire a detective. But they think it evil that he has so obviously insinuated himself into your confidence. And we agreed, the three of us, that it is against all standards of morality for the man to create false evidence. We agreed that you should be alerted. The man is an expert at winning women's trust. He specializes in it. He began by slashing your tires so he would seem to come to your rescue. Such acts are, of course, unconscionable."

Valery said nothing. There was nothing to say. She felt like someone who has been stabbed and can only stare helplessly at the wound.

At last she turned her eyes to Nikolas. She knew he could read her expression. He understood what she was hearing.

His face told her more clearly than John Upchurch's words. She had been betrayed.

He had betrayed her. And Tony.

Again she felt like someone who has received a mortal blow, someone dying.

She had been deceived, beguiled, caught in his snare. He was selling her life and her child's life to Thelma Bellarion. He was a vampire, a Judas.

"Valery," Upchurch said anxiously, "do you understand me? Do you realize what I'm saying? Evidence may be created against you that seems irrefutable. Nothing concrete was said, nothing that would hold up in court, but it was Paris's distinct impression that the Grady man will make sure that you'll be sentenced to life in prison."

"I understand," Valery said. Her eyes remained locked with Nikolas's. *You were the enemy all along,* she thought. *I thought you were Life. You're Death. You're worse than Death.*

"They're boxing you into a corner from which you can't escape." Upchurch's voice almost shook with urgency. "You'll be trapped."

She stood straighter. She put on the carefully controlled face she had worn, like a mask, since Charles had been murdered. She felt as if a part of her had died. Nikolas Grady had killed it. In cold, conniving blood.

"Thank you, John," she said with a calm that astonished her. "Thank you very much."

She set the receiver down carefully. She stood, still staring at Nikolas. Her gaze never faltered.

"I know the truth," she said.

And he knew it had happened at last. His time had run out.

Chapter Eleven

He stood before her, unmasked now, her adversary and a traitor. She squared her shoulders, lifted her chin higher. "That was John Upchurch. He says you're a detective. Hired by Thelma Bellarion. Is it true?"

His expression told her it was. Hardness mingled with resignation on his face. Something else was written there. Disgust perhaps. But she didn't know if it was for himself or for her.

He put his hands in his pockets. He leaned against the doorjamb. He shrugged, as if her accusations made little difference. "It's true."

Her hands clenched, unclenched, clenched again. She took three steps across the small kitchen, so that she could look directly up into his dark face. His expression was nearly blank, but his mouth had a slightly bitter curve. A nerve jumped in his temple.

"He says," she ground out furiously, "you came here to find evidence to make sure I'm convicted. So Thelma Bellarion can get Tony."

His dark eyes remained steady. The nerve in his temple twitched again. "Yes" was all he said.

"He says you've made a career of this," she denounced the danger rising in her voice. "It's your speciality—getting close to women, lying to them."

He raised one brow slightly. He gave the same indifferent shrug. "I've done it before. Yes."

"And I suppose," she said between her teeth, "that you

never lost your wife and child. You probably never even had a wife or child."

He didn't so much as blink. "I lied."

He was inhuman. Pain and disgust overwhelmed her. She drew back her hand and slapped him. She struck him full force across the face that was so handsome it seemed designed to charm women.

He didn't flinch. He didn't even take his hands out of his pockets. The curve of his mouth grew slightly more bitter.

His calm made Valery angrier and sicker still. Her breathing was ragged. "He says you planned this whole thing. You slashed my tires?"

"Yes." His face remained implacable except for the jumping nerve. His posture, leaning against the doorjamb, seemed almost casual. But the print of her hand branded his cheek.

Her eyes flashed with rage. "You scared my child to death," she said savagely. "He'd already been put through hell, and you frightened him. You made him cry. You bastard!"

He did not try to evade the blow when she slapped him again. He simply held still and took it. Her anger and hurt gave her unexpected strength. The slap stung like hate itself, but he didn't wince.

She stared at him in loathing and disbelief. He remained lounging against the doorjamb, hands in his pockets, looking coolly down at her. Her hand burned like fire, but he seemed to feel no pain. He really wasn't human, she decided. He was some sort of monster, a demon.

"How could you do this?" she demanded. Tremors ran through her, but she willed herself not to shake. "Why? Was it for money? You do things like this just for money? My God, what *are* you?"

His gaze held hers and didn't waver. "It wasn't for

money. It was for a woman I'm trying to find. Thelma Bellarion claimed to know where she is."

Now it was Valery who felt as if she'd been slapped. This man had not only deceived and betrayed her, he'd done it for another woman. The final humiliation. "You were willing to sacrifice me and my child," she said, her eyes narrowing, "for some woman. Well, she must be something for you to sink to this."

He stared down at her. The hate in her eyes cut him to the marrow. His smile faded. "She's nothing to me. She's a woman I had to get close to on another job. She didn't show quite the same spirit as you. She tried to kill herself, then she disappeared. I need to find her."

Resentment swept over her. "Why?" Her voice trembled with anger. "So she could finish the job? You did this to another woman, too, and she tried to kill herself? You are a bastard, Nikolas."

In cold rage she swung her hand a third time and struck him across the mouth. It hurt her so much she wondered if she had broken her fingers. She was satisfied to see a small trickle of blood stain his lower lip. He licked it away, almost meditatively.

"All right," he said, nodding. "I deserved that. Now listen. I was going to tell you all this—"

"Oh, certainly," Valery said with scathing sarcasm. "When? After you'd put me behind bars? Get out of my house. Get out of my life. Get out!"

He took his handkerchief from his pocket and wiped away the last trace of blood from his mouth. "No. I want you to listen."

"Get out!" she ordered between her teeth. "Damn you."

He shook his head. He wiped the blood again. "Not until you hear my side."

"I don't want to hear your side. I don't want to breathe the same air you do. I told you to leave, and I mean it."

"No, dammit. You're going to hear—"

"No, I'm not. There are junkyard rats with better scruples than yours. John said if you can't find evidence against me, you'll make it up."

For the first time, anger shone in his black eyes. "That's a lie. I never falsified evidence in my life."

"Of course you'd say that. John says otherwise. Thelma told Paris today."

His mouth went more crooked still. "Another lie. Thelma Bellarion fired me today. And she never asked me to falsify evidence. Somebody besides me has lied to you, Valery. You'd better realize it. And realize I'm not lying anymore. I want you to know the truth. Just not now. Later. When you know you can trust me."

"Trust you?" She laughed in disbelief. "Trust you? I'd be better off trusting the devil himself. How much of what's happened did you make happen? Did you write those Chrissy letters? Did you arrange this thing with the library book? Plant that jewel in the bottle somehow, so it'd look like Charles and I were stealing gems, and I killed him so I could have them all? Oh, you've got all kinds of proof against me now, don't you, Nikolas? Well, good luck with your lies, because I'll fight you. I'll fight you like you've never been fought before. I'll teach you the meaning of the word fight."

She started to turn from him. His hands snaked out and seized her. He pulled her to him. She stared up at him with shock and outrage. His face was frighteningly intent.

"I don't want to fight you. I want to help you," he said, his breath almost a hiss. "I didn't arrange any of this. It's just starting to make sense. I was supposed to see those letters from Chrissy. I understand that now. So I could testify that you'd withheld evidence. But I don't think either of us was supposed to find out this other stuff—about the jewel. I didn't make any of it up. Charles got into enough trouble to get killed. You're in trouble just as deep. The truth about me is out, but it's only part of the truth. I want you to know all of it. I can explain."

"Let go of me," Valery ordered. She tried to strike away his hand with her fist, but he captured her wrist before the blow could connect. She struggled so hard that he had to hurt her to keep her in his grasp, but he refused to let her escape.

"I'll never trust you," she said furiously. "Never. How could I?"

He pulled her against him so hard that she gasped. He brought his face near hers so that she had no choice but to look at him.

"Because I love you," he returned furiously. "Because I don't want you to go to prison. Or lose your son. Because I want you—more than I've ever wanted anything in my life. Thelma Bellarion can go to hell, because we belong together. And you know it. You've known it from the start."

His arms imprisoned her like iron, but when he tried to kiss her, she jerked her face away. "Are you insane?" she asked contemptuously. "Aren't you sick of lying? Don't touch me. I despise you."

He did not force the kiss on her, but nor did he release her. He had her backed against the wall, and she couldn't escape.

"Listen," he commanded, shaking her slightly. "A man came to Dallas. An investment kingpin. His name was Allen Epperson Fields. He started taking in money—lots of money from lots of people. Big investors. Small ones. One of his clients got suspicious. He came to me."

"Let go of me," Valery demanded, glaring at him.

"No, listen. I looked the situation over. I had the feeling Fields was going to take the money and run. Soon. I needed the truth, so I used his secretary to get it. I had no choice. But it backfired. I didn't mean to hurt her. I never promised her anything. I never took her to bed. I never said I loved her."

Valery's reply was scornful silence.

Nikolas gripped her more tightly. "I didn't have much time. I had to get into his records, his safe. Just when I thought I had him, Fields got wind of it. He split. He'd already turned his assets into jewels, I knew. He disappeared. After firing the woman and telling her what a fool she'd been. He made out that I was a corporate raider, after some kind of company secrets, and I'd used her to get them. She tried to kill herself. She survived, but then she found out the truth: Fields was a con artist, and I was law. She disappeared. I didn't mean to hurt her. She was an innocent victim. I'm not used to dealing with innocent people."

"Really?" she asked, venom in her tone. "Who were you used to dealing with? Were you even really a policeman? Was that a lie, too?"

He resisted the desire to shake her to make her listen, and the equally strong desire to kiss her and stop the talking because the talking wasn't doing any good.

"All right," he admitted angrily. "I lied. I was with the FBI. And when I went after women before, it was because I had orders to nail them. Government orders. With Penny Shaw, Fields's secretary, it was different. I lost her and I lost Fields, and I lost about twenty-million dollars. Twenty million stolen from people who trusted Fields. He got away, Valery. The guy was a master swindler."

"So it's down to money again," she retorted, her mouth twisted. "Can Mrs. Bellarion tell you where this Fields and his twenty million have gone? And the only price is my life—and my child's?"

He swore viciously and pulled her closer to him. "I told you. Listen. I wanted to find the woman. To help her. Thelma Bellarion claimed to know where she is. For all I knew, you were guilty. You were my only way of getting to Penny Shaw."

She looked up at him coldly. "Well, Nikolas," she said with deadly calm, "I hope you find her. I don't blame her for wanting to die. Did you tell her the same lies you told me? Or do you use a different set for each woman?"

"I never told her the things I told you," he growled. "I'm not working for Mrs. Bellarion any longer. Now she's claiming Penny Shaw is dead. If she is, I can't help her. But I can help you, Valery. I think something big is going on here, and it'll destroy you if you don't let me help. I mean it. I'll get you a new lawyer tomorrow. A whole team of lawyers."

She looked at him with icy fury. "No more lies, Nikolas. Go. If Penny Shaw is dead, you killed her. Now you're trying to do the same thing to me—take my life away. How can you stand yourself? You didn't even know me, and you came here to wreck my life and Tony's. Get out!"

"I came believing you were guilty," he said, his jaw tense with barely controlled emotion. "I think I knew you were innocent as soon as I looked in your eyes. I can't help Penny Shaw, but I can help you. I said I loved you. I'll prove it."

She tossed her head disdainfully. "How? More of your irresistible kisses? No thanks. You're despicable. Were you the one who had my house vandalized? That was a lovely touch. Oh, how I leaned on you then."

He still had her pinned against the wall. He took her jaw

in his hand and gripped it so she couldn't turn her face from his. "I'd like to kiss you, all right," he breathed. "I'd like to kiss every part of you. Don't worry, I won't. Just listen, will you? I didn't vandalize your house. Or plant those letters. Or the book or the jewel or anything else. Can't you believe that?"

"No," she stated flatly. She wished he'd move away from her, take his hands off her, because his words and his nearness and the intensity in his face were filling her with conflict as sharp as broken glass.

But he pressed against her more insistently, brought his face still closer. "Lies were told before I got here, Valery. Lies are still being told. But not by me. Why did those letters from Chrissy suddenly turn up everywhere? Why all of a sudden would Thelma Bellarion tell Paris she'd pay to have me falsify evidence? Why would John Upchurch tell you? And why would Thelma supposedly leak this story the same day she tells me to get lost and go back to Dallas? All of a sudden she doesn't want me here. She wants me gone."

"Stop it, Nikolas. Just stop!" She pushed futilely against his chest.

"You know what?" he went on relentlessly. "I think somebody wants us both gone, Valery. They want you to run, to incriminate yourself. They don't want me here to stop you. Somebody's getting scared. But if we stand together and stand tough, we might beat them."

She willed her body to be as stiff and unresponsive as stone. She looked at him with polar cold. She refused to answer him.

"They're getting desperate, Valery," he insisted, desperation creeping into his own low voice. "Trust me. Just a little longer. Please. If not for your own sake, for Tony's. I can help you. I can help him."

She only glared. He had no shame. Not a shred. She hated him.

"All right," he said at last. His grip on her loosened, his face hardened with defeat. "I know how you feel. But I'm not leaving town. And I'm not quitting. If you run, I'll run with you. You won't be able to lose me. In the meantime, I'm right next door."

"Yes," she hissed. "To serve and protect. I remember." Her contempt was like a double-edged knife, slicing into them both.

"Remember this, too," he said. He bent and kissed her before she had time to resist. His hands were on her tightly again, and his lips claimed hers passionately. There was fury in his touch, but tenderness, as well. The warmth and strength of him filled her like a forbidden drug.

She willed herself not to respond. He drew back. "Remember that," he said, "because that wasn't a lie."

He looked at her a long moment. All he saw in her face was the same coldness. It was as if she'd turned to stone. And he had done it to her. There was nothing more he could say. He turned and left.

Outside, the night was a velvety black. Crickets sang and a whippoorwill trilled its haunting cry in the darkness.

John Upchurch looked at the woman in the black veils and then at the inert little form on the library's leather sofa. His expression was one of pure horror. "You what?" he asked in disbelief.

"I have Tony Essex," she said, unbuttoning one black glove. She nodded toward the unconscious boy, nearly hidden under an afghan. "I took him from Willadene's. I drugged him."

"You what?" he repeated. Upchurch had always been a

tall, imposing man. Now suddenly he looked shrunken, old.

"I drugged him," she said with satisfaction. "I told you—I want Valery and Nikolas dead tonight. I'm tired of waiting. The boy is my guarantee that it happens. I know you, John. Your nerve is running out. You'd let them both get away if you could. We can't afford that. They're a threat to Dahlia Lee. To all of us. They have to die. Tonight. Or perhaps something will happen to this boy. You wouldn't want that."

He looked at the woman, his hands sweating. She looked like the Goddess of Death standing there in her black dress and gloves and her black feathered hat with its veils.

"I want to talk to Dahlia Lee," he said in a strangled voice. "Immediately. What you're doing will destroy her."

The woman stripped off one glove. She admired her pale hand. "Dahlia Lee isn't strong enough to cope with this, John. And you're the one trying to destroy her. With your cowardice."

"Paris," he said desperately. "Paris wants to talk to her. Paris will put an end to this. Because it has to end. It can't go on. You've gone too far."

"Paris is no longer in charge here," the woman said. She peeled off her other glove and tossed both beside the sleeping child. She flexed her long fingers and regarded their agility and strength. "I'm in charge. Finally. You know it, I know it, Dahlia Lee knows it, and the sooner Paris realizes it, the better."

"We have to talk about this," John Upchurch said, his voice shaking.

She walked toward him. She put her hands on his tie and adjusted the knot so that it slid upward, choking him slightly. "Dear John," she said fondly. "What could you say that would change my mind? You poor dear coward. You've always needed a woman to tell you what to do. It used to be Paris. Now it's me. I'm the new Paris around here."

"Listen," he said, trying not to flinch away from her touch at his throat. "We shouldn't do anything until we trace what Charles did with his share of the money. We've talked about this before. If it suddenly turns up, it could be incriminating."

She pushed the knot of the tie half an inch tighter. He grimaced slightly. "John," she said between her teeth, "you're such a worrier. Let's get Nikolas and Valery out of the way. Then we'll think about the stupid money."

She was starting to cut off his breath. He could feel his heart pounding dangerously hard and wondered if he was going to have an attack. "Listen," he said, patting her hands with false affection until she relaxed her hold. "Listen. I may know where the money is. I think I know."

She went completely motionless, her hands still on his tie. Then, slowly, angrily, she began to run her long nails up and down the expensive silk, almost clawing it. "Why didn't you tell me?"

"You didn't give me time," he answered, lying for all he was worth. He had to do something to stall her. Anything. The child asleep on the sofa terrified him as nothing else had. "Let's sit." He sat on the sofa at the boy's feet, as if he could guard him somehow. "Sit down. This is a long story."

The woman walked to the couch. She ran her hand over Tony's dark hair, stroking-it. "I have the boy. Why should I be interested in where the money is? And if you know, why didn't you say so sooner? Talk."

John Upchurch, pale and trying to hide his fear, began talking.

Nikolas lay on the worn sofa in his rented house, staring

at the ceiling and smoking. He didn't usually smoke. He remembered his first cigarette—in Vietnam, in the field, his first month. He'd watched medics carry away his best buddy, dead. He'd sat there numbly, and somebody had handed him a cigarette and lit it for him. He'd smoked it, feeling like a dead man himself.

He had that same feeling now.

He drew deeply on the cigarette. It tasted rotten, which was fitting.

He'd lost it all. If Mrs. Bellarion had ever known where Penny Shaw was, she denied it now. He wondered, darkly, if the girl was really dead.

He ran the tip of his tongue over the small split in his lower lip. The smoke stung the cut. Valery packed a punch, he thought. It wasn't so much the force of the slaps. It was the contempt they carried.

He'd told her he loved her. He supposed it was true. So what? What was truth to him? The truth had to do with the law, not with emotions. He had ruined her trust in him, and he knew when trust dies, it stays dead.

But maybe, just maybe, he could leave her with something. Maybe, like Cato Pike had said in the bar, the law could save Valery. And Tony. Maybe the truth of hard cold facts could rescue her. Maybe he could find those facts. He could give her that. It wouldn't make her love him, but maybe she'd hate him less.

He swore softly. The way she'd looked at him—he'd felt like the serpent in the Garden. Maybe he was.

But.

But he had to think.

Why had John Upchurch blown his cover? What was this cockamamy story about Thelma Bellarion's wanting evidence faked? Why, if she was going to do it, would she tell

Paris Talmidge, whom she had considered an enemy only a few months before?

It made no sense. Valery said that Thelma Bellarion had called Paris Talmidge today, telling her what Nikolas was supposed to be up to. But Mrs. Bellarion had fired him today. The firing made no sense, either.

He tried to remember the dates on the records of the phone calls Charmian had filched. There'd be no record of an incoming call from Mrs. Bellarion, but had one gone out to her today? He'd never had a chance to look. He could go back to Valery's, demanding to see the records, but she'd probably brain him with a skillet, and he couldn't blame her.

He tried to reconstruct from memory the little he had seen of the phone records. It was an almost impossible task, but his memory was good and it was trained. He could remember patterns.

He ground out one cigarette and, without thinking, lit another. Patterns. His mind resisted concentrating on patterns.

There were too many questions unanswered. Where had Charles gotten the emerald, and how many more had he had? Had he really stashed a secret pile of cash in some crazy account in New Jersey? And why was everything happening to Valery now that he, himself, was here?

Jewels, he thought. Patterns. Things happening now that he was here. No calls to Colorado when Dahlia Lee had been hurt and the Count had been killed. Instead, calls to Dallas. Dallas. When? A flurry of Dallas calls in February. When Dahlia Lee and the Count were in the wreck in Colorado.

Calls to Dallas, not Colorado. In February. Dallas. Where Fields had disappeared in February. Where twenty-million dollars of jewels had disappeared, as well. February. Dallas. When and where Penny Shaw had disappeared.

Jewels. Fields had disappeared with jewels in the middle of February. Shortly after that, Charles had started those flights to New Jersey, and then in April he was dead, leaving only a jewel behind for a clue. An emerald. Fields was reputed to be particularly fond of emeralds.

Patterns, he thought. He sat up. He ground out the cigarette, half-smoked. Fields had disappeared as if by magic. The Talmidges had been calling Dallas about the time he vanished. Charles, a pilot, could help a man disappear, literally to vanish into the air. And take him to New Jersey to fence jewels.

He stood. He put his foot on the sofa and adjusted his leg holster. Patterns, he thought, the blood hammering in his temples.

Everything suddenly fell into place. Charles had helped Fields escape. And gotten murdered for his trouble.

He remembered how Chrissy's signature had reminded him inexplicably of Penny Shaw's. Maybe Penny hadn't been quite as heartbroken as Nikolas thought. Maybe she'd faked the suicide attempt. And then joined Fields—in New Jersey.

He had to talk to Valery. He had to see the phone records and the flight log. If he was right, somebody was setting her up to take a twenty-million-dollar fall. And people with twenty-million dollars at stake play rough. They play unto the death.

He dialed her number, an unlit cigarette hanging from the corner of his mouth. Tomorrow, he was calling the FBI to have them check out everything: the account in Towaco, the emerald that showed up, how Chrissy's writing compared to Penny Shaw's, and exactly what Charles—and possibly the Talmidges—had been up to in Jersey.

He was also going to get Valery a fleet of lawyers, a change of venue, and protection. He wanted her and Tony both out of Constant and under guard.

Her phone rang emptily and repeatedly. He swore and threw down the unlit cigarette. She'd unplugged the thing. He'd have to go to her house and beat on the door and beg and plead for her to let him in. Well, if it took begging and pleading, he'd beg and plead.

For the first time things were coming together, leading somewhere. But even as they did so, the peculiar metallic taste of fear filled his mouth. If he was right about Fields, ugly possibilities arose.

For instance, he might have been sent to Constant because somebody wanted both him and Valery out of the way. He, the hired betrayer, might also be targeted for betrayal himself. After all, they were both caught up in the Fields thing—she just didn't know it yet. The old double double cross. He might be in danger himself.

He left his house, stepped out into the darkness, thinking, if somebody had wanted him here, wanted to set him up, why did they now suddenly want him gone? Why did they suddenly seem determined to make Valery panic and run? He didn't know, he didn't understand, but he didn't like any of it.

He took the back-porch steps two at a time and started beating on her door. "Let me in," he demanded. "It's important."

He knocked until his knuckles were raw. She finally came to the door. She refused to open it, but he could see her through its paned window.

"Open up," he shouted. "I want to see those phone records again. And the flight log."

He saw her hand go up, heard a noise and knew she had shot the bolt so that the door was double-locked now.

"Valery," he cajoled, "I think I know where Charles got that emerald. I told you Fields skipped with jewels. Right about the time the Talmidges were calling Dallas. I've got to know who they were calling. I've got to know if Charles went to Dallas about the time Fields disappeared. Let me in. I promise that's all I want."

Valery looked through the glass, amazed at his audacity. "If you think I'm giving you one more iota of information, you can think again," she said with chilling distinctness. "Go home."

He knocked again, so hard the door shook. "Open up, Valery. I've got to know. Did Charles fly to Dallas in February?"

She stared out the window at him. He was a shadowy figure surrounded by darkness. He was a prince of darkness, she thought, the king of tricksters. He had made a fool of her once, and now he was trying again.

"Valery," he said, and realized he was actually pleading with her, "did he fly out of Dallas on the fourteenth of February? That's when Fields made off with the jewels. If things are connected, you could be in deeper trouble than you know. The stakes are bigger than you think."

"The stakes," Valery said acidly, "are my life and my son. To me, that's big. Go away, Nikolas. I don't want to hear some hot-dog conspiracy story you've cooked up."

"Valery, please." He was trying to be patient, but he knew his voice was ragged with exasperation. "At least tell me what numbers in Dallas the Talmidges were calling. For your own sake."

Unshed tears stung her eyes. "I'm not telling you anything. Get out of here."

She turned her back on the door and walked away. She sat down again at the kitchen table, bending over the list of numbers once more. She tried to shut Nikolas out of her consciousness, but she could feel his presence, even through the closed door.

He pounded on it again, with brutal force. "Valery? Valery!"

She turned her chair so that her back was to the door. She squared her shoulders and vowed she would not cry, that she would never, ever, as long as she lived, shed one tear for Nikolas Grady. She would hate him until the day she died and, if possible, afterward. But she would not cry over him.

"Valery." His voice was edged, insistent. "Look. Do anything you want. Call the FBI. Tell them I'm here. Tell them a former agent is on your back porch telling you that you may be in the middle of a twenty-million dollar heist. Tell them that he says you're in danger. Or tell them I'm crazy. I don't care. Just get in touch with them."

She kept her back to him, her spine rigid. She looked at the numbers on the list and at the poem in the book. She tried to shut out his words, his existence. She stared at the circled page number and the *o*'s that had been inked in.

He was pounding again. "Valery, listen. Call the FBI. They know I'm working the Fields case. You can check me out. Call the Dallas police. You can call the White House and tell them I'm here, if it makes you feel better. But tell me those two things. Did Charles fly out of Dallas on the fourteenth? And what Dallas numbers were the Talmidges calling?"

She gripped her pencil tighter. She pressed her lips together. She remembered gazing at him in stupid adoration, as if he were her knight, her cavalier, her fearless rescuer.

She ignored him and kept looking stubbornly at all the little inked-in *o*'s in the poem.

He punched the door so hard the glass rattled and the dead bolt groaned. She stiffened, but refused to turn toward him.

"All right," he growled, and she could imagine his dark brows knit in frustration, the set of his angular jaw. "All right. You can hear me. I know it. Just tell me if they called any of these numbers: 214-555-3637, 214-555-4874, 214-555-8001. I'll say them again. Take them down and check them."

With painstaking slowness, he repeated the numbers. Valery pretended to ignore him, but she dashed them down beside her list. She didn't know why. He was only up to some trick. His tricks were just more desperate now.

At least he'd stopped his pounding. His breathing sounded heavy, as if he were out of breath, or out of patience, or both.

"Now listen," he said. "Listen carefully. Check the log. Check the phone numbers. But first call the Bureau and check me. Ask to speak to Mort Kurrski. That's a code. It'll get you through immediately to somebody who knows."

There was a beat of silence. She took a deep breath. She was filled with incredible weariness. She wished he'd go. She felt battered, hammered down, and it was taking all her strength just to hold herself together and keep going. But she intended to hold on. And she intended to keep going.

"Then call me within an hour." Nikolas's voice was still ragged, lower now, but no less urgent. "I think Charles knew about Fields. I think he helped him escape to New Jersey. Fields may be behind this frame. If he is, you've got a very desperate enemy. I mean it. Check and call. If you don't, Valery, I'm coming over here and I'll kick this door down to check things out myself. I'll shoot the lock off if I have to. And the only way you're going to keep me out is to kill me. Do you understand?"

Her back stiffened even more. His threats only made her steelier. She would do nothing he asked. If he tried to force his way in, she would stop him. She didn't know how, but the sheer force of her hate could bar him. It could create a wall of ice to keep him out, a barricade of snow to freeze him out forever

He still hadn't gone. She could feel him, as if he radiated some supernatural force.

"I mean it," he said again. "Check it. Call me. I think Charles helped Fields escape. Fields is free but Charles is dead, and you're going to pay for it. And I don't want you to, because you didn't do it. And because I love you."

The last sentence went through her like a knife. How stupid did he think she was? She bowed her head over the page. She knew. Exactly as stupid as she'd been. She'd actually thought she'd been in love with him. It made her sick with anger and shame.

She heard footsteps and knew he was gone. She allowed her shoulders to sag at last. Tears blurred her vision, but she blinked them back. She was alone again, but she wouldn't lose her will to fight.

She would go on until she dropped because she had to save Tony, and if she did drop, then she would get up and go on some more. Because she had to. There was no one else to do it. She had been foolish to believe someone would help.

She stared at the stupid little *o*'s. The tears smeared her vision again and once more she blinked them back. Almost idly, she counted the *o*'s.

Counting the one in the title, there were fifteen.

She forced herself to think about the number fifteen. She added it to the page number, which was 11.

The sum was 26. She turned to page 26. There was a short, sentimental, atrocious poem about the importance of smiling. If it contained any clue, any secret, she could not find it.

She sighed and subtracted 11 from 15. She turned to page 4. It was another sentimental poem, a longer one, but at least better, about an old oaken bucket that once hung in the well. But the well and the bucket were both dry, as far as Valery could discern. They contained no answers.

She sighed again. She rubbed her eyes and told herself she was only rubbing fatigue from them, not tears. She multiplied the 15 by 11. The answer was 165, and she rubbed her eyes again and turned to page 165.

It was a long poem called "The Garden of Proserpine," and it was all about weariness and death. The images, the very rhythm of the poem were sinister.

She shook her head, trying to clear it. She counted the poem's stanzas. There were 12. She looked at her list. The number 12 appeared twice, at the end. She looked at the first entry on the list: 5-2-3

She gnawed her pencil. Perhaps 5 was the number of the stanza, 2 the line, and 3 the word within the line. Perhaps the code was as simple as that.

She counted it out. The third word of the second line of the fifth stanza. When she found it, she stared at it in frightened shock. It made sense. Terrifying sense.

Quickly she went to the second number on the list and found the appropriate word in the poem. It fit with the first. The words were forming a sentence. Nervously she found the third word. It stared at her from the page like an evil omen.

She took in her breath sharply. But she wrote the word down. The sentence seemed complete. She stared at it. She recalled Nikolas's words: "Fields is free."

But the words hidden in the poem conveyed different information, a message unexpected and chilling.

It didn't say, "Fields is free."

It said, "Fields is dead."

Charles was not the only man who was dead. She felt the night close in around her.

Chapter Twelve

"So, you see," John Upchurch improvised, watching the woman in black carefully, "we'd be foolish to move now. Valery and Grady have uncovered something about Charles's share of the money. They'll probably make a move toward it tomorrow. Let them find it for us. Then take care of them."

She stood over the boy's silent form. She was unwinding the layers of her black veiling. He almost wished she wouldn't. He wasn't sure which would be more unnerving— her shrouded face or her uncovered eyes, blue as ice and not missing anything.

"They know where the money is?" she asked dubiously. She drew the last veil away and took the feathered hat from her head. She set it beside the gloves on the mantel. Resting in its own coiled veiling, the hat looked like a black bird lying dead in its nest.

She came back near the boy. She sat on the arm of the couch. She began stroking the child's hair. "Just when did this develop, John? And who says so?"

"The police," he said quickly, hoping the answer wasn't too quick. "Both Cameron Carter and Dennis Finch. There's been a flurry of strange activity today. They think Valery and Grady may have uncovered something over in Corday. There was no other earthly reason for them to go to Corday."

She turned her white face toward him. Her waxy features were almost perfect in the lamplight. Almost, but not quite. The blue eyes were too small, too pallid, too cold. She held her head with the arrogance and self-assurance he found so frightening.

"Corday?" She gave a short bitter bark of laughter. She folded her arms. "You're making this up, John. Who'd hide anything worth anything in Corday?"

"Don't you see?" he asked anxiously. "That's the point. They went to the post office. They picked up something there. It could be anything. A name, an address, a safety-deposit-box number." He paused. He gave her a measuring look. "We have no idea what.

"Perhaps," he said carefully, "we should take the boy back to Willadene. I'll tell you the rest on the way. Really, we must be patient—as planned. Everything will look more natural, and we have a chance of finding the money, besides. We don't want anybody else finding it. Who knows what might happen? It's the one loose end we don't control."

She went to the bar and poured herself a drink. Upchurch was glad she had moved away from the still form of the child. Something about the way she liked to hover over the boy was ominous.

She turned and regarded Upchurch through narrowed eyes. "The boy stays here," she declared. "I don't believe you. Nikolas is good, but he isn't that good. He can't have sniffed out Charles's money already. Not after all the time we've been trying."

Upchurch swallowed nervously. He had once thought Paris Talmidge was a strong woman, but she was nothing compared to this one. This one could twist his conscience raw and make him agree to anything. He had done terrible things for her, promised to do more, and it had to stop. But he truly feared he was too weak to stop her. He could only delay her. He thought of the little boy lying drugged beside him. The thought made him slightly ill.

"It's true," he said. "It was Cameron's day off. He followed them in the pickup. He even thought, for a moment on the way back, that Grady spotted him. We're very foolish if we move against them tonight, before we know what they've found."

She stared at him. She touched her chiseled chin lovingly. He was scared. But she had made his cowardice work for her before. She would not allow it to work against her now. She was in charge.

"You have," she said, raising her glass toward him, "until the end of this drink to convince me." She took a sip and savored it. "Otherwise Valery and Grady die tonight. And the boy—who knows? Maybe he should die, too." She smiled thinly. "I'm beginning to like the idea. Try to persuade me otherwise, dear, dear John."

Nikolas vowed he would be damned in hell before he'd ever again spend the night anywhere without two phone lines. He waited impatiently for Valery either to call him or to appear at his door. She had done neither.

He couldn't say he blamed her.

In the meantime, he had smoked two more cigarettes, each of which tasted like ashes from the stalest pit in Hades. He supposed he was going to have to do it: add insult to injury. Kick down her door and force his way in to get to the records. He hoped she wasn't over there sharpening arrowheads or boiling oil to welcome him.

He couldn't say he blamed her for that, either.

Just before he went, he'd call the Bureau and tell them all he suspected and all he wanted checked. The more he thought about everything, the less he liked it and the edgier he felt.

He was at the point where he wouldn't mind somebody

backing him up. Not so much for his sake as for Valery's. He'd already changed the leg holster, which he hated, for the shoulder holster. He didn't know who might come out shooting, but that was part of the trouble. It could be anybody, including the police.

The police were in this somehow; he'd bet money on it. Some kind of cover-up. So was the Perry family. There were so many of them appearing at too many important junctures. The Talmidges or John Upchurch were mixed up in it, too. They had blown his cover with Valery, and he suspected it was because they were scared of something.

He lit another cigarette, rechecked his automatic, and squinted at his watch. It seemed like he'd been waiting forever.

He remembered the sight of her turning her back on him, and the image hit him like a blade between his ribs. She had trusted him. She had been in love with him.

Or in love with what he had pretended to be, a kind man who cared deeply for her.

He swore for approximately the thousandth time that night. He *was* a man who cared deeply for her, although he was not kind. If fate had given him a fairer chance, he might have been. For her, he would have wanted to be kind. Instead he was going to have to kick her door down.

He shrugged. Fate wasn't fair, and he couldn't afford to be gentle. He could serve her best by being what he had been trained to be: ruthless. Maybe she'd understand that someday.

He glanced at his watch again. He hadn't been waiting anywhere close to an hour. He itched to call the Bureau. He was starting to smell danger everywhere, as if the whole world had broken into nervous sweats.

He stood up, pushing his hand through his hair. Restlessness triumphed. He was going to call the Bureau now. Then he'd go over and take his chances with Valery. It didn't matter if he did it now or forty minutes from now; it had to be done. She was going to hate his guts for forcing his way in.

He couldn't blame her. He had mortally wounded the two women in the world he wanted most to help. Poor, plain, plump, shy Penny Shaw, whom he pitied. And Valery, whom he loved. He supposed he would be well advised never to pity or love anyone again.

He reached for the phone.

Breathless, Valery stood before Nikolas's front door, her heart pummeling. The scent of roses was heavy on the night air. She raised her fist hesitantly, paused, then knocked. The sound echoed hollowly in the darkness.

A long moment passed before he swung the door open. The light behind his tall figure made her blink painfully. Against the light, he looked shadowy, but she thought he was wearing a shoulder holster. A gun, she thought in alarm. But of course. Detectives always had guns.

"You came," he said. He opened the screen door and reached out, taking her by the wrist. He drew her inside. His touch sent her pulses skipping wildly, like small frightened animals.

She looked up at him apprehensively. His dark hair was mussed, his face was taut, and there was an unlit cigarette hanging from the corner of his mouth.

He took it out and flicked it away. "I didn't think you would." He took a deep breath, gripped her wrist more tightly. "I was going to call the Bureau, then come over. Something's going on, something big. Do you believe me?"

She felt her heart hammering and his hand like a brand

of fire around her wrist. She was taking a gamble, trusting him. But all she could do at this point was take chances, no matter how dangerous.

"I don't know if I can believe you or not," she said. It was the truth.

His eyes held hers, willing her to renew her faith in him, if only for a little longer. "Did you check the dates in the log? Did Charles fly out of Dallas on the fourteenth?"

She swallowed hard and nodded. "Yes. The day Fields disappeared?"

He released her hand so that she could show him the records of the calls. He scanned the dates and numbers, setting his jaw. "They called Fields's private office once. They called Penny's desk once. But they called her apartment *eleven* times. In one twenty-four hour period?" He shook his head.

"Maybe she made the arrangements for it all," Valery suggested. "For Charles to come and pick them up." She didn't understand the Talmidges' calls to Penny Shaw, either.

He pushed his hair back from his forehead impatiently. "At least this shows how Thelma Bellarion knew all about Penny. The Talmidges must have told her, sent her the cards and notes. Thelma may never have seen her. She may never have known exactly where she was."

Valery studied his profile. She bit her lip nervously. "You said Penny Shaw tried to commit suicide."

He stared at the phone numbers, his mouth cynical. "She swallowed some pills and ended up in the emergency room. She was released the next day. Maybe she faked the whole thing. For somebody whose heart was breaking, she was keeping long distance plenty busy. Are there any more calls to her number or Fields's? Before this cluster when they both disappeared?"

"Yes." Valery tried to keep the anxiety out of her voice.

"But only to the Penny Shaw number. Once a week. Every Sunday afternoon at two o'clock. For the whole year."

He swore softly. "What the hell?" he muttered. "Was she involved with Fields in some way I didn't understand? Was she actually two-timing him with me? Or what? How did she get mixed up with the Talmidges? What's she to them?"

"I don't know." She shrugged helplessly, wondering how much of the rest she could safely tell him.

"And why would the Talmidges help Fields escape?" Nikolas mused, frowning. "Why hide him here, then take him to New Jersey? Did Penny go with him? And why? Did he have something on them? Is that why they helped him go free?"

She took a deep breath. "He isn't free. He isn't in New Jersey. He's here. In Constant. And he's dead."

He jerked his attention from the telephone records and stared at her in disbelief. "What?" he demanded. For the first time he noticed that she'd brought the mutilated book of poetry with her.

His astonishment, Valery thought, her mind racing, seemed genuine. But then, he'd always seemed genuine. It was his genius. She plunged on, feeling reckless and unprotected as she did so. "The numbers on the list Charles left," she said, trying to explain, "meant words in a poem. I found the poem. The numbers were a message. Fields is dead. And Charles knew."

"Fields is dead?" Nikolas repeated, looking truly dumbfounded. How could he be dead? Nikolas had been sure Fields had skipped to some foreign beach where he sipped champagne and smoked Cuban cigars.

She opened the book to the poem and took out a folded sheet from a notebook. "Look," she said softly, unfolding the paper. She pointed to the list of numbers. Beside each entry was a word from the poem. As he read the message, she read it again herself, still in disbelieving shock.

"Fields-is-dead Dead men rise up never-from-the-garden-of darkness-with-pale-green-roses Only sleep eternal-in eternal night."

"What is this?" Nikolas muttered, shaking his head. "Dead men rise up never from the garden of darkness with pale green roses? Only sleep eternal in eternal night?"

Valery mentally tallied the scoreboard. Nikolas had told her correctly about the dates of the flights. He had told her what numbers the Talmidges were calling. He seemed astonished at the news that Fields was dead. They were points in his favor. He didn't hide everything and he didn't know everything . . . maybe.

She would push him now, see precisely how much she could trust him. "I know what it means," she said. "I know where his body's hidden. I can take you there. Give me your car keys."

His dark eyebrows shot up in displeased surprise. "What?"

"Give me your car keys," she said, holding out her hand. "I can take you there. I know what he means by the garden. By the green roses."

"How did you figure this out?" he shot back. "What do you mean you'll take me there? Listen, I was about to call the Bureau. I'm going to call them now. I want somebody else to know this."

"No," Valery said tersely. "You don't tell anybody yet. You could call Thelma Bellarion. You could call the police. You wanted me to trust you. All right, then do as I say. Give me your keys. We'll go. We'll look. If it's Fields and he's really there, then we get Tony, and together, all three of us go to the state police. I tell them everything I know. You tell them everything you know. Give me your keys."

He drew back slightly, staring at her. "You want my car keys so you can drive me to some garden in the middle of the night to look for a dead guy?"

"I have to know," she said, her jaw stubborn. "I have to know it's the truth, not something somebody made up. For the first time, this is a piece of evidence that might incriminate somebody other than me. If it's true, then I can prove I'm innocent. Somebody else had a reason to kill Charles—Fields was dead, and he knew it."

"Valery, have you ever looked for a dead man before? It isn't pleasant. Especially if you find him."

"I have to know," she repeated desperately. "And I have to know about you, too. You claim to be on my side. All right, prove it. Come with me. Help me look."

He stared at her. She was a woman who'd been pushed to the edge, and now she was pushing back. He'd seen the strength of her will before, and he knew she meant what she said.

"It's crazy," he said, knowing it would do no good. "It's dangerous. This is not something you really want to do."

"I have to know."

He looked at the determination in her face and sighed harshly. She had to know if the message from Charles was genuine. And she had to know if Nikolas was genuine. He supposed, in its reckless way, what she asked was fair. She'd been told enough lies. She had no reason to trust anybody.

He dug his hand into his pocket. He withdrew his keys. "Here," he said brusquely. "Okay, beautiful. Take me away to the garden of darkness. Have it your way."

She took the keys. She held out her hand again. "That's not all I want. I want your gun, too."

"What?" he almost yelled. "You want what?"

"The gun," she answered, looking him in the eye. "There

are a lot of things I don't know about you, Nikolas. Such as, should I trust myself to go someplace deserted with you when you have a gun? I'd feel safer if I carried it. I'll take it, please."

He shook his head. The muscles in his jaw were rigid with resentment. "I don't go digging up some grave at night without my gun. When it comes to trust, do I need to remind you that you're the one accused of murder, not me? But you want my gun. No. Flat no."

Anger flashed from her eyes. "If you really believe I didn't kill Charles, you won't be afraid to give me the gun. Either hand it over or stay here. I'll go look for Fields alone."

He mumbled something profane and handed her the gun. If John Upchurch hadn't blown his cover, he wouldn't be in this mess. Valery would have found out Fields was dead, and like sensible people they could have gone hand in hand to the nice authorities, and later he could have told her he'd once been a little bit involved with Thelma Bellarion, and maybe she would have forgiven him. Now he had no choice.

He looked at her, awkwardly slipping the gun into the pocket of her skirt. "Do you even know how to shoot that thing?"

"I suppose I could do it if I had to," she answered, implacable.

He wondered if she really could.

The woman in black sat on the arm of the couch again. Upchurch tried to keep from shuddering as she reached out once more to stroke the sleeping child's hair.

She had almost finished her drink. "If Valery and Grady are on to something about Charles's cut of the money," she said, "we'll find out later. We can search their places. But first I want to take care of them."

"They could lead us right to it," Upchurch said, almost pleading.

"Why take the chance?" she asked with a yawn. Then she darted him a chilling little smile. "Isn't this a handsome little boy? I never realized what a handsome little boy he is. It'd be a pity for something to happen to him, wouldn't it, John?"

Upchurch felt a surge of sheer cold panic. He'd been involved with murder before, and he'd agreed, out of fear of this woman, to be involved in it again. But he had never imagined she would drag the child into it. Never.

"But," she almost crooned, "maybe, as nice as he seems, he never should have been born. What if Dehlia Lee had married Charles? I think she would have been happy, don't you? She could have had lovely children herself. She could have made Charles happy, too. Valery never did."

Upchurch felt almost strangled by his anxiety. "That was long ago. Charles was weak. Dehlia Lee wouldn't have been happy with him. If she wanted him that badly, why didn't she say so? Why did she hide it? Why did she resent Valery all those years?"

The woman stopped stroking the boy's hair. She laid her hand possessively on the back of his neck. "Dehlia Lee was shy," she said acidly. "Dahlia Lee was proud. The poor girl had practically no defenses at all. Charles never looked at her. What was she supposed to do? Throw herself at him?"

Upchurch sighed. He shook his head. "Why," he asked hopelessly, "do you want Valery and Grady dead tonight? Why can't we stay with the original plan? Take more time? Plant the other letters? Let Grady be seen with her more?"

The woman's hand tightened on Tony's neck. She glared at Upchurch with her ice-cold eyes. "Because it takes too long," she snapped. "Grady hurt Penny Shaw. He as good as destroyed her. And he's in a position to destroy Dahlia Lee.

Dahlia Lee will inherit the controlling shares of the Talmidge Corporation. If anything happens to her, the whole company shrivels up and dies. And we all go with it. You, me, all of us."

He looked at the woman. Her hand grasped the back of the boy's neck like a claw. She was getting drunk on her own ever growing power. Now she had decided that Penny Shaw must be avenged and that Dahlia Lee must be protected. Murder, cold-blooded and immediate, was the only way to achieve what she wanted. She wished for more murder. And she would have it.

"Where in hell are we?" Nikolas demanded, his jaw taut. Valery had parked on a side road, led him through a gap in a tall iron fence and into this garden, shadowy in the weak starlight. He had a shovel from the trunk of the Lynx, and he had a gnawing feeling in the pit of his stomach that he was going to find exactly what he was looking for, and it was going to be the stuff of nightmares.

"The west side of the Talmidges' grounds. The west garden," Valery answered. She whispered instinctively. The gun felt like a stone in her pocket, and she wondered if she should have let Nikolas keep it.

She led the way down a pebbled walk, and he followed her through the darkness. "The Talmidges' rose gardens? You're telling me that Fields is buried right on the Talmidges' grounds? In their garden?"

Valery stooped to avoid an overhanging bow. "Paris and Amanda's father bred roses. He bred a green one. Greenish white. He called it Pale Jade. It was popular as a curiosity for a while. The original bed is here. People say it's massive now. And nobody's ever allowed to attend it except Amanda or Paris."

"Sounds like a promising place to bury a body," Nikolas said without enthusiasm.

"That's what I thought." She paused, listening again to the bark of a dog. It sounded closer this time.

Nikolas followed her through the darkness. Her white blouse was a bluish blur, and her long hair looked as black as a shadow. "How far is this thing?"

She stopped, breathing hard. "No farther. We're here." They stood together, silent a moment, staring at the ancient rosebushes with their gnarled branches. The pale blossoms were dying and nodded, ghostly in the slight breeze. A semi-circular low wall of ornamental stone stood directly behind them, framing them. Immediately behind the wall was a thick grove of rustling cherry trees.

The wall seemed almost to embrace the old bushes with their fading pale blooms. Between the bushes and the path were flagstones with some sort of low, creeping flowers pushing up between them. If Fields were buried close to the green roses, the logical place was beneath the stones.

Valery felt a chill. The spot was too perfect. The flag-stones were heavy and would protect anything hidden beneath. She looked up at Nikolas's shadowy face. She could tell he was thinking the same thing. She shivered.

Nikolas clenched his teeth, studying the flagstones. He sensed Valery's uneasiness, felt the same emotion stirring deep within. Somewhere, closer still, the same dog barked again, wildly, with alarm, then stopped abruptly.

"You're sure," Nikolas said, "that you really want to do this?"

Valery swallowed hard. "Yes. I'm just kind of afraid to use the flashlight. Do you think we can do without it?"

He looked up at the sky, strewn lightly with stars. The moon was new and determined to stay hidden behind a silvery bank of clouds. "We can try."

He bent and curled his fingers under one of the stones nearest the path. "I suppose if they went digging around, they wanted to stay as far from the roots as possible," he hazarded. He groaned as he heaved the stone out of place. It made a wrenching, scraping noise.

The sound, combined with the smell of fresh bare earth, made Valery step backward involuntarily. She held the unused flashlight in both her hands. The weight of the gun seemed to tug at her. She watched as Nikolas bent again, made another sound of exertion and lifted a second stone out of place, then a third.

"I should have brought a crowbar," he grumbled, prying up a fourth stone. "But they move easier than I would've thought. I think somebody else has moved them. Not long ago."

"Nikolas," Valery said timorously, "do you really think he's down there? Fields?"

He strained to lift a fifth stone and roll it to the side. He had already cleared an area almost as large as a man's body. He stood and ran his forearm over his brows, wiping away the sweat of exertion. "We'll see. Remember, this is your idea of a good time, not mine."

He picked up the shovel and started to dig. Valery began to feel distinctly squeamish, and Nikolas sensed it. "Don't worry," he consoled her sardonically. "If anybody's down here, he was put here by expert gardeners. They most likely covered him with quicklime. We'll probably find a nice, tidy skeleton, that's all."

That's all, he thought to himself with dark humor.

That's all, Valery reflected bleakly. A lump of fear seemed to have settled permanently on her throat. "If all we find is a—" she faltered momentarily "—skeleton, how will we know it's Fields?"

"He had a gap between his front teeth," Nikolas said, shoveling away the pungent earth. "And his fillings were all gold. He had a grin like a charm bracelet. You don't find many people with gold fillings nowadays."

Valery was beginning to hope they wouldn't find one now, either, but at that moment Nikolas's shovel struck something with a dull thunk. A fresh wave of fear jumped through her like a charge of electricity.

"Nikolas?" she said, her voice wavering.

He knelt before the shallow hole, and began to brush dirt away with his hands. He said nothing. The only sound was the breeze rustling in the leaves and the faraway call of an owl.

"What is it?" she asked.

He didn't answer. He kept digging gently with his hands.

"Nikolas, answer me. What is it? Is it a body? Is it him?"

"Hand me the flashlight," he said brusquely. She leaned over, trying to give it to him without stepping any nearer the raw opening in the earth.

Nikolas pulled out his shirttail and wrapped a layer of cloth over the light before he switched it on. It gave off a dim but serviceable glow. He shined it into the hole.

He said something in a language that she didn't understand, Greek perhaps. It could have been a prayer or a curse.

She forced herself to take a step nearer. She looked at the spot where the light was shining.

Her knees started to tremble. In the dark gash in the earth, she saw a pale gleam. It was bone, a human skull.

It grinned blindly up into the light. It had a large gap between its upper teeth. Gold dental work twinkled in the flashlight's beam. A neat bullet hole punctured the center of its forehead.

Chapter Thirteen

Nikolas bent over the grave, shoveling with all possible speed and strength. He switched the light off, and darkness enshrouded them again.

"I suggest," he said, heaving a flagstone back into place, "we get out of here fast as possible, get Tony and get out of town. There's no way I can hide that this has been dug up."

Valery leaned against the stone wall, her eyes closed. She heard Nikolas's groan as he hoisted another stone and let it fall back into place. "This must not seem too smart to you right now," she said shakily.

"You wanted to know. Now you do. So do I. Lord, who moved these stones? It wasn't Paris or Amanda."

She heard the scrape and thunk of another stone as he put it in place. She turned, forcing herself to look at the spot again.

Charles could have moved those stones the first time, she thought numbly. How did he know where the body was buried unless he had helped put it there?

The pale roses bobbed in the breeze, scattering their dying petals.

"I—I don't think Charles could have killed anybody," she said weakly. "I don't think he killed Fields."

"I don't think so, either," Nikolas returned, gasping slightly as he forced the last stone into place. "But he probably knew who did and tried to blackmail them. That's the only answer that makes sense. Why else would he leave that code lying around? He thought it would protect him. It didn't."

Valery folded her arms around herself, shivering, although the night air was warm.

Nikolas made an unsuccessful attempt to restore some ruined moss roses into place. He gave up and stood, wiping his hands on his slacks.

He took her arm. "They've probably been wondering what he did with the money he got. Let's hope they don't figure out we know. Let's get out of here. Fast."

He started to lead her back down the path when a light flashed in their eyes. A strong light. Valery, frightened, threw her hand up to protect her eyes, and Nikolas stepped in front of her, as if to shield her with his body.

"Mr. Grady, Mr. Grady," said a man's voice, sounding infinitely sad. "Put your hands up, behind your head. You, too, Valery. Immediately."

Nikolas hesitated for a split second. His instinct was to dive into the darkness for cover, but he couldn't do that; Valery would be left unprotected. He knew his gun was in her pocket, but he didn't know how to go for it without endangering her.

"I said, hands up, Grady. We have you covered. We'd shoot you in a moment. Both of you. Now comply."

Reluctantly Nikolas raised his hands. He put them behind his head. He kept his body between Valery and the faceless man with the gun.

Valery's heart knocked against her ribs. She could not see who held the light. No, she amended, lights—there were two of them shining with blinding intensity.

But she recognized the voice. It sounded strained, affected, but nervously determined. It was the voice of a desperate man.

"John Upchurch," she said. Her hands were locked behind her head, and her arms trembled. Nikolas's broad back stood like a protecting barrier between her and Upchurch's voice. She wondered wildly if there was any way to get Nikolas's gun to him.

"Step up beside him, Valery," Upchurch said. "Stand where I can see you both."

She had no choice but to obey. She stepped beside Nikolas, her eyes narrowed against the glaring lights.

"Upchurch?" Nikolas said, although he could barely see the man through the blinding rays. "Do the Talmidge sisters know they have a body stashed in their garden?"

"The unfortunate thing," Upchurch returned, his voice steadier now, "is that you know it. The gardener heard the guard dog barking and saw someone moving among the rose beds. He reported it immediately. We dismissed him—we knew it would be you. A pity. We've been watching. Right up until you refilled the hole."

Valery sensed Nikolas's taut alertness beside her. He spoke. "Who's *we*, Upchurch? It looks like a woman next to you. Did you two kill Fields? Did Charles help you, then want a bigger piece of the action? So you killed him, too?"

Upchurch sighed. "Close enough, Mr. Grady. You're too smart for your own good. And both you and Valery are too tenacious. Neither of you ever learned to quit. It's our unfortunate task to teach you."

"Who's *we*?" Nikolas demanded again. He didn't like the note in Upchurch's voice. The man sounded as if his back was against the wall. Such men were dangerous. He took pains to keep his own voice level, even lazy. "That wouldn't be Penny Shaw beside you, would it?" he called.

There was a beat of silence. "No," Upchurch replied, an edgy weariness in his voice, "it isn't Penny Shaw."

"Where is she then?" Nikolas challenged, wondering just how nervous Upchurch was. The more scared the man was, the quicker he might pull a trigger.

Another beat of silence pulsed. Valery stared into the lights, trying not to blink in pain.

"Penny Shaw's alive. She's safe," Upchurch said. "But she's hidden. She must stay hidden. Because of you."

Valery stood straighter, willing herself to stop trembling. She made out Upchurch's figure, a shadow nearly obscured by the brightness of the light he held. She could barely see the figure of the woman beside him, but it looked familiar to her.

"Dahlia Lee?" she said, struggling to keep her voice even. "It's you, isn't it? But why?"

"It's not Dahlia Lee," the woman replied, her voice deadly flat and without emotion. Its coldness and the strength of its hate were its most marked characteristics.

Valery had never heard such power and hardness in a woman's tone. Dahlia Lee had a shrill voice with a nervous quiver to it.

"Dahlia Lee is resting," said the woman, with that same chilling flatness. "She has to rest most of the time. She's had a great shock. And soon she'll have to run the Talmidge Corporation."

Valery chewed her lip in confusion. The woman sounded like Dahlia Lee, and yet she did not.

The woman spoke to Upchurch. Her tone could have shriveled every flower in the dark garden. "Tell them what's going to happen to them."

"We're going to take you back to your house, Valery," Upchurch said, the same tired despair marking his utterance. "Both of you. I'm sorry. There you'll have to die."

All she could think was Tony. Who would take care of Tony? It seemed as if her heart had already stopped beating, had turned to a lump of ice. She couldn't breathe.

Nikolas shifted his weight slightly, testing the reflexes of the two people who held them prisoner. Upchurch's reaction was frighteningly immediate.

"Don't move! You can die here as easily as anywhere."

"So I'll die," Nikolas said laconically. "Satisfy my curiosity; Who's the woman? She sounds like she'd enjoy killing."

"You don't know me, Nikolas, dear," the woman said, her icy voice somewhere between a growl and a purr. "You and I never met. Not officially. Nor you and I, Valery. I'm a stranger. Or perhaps I'm not."

She suddenly turned her light upward, so that it shined onto her face. The odd angle of the light was eerie, casting shadows in unnatural places. The woman's face was delicate, with an almost unnatural evenness of feature. It was a face that neither Valery nor Nikolas had ever seen before, yet beneath its artificial perfection, each found it familiar.

She was not Penny Shaw.

She was not the Countess Dahlia Lee Talmidge Corelli.

She was both.

"Dahlia Lee," Valery breathed, frightened at the change in the woman's face. Surely only surgery could have accomplished such alteration. She had heard that Dahlia Lee had been cut up in the accident, knew she'd had operations, knew nobody but members of the Talmidges inner circle had seen her since, but still she was shocked. "Dahlia Lee, what's happened to you? Why are you doing this?"

Nikolas took longer to recognize the ghost of the plump, undistinguished features of Penny Shaw hidden beneath the altered face of the woman before him. He darted Valery a startled glance when she murmured Dahlia Lee's name. Dahlia Lee? The woman was Penny Shaw. He could swear to it.

She had the same small, close-set blue eyes, the same washed-out complexion, the same pronounced widow's peak. She was thirty pounds lighter, and her features had been refined by some surgeon's expert knife, but it was Penny Shaw.

And it wasn't.

"If it's Dahlia Lee," he said out of the side of his mouth, "she lives a double life. That's Penny Shaw."

He addressed the woman, who still grinned at them over the light that illuminated her face so ghoulishly. "Hi, Penny," he said flippantly. "I've been looking for you. Didn't you hear?"

The woman swore at him. She spun the light away from her own face and leveled it so that it shone with dazzling intensity into Nikolas's eyes. "You smug, fast-talking bastard. Penny's not here. She's hidden. She has to stay hidden forever. You tricked her, and you hurt her, and you nearly got us all killed. She would have committed suicide, if I hadn't stopped her."

Nikolas shrugged, seemingly unimpressed. Valery watched him numbly. Wasn't he frightened? she wondered desperately. Wasn't he as bewildered as she was? How could this woman be both Dahlia Lee and Penny Shaw, and yet be neither?

"Glad you saved her, pretty thing," he drawled. "I'm sorry she's hidden. She was nice. But you're looking good. Really great. What do you call yourself? What's your name?"

"It doesn't matter," she retorted, her words as edged as blades. "Most of the time I have to use Dahlia Lee's name. But I'm not her. I'm the keeper. I take care of the others. I'm like Paris. I'm the new Paris. I control everything, and I take care of everything. I'm out now, and I intend to stay out, because I'm the only one strong enough. Dahlia Lee's too weak and always has been. We thought Penny was strong enough, but she wasn't—you proved that, Mr. Grady. Now I have to keep her locked up inside with the others."

"Surely a lady as distinctive as you has her own name," Nikolas offered, almost smiling.

The woman was silent a long tense moment. "I call myself Dahlia Rose," she said at last. There was immense satisfaction in her voice.

"Nikolas," Valery pleaded, her voice barely a whisper.

"Multiple personality," Nikolas explained. "She's both of them. And this one, too—whoever it is."

"I heard that!" the woman snapped. "Just shut up, Nikolas. There's nothing wrong with it. When the others ran out of hope, *I* was there, and I'm strong and getting stronger every day. Stronger than *you* this time. Much stronger."

Valery's brain reeled drunkenly. Dahlia Lee was insane. That was the only answer. Valery had heard of people with multiple personalities before. It was like *Sybil*, or *The Three Faces of Eve*, or the man in California who had at least ten personalities—including one that murdered.

She tried hard to remember what she knew. Two or more distinct personalities could live within the same body. They might be completely different from one another. Some didn't even know about the others. One personality might dominate for years, then in crisis, give way to a second, who would come out and take over. Sometimes they would emerge, one after the other, changing control with bewildering rapidity. There were at least three distinct people in Dahlia Lee. This one was a killer.

"I didn't say there was anything wrong with it," Nikolas asserted casually, his hands still clasped behind his neck.

"We all have different sides. So tell me—did Penny kill Fields? Or did Dahlia Lee? Or was it you, sweet thing?"

"You don't have to say anything," John Upchurch urged her. "Enough talking. Let's just get on with it."

"Shut up," the woman snapped at Upchurch. She held the light so that it shone even more brilliantly into Nikolas's eyes. He squinted helplessly.

"I killed him," she said with obvious satisfaction. "Between you and Fields, you nearly destroyed Penny. Fields figured out what was going on. He knew somebody'd been in his safe. He knew Penny let someone in. He interrogated her. He was merciless. The whole story about you came out. Then he swore at her and told her she was a fool and started unloading the jewels from the safe. She knew he was going to run. She realized then that he must be crooked and that you had to be the law, and that both of you had lied to her. Lied and lied and lied. Penny tried to be so good, but everybody just used her. Well, they won't use her anymore."

"Be quiet," Upchurch said. "Please. Don't say any more. Get them into the car."

"I'll say what I like," the woman sneered. Valery sensed that Upchurch quailed. The woman called Dahlia Rose dominated him; her character was stronger, ruthless and fearless.

Nikolas seemed as at ease as a man starting a casual flirtation. "When a woman's boss turns out to be a crook, isn't that his problem, not hers? Penny wasn't a partner in his scams, was she? She was guilty of nothing. Why murder the guy? Or are you just very intense about business ethics?"

Valery held her breath, afraid Nikolas was going too far. Dahlia Rose—the woman truly did not seem to be Dahlia Lee—was dangerous and unpredictable. Nikolas shouldn't toy with her.

But the woman who had taken over Dahlia Lee and Penny Shaw seemed to enjoy parrying with Nikolas, playing cat and mouse. "No, Nikolas," she said, her tone almost coquettish. "Penny wasn't his partner. She was his victim. She'd coaxed Amanda into talking Paris into investing over four-million dollars of Talmidge Corporation money with Fields."

Nikolas said, "I read you. It wasn't the principle of the thing. It was the money. I applaud the sentiment. So he suckered Penny, too. But how did Penny hook Amanda?"

Valery cringed. Nikolas really was pushing, taunting, almost teasing. Perhaps he was playing for time, but perhaps the woman would simply grow tired of his gibes and gun him down here in the darkness of the garden.

"Penny had a better business mind than Dahlia Lee," the woman explained, as if Nikolas was stupid not to know it. "She was more than Fields's secretary. She was his executive secretary, almost his assistant. She was learning, so she could run the Talmidge company one day. Dahlia Lee couldn't, so Penny had to learn. She'd come back and take Dahlia Lee's place. Nobody would ever know the difference. But you ruined it. You and Fields. The two of you showed her she knew nothing. She didn't know that Fields was a thief, and you were a liar."

"Let's get this straight," Nikolas said. He sounded so calm that he might be about to yawn. Valery gritted her teeth. Nikolas had charmed many women in his time. Surely he didn't think he was going to bewitch this monster, this aberration?

She watched dubiously as he cocked one brow in concentration. "The family—the Talmidge sisters—and our friend Upchurch here have always known about this little condition of Dahlia Lee's. That she's three or four or five people. They knew she'd assumed the personality of Penny and was training to take over the reins of the family business. Penny would just come back and pretend to be Dahlia Lee—new and improved."

This time it was Upchurch who answered. His tone was fraught with impatience. "We had no choice. We were pleased with how well Dahlia Lee was turning out as Penny. When she advised Amanda to invest with Fields, Amanda was glad to do it, as a gesture of trust. Paris was unhappy, but she loves Amanda. But to lose those four million would ruin us, Grady. Penny not only failed, she failed miserably. Now that it's all clarified, let's be on our way."

"I'm sorry," Nikolas said, and Valery was appalled that he had the audacity to smile. "It's not clarified. How long have you known about Dahlia Lee's personalities?"

This time it was the woman who answered. "Since college. Since Valery ran off with Charles. He broke Dahlia Lee's heart. She was shattered. Somebody else had to come and take over for her. The playgirl—Rosalee. But Rosalee only got Dahlia Lee into deeper trouble. Dahlia Lee had to come back and then go rest. And that's where she met Penny."

"You've boggled my mind again, pretty thing," Nikolas hedged. "How could she meet Penny and *be* Penny? Because there really is another Penny Shaw. A relative of Mrs. Bellarion's."

"Not anymore," Dahlia Rose said with great satisfaction. "*I* came then. Because Dahlia Lee was still so weak. I saw that Penny had the qualifications Dahlia Lee needed. She was smart, she liked business, she behaved herself, but she was a workaholic—that was her only problem. That's why she had to rest, too. It was a very special resting place for tired people. Dahlia Lee met her. They found out they knew someone in common—Thelma Bellarion, Charles's mother and Penny's cousin by marriage. They became friends. When they were released, Dahlia Lee took her to the Bahamas. One day Penny just disappeared. She might have drowned. She might have broken down again and run off. But she was gone without a trace, and so we could use her. She had hardly any family. Hardly anyone to miss her. Or care. So we became Penny Shaw."

Valery shuddered. She had no doubt that the real Penny Shaw was dead and that this woman had done it, in cold blood, to take her identity.

Nikolas clenched his jaws He knew as soon as the woman spoke that Penny Shaw was dead. Dahlia Lee—or the killer Dahlia Rose—had become another Penny Shaw. One not afraid to eat too much or be frumpy or work herself to a frazzle to learn everything she could about business.

The real Penny was dead long before he had ever met this woman who had stolen her name. None of the other personalities must have suspected that someday drudging, dumpy Penny Shaw might fall in love with a man like himself, who would send the fragile structure of her personality caving in like a house of cards.

"And Mrs. Bellarion?" he asked. "How did she fit into it all?"

"Thelma Bellarion's a jealous, possessive old fool," the woman said between clenched teeth. "She wanted Valery convicted. And I wanted Valery gone. If that fool judge hadn't let her go free until the trial, things might have been fine. But Valery kept nosing into things. I hated her being free, and I hated her making me nervous.

"I called Thelma, posing as Dahlia Lee, and gave her your name, Nikolas. Because you wouldn't quit, either. You wouldn't stop trying to find Penny and Fields. I guaranteed Thelma that you could find the evidence to put Valery away.

"I gave her all the information she needed on Penny. As far as she knew, she was telling you about the real Penny—she'd never bothered to keep track of her. She didn't mind twisting the truth to get you. And here you are. Mine. At last."

"Here I am. Yours. At last." Nikolas's voice was mocking, but almost friendly. "So the question is why? You want me to guess?"

Valery gnawed her lip harder. Nikolas actually was flirting with the woman. It was buying them time, but if he had any other purpose, she could not fathom it.

"Yes. Guess. You've always been so smart. Guess."

He shrugged slightly. "Penny screwed up. You emerged and killed Fields. Then you called home. Because you were in trouble, big trouble. Your aunts sent Charles to get the body and help hide it. They probably sent you, too, Upchurch. Right?"

Upchurch said nothing, so Nikolas shrugged again. "You faked suicide—"

"I didn't fake it," the woman nearly snarled. "I *stopped* it. Penny really wanted to do it. I let her take a few pills because it gave her a kind of alibi—she was in the emergency ward when John and Charles smuggled the body out of Dallas. But she would have really done it, if I hadn't been there to stop her."

"Sorry," Nikolas said pleasantly. "No insult intended. Anyway, the next day Charles went back to Dallas and got you. Then he helped Upchurch fence the jewels in New Jersey, so that the Talmidge Corporation got its money back—with a tidy profit, I imagine. And Charles got a nice bonus. But he got greedy, blackmailed you for more, and you killed him. And the most convenient person to frame was Valery."

"Charles tried to put pressure on Dahlia Lee," the woman sneered. "He didn't count on *me*. On that last flight I simply slipped his pills out of his shaving kit, locked myself in the rest room and refilled them with Parathionex. He was dead that night."

Frightened as Valery was, she felt anger flare within her. "You killed my husband. Just like that." She shook her head in disbelief. "You caught him up in your dirty games and then you actually murdered him."

"And saw that the police found the jar of Parathionex in your backyard. I saw to it that the evidence boxed you in, whichever way you turned. But you wouldn't stop fighting, and you wouldn't stop asking questions. And neither would our darling Nikolas here."

"So you arranged that we cancel each other out, didn't you, sweet thing?" Nikolas's voice was so calm that it took Valery a few seconds to understand the import of what he said. "It'll look like she discovered the truth about me and knocked me off. And as if I took care of her in self-defense. The case on Charles is closed, the chief suspect dead, but with one more victim to her credit. And nobody ever finds the link between Fields and Penny Shaw and you."

The woman sounded immensely satisfied with herself. "That's right. You cancel each other out. And nobody connects me to Penny Shaw. How could they? I don't even look the same. Dahlia Lee was conveniently away from home the whole time Penny was learning how to take care of business. She was married to her Count. Except there was no Count. So we simply said he died and brought Dahlia Lee home where she's safe and I can take care of business for everyone. I'm the keeper now. The guardian. The final flower of the Talmidge family—Dahlia Rose."

"Dahlia Rose," Nikolas said reflectively. "And just how did Dahlia Rose get the police under her thumb? And Mr. Upchurch here? And all those other people who just happen to be in the Perry family?"

Upchurch spoke to the woman, his voice quavering with anxiety. "If you want to kill them, let's get them out of here and kill them," he almost pleaded.

"Be quiet," commanded the woman. "I like this. Nobody ever gets to see the real me. I always have to pretend to be that prissy, stupid Dahlia Lee. Nikolas thought I was poor, pathetic Penny Shaw. He'll see who's pathetic now."

"How did you do it?" Valery demanded. "How did you turn everyone against me? Even people who hardly knew me."

"It's simple," the woman retorted, her voice icy, "you're expendable. Dahlia Lee is not. When she's thirty-five, she'll inherit over forty percent of the corporation. Paris and Amanda have controlled it for her. They'll leave her another twenty-five percent. That means Dahlia Lee will control sixty-five percent of the company. She'll *be* the company."

Valery shook her head, puzzled. "But the other people—Sheridan Milhouse, Tammi Smith, Cameron Carter, even the chief of police—"

"They own the other thirty-five percent," the woman said sweetly. "Darling John here owns the most—a whole twelfth of the stock. But the rest is down to dribs and drabs. Sheridan Milhouse owns a thirty-second of it. Cameron Carter the same. Tammi Smith a sixty-fourth. It brings them only a few thousand a year. Twenty or forty—I forget, exactly—but enough to be crucial to them. Enough to make them very, very protective of Dahlia Lee."

Again Nikolas shifted his weight slightly. Again he heard John Upchurch move in immediate nervous response. There was no way for Nikolas to get to the gun without getting himself shot, and probably Valery, too. But Upchurch was uneasy, and the woman was arrogant, and he could only hope somehow he could make those factors work in his favor.

"Why," he said, "should any of them bother to protect Dahlia Lee? Why should they give a damn what happens to her so long as their stock is safe?"

"I told you," the woman snapped, shining her light more directly into his eyes. "Dahlia Lee *is* the Talmidge Corporation. Her grandmother was Bartholomew Talmidge's second wife. She went mad. Of their two sons, one died by his own hand. Royce, Dahlia Lee's father, wasn't the most stable of men, and he knew it. He was afraid of the old notion of tainted blood. That's why Dahlia Lee can't inherit her share until she's thirty-five. To ensure she's free of that taint."

"Wait a minute," Nikolas said. "You're saying Dahlia Lee can't inherit that forty percent if she's mentally unstable? What happens to it?"

"Royce was a fool," the woman practically spat. "If Dahlia Lee becomes ineligible for her inheritance, it goes to GreenWorld."

"GreenWorld," Valery said, drawing in her breath sharply. GreenWorld was an environmental group, an active and aggressive association of which her father had been a member. "GreenWorld would shut the company down in a minute. It's against pesticides. They'd dissolve the corporation, put it out of business."

"Precisely," the woman replied with bitterness. "I said he was a fool. Dahlia Lee had enough money from her mother's side to ensure she was always taken care of. But Royce was sick of life and sick of family and sick of the company, and he made sure if his own child wasn't fit enough to benefit by it, he'd see that it was destroyed."

"But," Nikolas said carefully, testing her reaction, "Dahlia Lee isn't fit. She isn't stable. In fact, according to you, she isn't even here."

"She's fine!" the woman retorted with such fury that Valery winced. She was afraid that Nikolas had finally pushed too hard and too far. "Dahlia Lee is perfectly fine, because *I'm* here to take care of her. And all the people who want to keep their Talmidge Corporation profits rolling in had better damned well make sure that she stays fine. And nobody ever says she's not sane. Nobody ever says it. Even when she had to go away that time, it was to rest—that's all."

"I understand," Nikolas said with disarming sincerity. "Forgive me. But, sweet thing, one thing's still got me puzzled."

"Precisely what's that, dear, darling Nikolas?"

"What makes you think we're going to let you take us back to Valery's and kill us without a struggle? You may own a few people in the police department, but you don't own it all. If we put up a fight, you've got a very suspicious scene on your hands. Especially since I've just been in touch with the FBI about the connection between Fields and Penny Shaw and the Talmidges."

Valery took another deep breath and held it. Nikolas was getting ready for something. If he mentioned struggle, he meant for her to struggle. The one thing Dahlia Rose didn't know about was the gun. Valery knew that she must stay attuned to Nikolas's slightest nuance, his least hint, his smallest move. She tensed herself.

"You won't struggle," the woman said, pleased at her own confidence. "And if you called the Bureau, why are you prowling in our garden like common thieves, disturbing evidence? No, I think you're lying. And I *know* you won't struggle. Do you know why?"

Nikolas gritted his teeth. She was tough, this one. She was smart, too. Damned smart. He said what she wanted him to say. "Why?"

"You won't put up the slightest fight," she returned sweetly, "because I have the boy. I have little Tony. We were just about to take him to the car when you turned up."

She turned the beam of light from their faces to the ground. There lay Tony, still wrapped in the afghan, as inert as if he were dead. The woman had one high-heeled foot resting on his back as if she were the huntress and the boy were her kill.

Chapter Fourteen

Tony was breathing. Valery, almost numb with panic, had been able to establish that much during the ride to her house. She was sitting in the front beside Nikolas, who was driving, and she kept looking into the back seat.

Tony was alive, but he must have been drugged. Dahlia Rose sat there beside John Upchurch, the child draped across her lap. She had an automatic aimed at the back of Nikolas's head. Upchurch, too, held a gun, and kept it trained on Valery.

"Face the front," Dahlia Rose ordered Valery.

"I just want to know he's all right," Valery said.

"He's all right as long as you do exactly what I say," Dahlia Rose retorted. "I told you. Cooperate and back to Willadene's he goes. He'll never know what happened. Now face front."

Valery obeyed, her heart beating rebelliously. She no longer had the gun. John Upchurch had frisked them both before ordering them into Nikolas's car. He had found the gun and taken it. Dahlia Rose had laughed out loud at the despair on Valery's face when Upchurch drew the gun from her pocket. Valery knew Nikolas would have lunged for the woman at that moment if he hadn't feared for her safety and Tony's.

"How much stock in the Talmidge Corporation does Willadene own?" Valery asked bitterly, staring out into the night. "How much did it take for her to sell my child?"

Dahlia Rose sighed. "She and her sister each own a

248

sixty-fourth. I suppose it will go to the twins someday. It brings a tidy-enough sum. What is it actually, John?"

"They each clear about twenty thousand a year," Upchurch muttered.

Twenty thousand, Valery thought, breathing hard. That's what somebody else's child was worth to Willadene Davis. Twenty-thousand dollars.

"And Osgood Perry? How much was he getting to make sure I went to prison?"

"Osgood sold his shares years ago," Dahlia Rose answered smugly. "Dahlia Lee's mother bought them from him for her, but her father tied them up in that stupid will. Along with the shares she bought from Lulu Upchurch. No, it was simply our good luck that Osgood was appointed your attorney. Fate couldn't have been kinder. The man's incompetent. He's too stupid to conspire against anyone."

Conspire, Valery thought darkly. Charles had blundered into a conspiracy to protect Dahlia Rose from charges of murder, then she had murdered him, as well, and the others had conspired to protect her again. This time the conspiracy was against her and Nikolas. The best she could hope for was that Tony would be spared.

But as Nikolas pulled up in her driveway, she felt her fear giving away to anger and the desire to retaliate. She had fought this hard and this long to save herself and Tony. She could not stop fighting now. She must stay alert, looking for any chance, any opportunity.

"Get out," Dahlia Rose ordered. "This is very convenient, really. Now nobody has to see our car here. We were about to load Tony into the Rolls when the gardener said someone was in Amanda's rose bed. I knew it had to be you. How fortunate we had the boy, isn't it, John? And you thought I'd done the wrong thing. You always did have to have a woman to think for you."

Upchurch climbed out of the back seat. He had Tony's limp body under one arm, as if the child were a sack of grain. In his other hand he held the automatic, which he kept aimed at Valery. "Get out," he said tersely.

She got out. From the corner of her eye she saw Nikolas, his long body uncoiling from the seat while Dahlia Rose kept her gun trained on him. She was careful to keep a safe distance from him.

"Into the house," Dahlia Rose ordered. "And then, Valery, you're going to make Nikolas a nice cup of coffee."

Valery went up the porch steps on numbed legs. She fumbled with the lock. The door swung open.

She entered, John Upchurch right behind her, his gun pressed against her back. She switched on the light.

Upchurch nudged her toward the living room. She turned on a table lamp and went to stand by the mantel. Nikolas entered the living room, his hands up, and Dahlia Rose followed, her gun still aimed at the back of his head.

Dahlia Rose looked at the smashed television set. "What happened here?" she demanded. "This is going to look like somebody struggled. Well, so what? Two people dying—of course, things get broken."

John Upchurch looked uneasier than before. He dropped Tony unceremoniously on the sofa. Dahlia Rose went and sat beside the boy. She adjusted the afghan carefully so that it covered the sleeping child to his thin shoulders.

"I thought you'd know what happened, sweet thing," Nikolas said, watching her every move. He nodded at the broken television set. "Your goons were here today. Probably one of the cops. Harassing Valery. They've gotten good at it."

"Nobody gave any such order," Dahlia Rose bit out.

"You're Lying. You're determined to die lying, aren't you, Nikolas?"

He smiled. "I'm not lying. Somebody was trying to scare her out of town. And Mrs. Bellarion fired me today and ordered me back to Dallas. Did you know that? You're lucky I'm still here. But you've been a lucky lady all along."

"Thelma Bellarion did nothing of the kind," Dahlia Rose snapped. "I wanted you here, and I've got you."

Valery watched Upchurch's reaction. He was growing visibly more nervous. She suddenly understood what Nikolas was trying to do.

"Sweetheart," he said to Dahlia Rose, "you ought to know you're not quite as much in charge as you think. Somebody in the organization isn't as loyal as you'd like. I think it was Upchurch here. He was trying to get rid of both of us. Before you started another round of Stack the Corpses. Did he tell you they found more letters from our friend Chrissy? You signed them, didn't you? But I bet you didn't plan on them turning up this early. Or maybe at all, if Valery's going to be so conveniently dead."

Dahlia Rose's face went terrifyingly cold. She stared at Nikolas as if he were some form of insect. The mention of the second batch of letters obviously startled her.

"Your friend Upchurch looks jumpy, sweet thing. I think he's been trying to double-cross you. Cheat you. He blew my cover, too. Called Valery tonight and told her I'd been working for Mrs. Bellarion."

"Shut up," Upchurch ordered, but the gun in his hands had begun to shake slightly.

"Yes," snapped Dahlia Rose, throwing Upchurch a venomous glance. "Shut up, Nikolas. You're trying to play divide-and-conquer, but it won't work. If John's been naughty, I'll deal with him later. Now it's you I'm taking care of. You and Valery. Valery, go make him coffee. John, keep her covered. If she tries anything, shoot her. It doesn't really make any difference who dies first."

Valery went to the kitchen. She tried to think straight. Nikolas had rattled John Upchurch and rattled him badly. But she could make no move from within the kitchen. Nikolas and Tony were still in the living room, and Dahlia Rose would shoot them both at the slightest provocation.

She made the coffee. She willed her hands to keep from shaking as she spooned the powder into the cup. "You did, didn't you?" she asked Upchurch softly. "You tried to scare me out of town. And make Nikolas go, too. That's why you called and told me the truth about him. To make me desperate enough to run. And force him to leave. Isn't it?"

Upchurch looked resigned. "I tried, but I failed. You were both too stubborn. I have no choice in this, Valery."

"Everybody has a choice," she said. "Everybody has responsibilities. You could stop this."

"Nobody can stop her," Upchurch said, his mouth working nervously. "It's too late. You didn't go when you could. I'll try to save your child. It's the best I can do."

She set down the spoon. She looked him in the eye. "If anything happens to him, it's on your head. If anything happens to that child, you'll burn in hell for eternity, John Upchurch."

But the look on Upchurch's face told her he had accepted his fate. He was a man with nothing left to lose. "I'm going to burn in hell already, Valery. We both know that." Any moral light within him had been quenched. His soul belonged to Dahlia Rose now, completely and forever.

He glanced at the counter, saw the emerald twinkling. "Ah, part of Charles's payoff. He obviously left a message for you. Where's the rest of it?"

"You'll have to find it," Valery challenged.

He pocketed the gem. He looked down at the kitchen table where her notes and scribbles and the atlas still lay. "I imagine it's all here," he said. He sighed again. "We'll find it. All of it. Ah, Valery, why didn't you run? Why did you walk right into our hands?"

"Get in here!" Dahlia Rose ordered from the living room. "Stop talking."

John gestured toward the living room with the gun. Valery gave him another cold look, picked up the coffee and carried it into the living room. Nikolas sat in the old green armchair. He still had his hands clasped behind his head.

"Set the coffee down. Over there." Dahlia Rose nodded toward the small table near the arm of the chair, and Valery did as she was instructed.

Dahlia Rose reached into the pocket of her black dress and drew out a vial. She tossed it so that it landed at Valery's feet. "Pick it up," she ordered. "Wipe it off so that only your prints are on it. Then put it in his coffee. All of it."

Valery picked up the vial. "What is it?"

"Parathionex cut with sugar. It's going to look as if you poisoned him, just as you poisoned Charles. You found out he was working for Thelma Bellarion, so you murdered him. Wipe off the vial and pour it in his coffee."

Valery rubbed the vial lightly against her skirt. She removed the cork.

She needed to act. She began to breathe hard. "I—I—I'm scared," she almost sobbed. She put her right hand into her mouth, as if gnawing her nails. "I don't want to kill anybody. I don't want to die. Please, Dahlia Lee. Please don't make me do this."

Nikolas looked at her carefully. He looked at the coffee and back at her.

"I'm not Dahlia Lee," the woman in Dahlia Lee's body said. "I'm the keeper, I told you. The guardian, the double blossom, Dahlia Rose. Stop sniveling, Valery. It's disgusting. Put the poison in the coffee."

"I'm frightened," Valery said, beginning to sob in earnest.

"Do it now, or I'll shoot you first. You can die at his feet like his dog," Dahlia Rose cried angrily.

"I'm doing it." Valery wept, her face pathetic with fear. "I'm doing it. It's just I'm so scared."

She turned, shaking, and emptied the vial. She knew her body blocked Dahlia Rose's view at least partly. She did not know how clearly John Upchurch could see her. She tried to pour most of the poison so that it landed in the saucer, not the cup. She gripped the vial so that her moistened fingers and thumb caught some of the powder. She could feel it, gritty, sticking under her nails.

Nikolas's face betrayed nothing. Valery kept pretending to sob.

"John," Dahlia Rose said sweetly, "check the cup. Make sure she didn't spill any."

Valery almost stopped, mid-sob. She saw the steeliness in Dahlia Rose's eyes, though, and kept up her pretense. She knew instinctively that Dahlia Rose liked seeing her cry and would savor the enjoyment as long as possible. "I'm—so—scared," she wailed again.

She dropped to the floor beside Nikolas and held out her clasped hands toward Dahlia Rose. "I'm begging you," she said. Dahlia Rose only smiled.

John Upchurch stepped to the table. He looked at the cup and then down at Valery, whose hands shook as she held them toward Dahlia Rose. Wordlessly he picked up the cup and set it on the table. Valery looked up at him, sobbing harder. "Please, John," she begged. "You won't let me die, will you?"

He said nothing, only gave her a cold look. Then he poured the poison from the saucer into the coffee. Her ruse had failed. She had kept only a minuscule amount of poison from the cup.

Valery fell forward slightly, her hands on the floor, as if she were too weak to support herself otherwise. "Please don't do this." She hoped she looked too helpless to defend herself.

"Now, Nikolas," Dahlia Rose purred, "drink it. It won't kill you right away. It'll take a good five minutes. They'll be a painful five minutes. But then it will all be over. So drink. Drink to dear little Penny Shaw. Drink in her honor. For me."

Nikolas locked eyes with the woman. Five minutes wasn't a lot of time, but it could be enough. She wasn't going to expect much action from a dying man. But she couldn't kill him more than once. If he could take her out first, then all he could hope was that Upchurch didn't have the guts to kill, or at least to kill fast, and he could take him out, too. Before either Valery or the kid got hurt.

The woman's guard should be down once he drank the poison. Upchurch's, too. But a determined man could do a lot with five minutes of life left.

"Cheers," he said, and smiled at Dahlia Rose.

He took the first sip and grimaced. The stuff tasted like hell. He could already feel it burning.

He looked at Valery, who still pretended to be too frightened and supplicant to do anything. His eyes sent her a message. *When I move, you move. And do it fast. Your life depends on it.*

Valery watched in horror as he took the second swallow.

She understood precisely what he was doing. He was sacrificing himself so that he could take Dahlia Rose by surprise. If he could.

He was going to die for them. *No!* she thought. *Nikolas, don't. For God's sake, don't.*

Her fingers closed on something half-hidden beneath the green armchair. It was a little metal car, one of Tony's, no larger than a matchbox but surprisingly sturdy.

"Drink up, Nikolas," cajoled Dahlia Rose. "Drink it all down, like a good boy, and I promise you Valery will die fast. But if you dawdle, well, they say being shot in the stomach is a terrible thing."

"You promise she won't suffer?" Nikolas asked, raising the cup to his lips again. "You give your word?"

"I give you my word. See how frightened she is?" Dahlia Rose nodded at Valery, who still crouched beside the chair, looking helpless. "She won't suffer long. I promise."

"And the boy?" Nikolas demanded. "The boy is safe?"

"The boy goes back to Willadene's. I promise that, too."

Valery no longer believed her, nor believed in John Upchurch's power to protect Tony. Dahlia Rose and Upchurch were watching Nikolas raise the cup to take another drink.

With a little cry she rose up on her knees and pointed to the windows. "Lights," she cried, with a strangled sob. "I saw lights out there! It's my aunt! She'll walk right in. She has a key. Oh, please, don't kill her, too. Please!"

As Dahlia Rose and Upchurch glanced nervously toward the windows facing the drive, Valery pitched the toy car across the carpet so that it hit the foyer wall and bounced out of sight, rattling and clattering.

"Oh," Valery wailed wildly, "she's letting herself in!"

Both Dahlia Rose and Upchurch looked toward the

foyer, their attention drawn by the scrabbling noise. Dahlia Rose's gun swung toward the entryway, to the corner around which Charmian might appear.

Nikolas was on his feet. His fist connected with John Upchurch's jaw. Valery sprang as hard as she could, hurling herself against Upchurch's legs. He staggered, fought for balance, then tumbled backward.

Dahlia Rose gasped, but Nikolas was already on her. He stumbled slightly, one of his trick knees buckling momentarily. He regained his momentum, seized her by the wrist. As he tried to wrestle the gun from her, she leveled it and pulled the trigger. The shot nearly deafened him and struck him in the shoulder. He jerked backward, then went for her again. This time he knocked her to the floor. She was an amazingly strong woman, all lean muscle.

Valery had fallen on the dazed John Upchurch like a wild thing. "Give me that, you coward." She wrenched at the gun as she smashed her hand across his face with all her might. Frightened and surprised, he lost his hold on it. He tried to snatch the gun back, but she kicked and slapped at him, knocking him backward again.

He tried to rise, but she struck him across the forehead with the gun. "That," she cried out, tears of rage stinging her eyes, "is for letting her take my child!" He fell back, groaning.

Valery scrambled to her feet. John lay groggily at her feet. He tried to rise again. He almost made it, grasping desperately at her skirt. With a strength she didn't know she possessed, she picked up the broken television set and brought it down on his head. Glass and plastic shattered. He moaned and fell backward again, and was still. She wondered if she'd killed him, and knew that she didn't care.

She took three steps across the room and stood so her

body shielded Tony's sleeping on the sofa.

She trained the gun on Dahlia Rose, who still struggled with Nikolas. The woman fought as if she were possessed, and Valery was afraid to fire at the tangled bodies.

"Let go, Dahlia Rose," she cried. "You're not in charge any longer." She held the gun in both hands and kept it aimed at the figures writhing on the carpet.

She was alarmed at how violently Dahlia Rose fought, and how much blood stained Nikolas's shoulder. His face was white and his teeth clenched. She knew he was feeling the first effects of the poison.

"Just shoot," Nikolas ordered, trying to keep Dahlia Rose from leveling her own gun again. "Shoot, dammit, Valery. If you get me first, then shoot again. It doesn't matter. Get her."

But Valery could not. She was not sure she could shoot at all.

Dahlia Rose managed to pull away slightly from Nikolas. The gun spun out of her hands, skittering toward the foyer. Awkwardly Dahlia Rose scrambled away, kicking at Nikolas's wounded shoulder with her spiked heel. She landed two blows. As he shuddered from their impact, he doubled up convulsively. The poison had hit, hard. Dahlia Rose scrabbled on her hands and knees to snatch the automatic from the floor.

"Stop!" Valery commanded. She forced herself to shoot, but the shot went wild. It shattered a window. The recoil almost knocked the gun from her hands, but she hung on, trying to aim again.

Nikolas, gritting his teeth, lunged for Dahlia Rose again. He caught her by one ankle and began to pull her back to him. Dahlia Rose kicked and squirmed, reaching for the gun.

"Don't!" Valery cried. "Touch it and you're dead. I told you. You're not in charge anymore."

Dahlia Rose fell flat, then tried to rise to her hands and knees again. Nikolas, grunting with pain, pinned her legs down. She drew herself up and pitched herself forward, toward the gun. Nikolas still held her legs, but it seemed to be costing all his strength. His face was contorted with pain. He threw himself higher, so that he pinned her waist and left shoulder to the floor.

Dahlia Rose would not stop fighting. The gun was just within her reach. But if she got her hands on it, it would be almost impossible for her to fire it effectively at either Valery or Nikolas, so awkward was the position in which Nikolas had her pinned. She struggled anyway.

She glared crazily around her. "I'm still in charge," she hissed. "I'm still in control. And you can't take us."

She reached for the gun. Before Valery could fire, she had it. Nikolas lunged again, so that now her right shoulder was pinned instead of her left. Dahlia Rose could turn the gun nowhere except on herself.

Nikolas reached to snatch her hand. She eluded his grasp. "I'm still in charge," she hissed again. "I'm the strong one." She aimed the barrel at her own chest and pulled the trigger.

Her body jerked. Then she slumped lifeless to the carpet, facedown, a bullet in her heart.

There was a moment of echoing silence.

"See to Tony," Nikolas managed to say. He forced himself to rise, to take two staggering steps toward the boy. He crumpled to the floor at the foot of the sofa.

Tony groaned softly and stirred. He was breathing regularly, as if he merely slept. His color was good.

Nikolas managed to sit up, but didn't try to get to his

feet again. He put his hand against Tony's cheek. "I think he's all right," he rasped, breathing hard. "I think—he's all right."

He groaned. "Oh, God." He doubled up. He clutched his midsection convulsively, his face twisted.

Valery had been standing as if paralyzed. She dropped the gun and fell to her knees beside Nikolas.

"Nikolas!" she screamed. She took him in her arms. His chest was covered with blood, sweat beaded his upper lip and forehead, and his hair was damp.

"I think," he said between his teeth, "I think . . . he's all right. Valery, I think . . ." He doubled up again, grimacing and clutching his stomach. "I think . . ." he repeated, his voice strangled.

Tears half blinded her. "Nikolas? Nikolas? I'm calling an ambulance," she told him. "Hang on, do you understand me? Hang on. For God's sake, hang on."

She forced herself to let go of him, to rise. She stumbled to the phone, dialed the emergency number with trembling fingers.

She heard her own voice and was surprised it sounded so rational as she asked for an ambulance. It was as if something of her father's unshakable coolness of purpose came to her in a time of emergency.

She hung up and ran to the kitchen. Her hands shaking again, she filled a large glass with water to dilute the poison.

"Check the kid," Nikolas panted when she tried to force him to drink the water. "Is he all right?"

"Drink," she ordered.

He drank, then repeated his demand. "Check the kid. I'm fine." He tried to rise again.

He wasn't fine, blood was everywhere, but he was trying to rise again. Desperate to set his mind at ease and keep him still, she quickly examined Tony.

"He's all right, Nikolas. I swear. Be still. Don't move."

He took a deep breath, as if he were going to say something. A strange look passed over his face and he made a sound deep within his throat. He fell to the floor. Anguish twisted his mouth.

She was on her knees beside him. "Nikolas?" she cried. She held him, his head in her lap. She watched helplessly as he tossed back and forth, teeth clenched, fighting the pain. She ran one hand through his damp hair.

"You're going to be fine," she kept saying. "You're going to be fine."

She knew she had to keep him conscious; that way he had a chance. But suddenly he had another convulsion and blacked out. He went as still as death in her arms.

She held him as tightly as she could, doing for him the little that she could. But he was slipping away, farther and farther.

The ambulance attendants had to pry her apart from him. "You got to let go," one said brutally at last. "Let go, lady. The man's dying. Let him go. You can't do him any good."

Chapter Fifteen

Nikolas refused to die. That was how the doctor had explained it to Valery. The man should have died, but somehow he hung on. Deep within him, some mysterious force stubbornly refused to give up.

Valery stayed by him as much as possible. He was in intensive care for three days, and they would allow her only fifteen minutes with him an hour. He was in a coma.

He was moved to a private room on the fourth day when he began to have brief islands of consciousness. Then he would drift away again, as if borne away on some dark private river. Valery held his hand and prayed.

On the sixth day he groaned and tried to say something. He could not. But his hand seemed suddenly to come alive in hers, to hang on to her as tightly as she did to him. "Please, Nikolas," she begged, "come back to me. Please."

Unconsciousness claimed him again, but his hand still gripped hers as if some part of him knew she was there and would not let her go.

On the rainy afternoon of the seventh day, he stirred uneasily and his fingers tightened around hers with still more force. With her other hand she smoothed his hair. His eyes flickered open.

Valery held her breath. He looked at her, slightly dazed. "Nikolas?" she whispered.

The dark eyes blinked. He frowned. The pressure on her hand tightened. He drew her toward him with surprising strength.

"Nikolas?" she said again, her voice trembling. Her face was only inches from his.

He gave her a slightly crooked half smile. He turned his head so that his lips were as near as possible to hers. She knew what he wanted. She kissed him. She kissed him a long time.

"Welcome back," she said against his mouth, then drew back so she could drink him in.

"You—you're all right?" he asked, his voice raspy, cracked. It seemed an effort for him to talk. "You're okay?"

She fought back tears of relief. She ran her hand over his dark curls again. "I'm fine. How are you? Do you want a doctor?"

"I want you." He shook his head slightly, as if his thoughts were still cloudy. "Tony. How's Tony?"

He tried to raise himself, then fell back with a groan. When he tried a second time, she put her hand on his good shoulder to keep him still. "Tony's fine," she said, trying to keep her voice steady. "He's perfect. He woke up the next morning with a headache, that's all. Oh, Nikolas, we've been worried to death. How are *you?* Are you sure you don't want a doctor?"

He kept his fingers laced through hers. "I've got what I want. Stay here."

"How do you feel?"

He grimaced. "Like hell. How long have I been here?"

"A week."

"I feel like I've got a grand piano on my shoulder." He grimaced again.

"It's a cast. You were shot badly, Nikolas. It's going to take a while to mend."

His face darkened as memories came coursing back. "Dahlia Lee—Dahlia Rose. She's dead."

It was a statement, not a question. Valery nodded. They were both silent a moment.

"Upchurch?"

"In custody. He's told everything. Shh, Nikolas, I don't think you should talk anymore."

Pain etched his face, but it was soon replaced by determination. "What else? What about the Talmidge sisters?"

She could see he didn't intend to take advice and that he was probably going to be a rebellious convalescent. She smiled ruefully and fondly. "Can't you rest, Nikolas? What is this? Once a lawman . . ."

". . . always a lawman," he finished for her. He shifted slightly, gritting his teeth. "The Talmidges?" he asked again.

She shook her head sadly. "It's nearly destroyed them. They tried to protect Dahlia Lee all these years. They'll be tried as accessories to murder. I don't know how they'll stand up to it."

"Hey," he said roughly. He let go of her hand and touched her face. He traced the outline of her lower lip with his thumb. "Don't waste your pity. They were willing to sacrifice you. At their age, the worst they'll get is a stretch in some country-club prison. What about the others?"

She caressed his cheek and cradled his head. She couldn't seem to touch him enough. She wanted to keep assuring herself that he was really there, had really come back.

"The indictments are raining down," she told him. "Terry Perry. Cameron Carter and Dennis Finch—the two highest-ranking men in the police department. Willadene Davis. And lesser charges against people like Sheridan and Melissa Milhouse and Tammi Smith. All the ones who gave false evidence."

Her face was grave. "There were so many of them, Nikolas. It really was a conspiracy. They were all covering for Dahlia Lee. They all lied—to save their shares of the Talmidge money. All of them but Freddy Perry."

"What?" He frowned. He never had quite figured out the bartender's place in the whole business.

"He was the one person who told the truth," she explained. "They told him to lie to you, but he didn't. He told the police that he knew everybody couldn't keep covering for Dahlia Lee forever; it would all blow apart someday. He's got a good business and he wasn't going to be caught up in conspiracy or perjury or anything else. What he told you about Dahlia Lee was the truth. Only I didn't know it. I thought it was nothing but rumor."

"Lord," Nikolas grumbled. "No wonder I couldn't quite get a hold on it. One of them was telling the truth. Actually being honest. Well, the kingdom's fallen, with Dahlia Lee gone."

She nodded solemnly. He took her hand again.

"Valery?" His own face was somber, almost harried.

"Nikolas," she soothed, "you really shouldn't talk. It's all over now. The authorities identified Fields's body, they're tracing the money, they've established that Dahlia Lee assumed another identity. They even found out Cameron Carter was making those calls to me. But now it's over."

He shook his head. "No," he said. "Mrs. Bellarion."

The name hung between them for a moment, like a dark cloud. "The Talmidges used her to get you here," Valery said at last. "That was all. Then John Upchurch told her to get rid of you. She never knew what was really going on. I hear she's furious with everyone. But I don't think she'll ever bother us again. She knows I didn't kill Charles. That the Talmidges tried to victimize all of us."

He was silent. He licked his cracked lips. "That's not what I meant," he said at last. He didn't look at her, but he kept holding her hand tightly.

The silence between them grew awkward. She looked down at their linked hands and bit her lip. "Nikolas, I don't know if you can ever forgive me—"

He cut her off. "What?" His black eyes flashed disbelief.

"It's my fault you're in here," she said guiltily. "If I hadn't insisted on looking for Fields, if I hadn't taken your gun . . . I nearly got you killed."

"It wasn't you," he said gruffly. "It was me. My reflexes were off. I think my knee went out. She never should have been able to get that shot off at me. I'm getting too old for this kind of thing. Besides, they were coming for us anyway. The lady was out for blood. She meant to have it."

"I'll never forgive myself."

"Listen." His hand went to her shoulder, pulled her toward him. "You did what you had to do. You handled yourself like a good soldier. You never lost your cool. Not once. You had no reason to trust me. None. It couldn't have been different. Understand? I never want you to feel guilty. Do you hear me? Never."

She nodded but couldn't obey. She still felt terrible. She said nothing.

He, too, was silent, his face haggard.

"The question is," he finally said, "will you ever be able to trust me? After what I did to you. The lies. Working for Thelma Bellarion. The whole thing."

She looked at him in amazement. "Nikolas, trust you? You were willing to *die* for Tony and me. You were willing to die three times over. You took the poison. You told me to shoot when you knew I could hit you. You didn't even want me to help you afterward—all you could think of was Tony. How could I not trust you?" Tears shimmered in her eyes again.

His hand moved to the back of her neck. His voice was husky. "Does that mean that maybe you'll forgive me?"

Her face told him as much as her words. "I've forgiven you everything. When you were lying in my arms that night, looking like you were going to die, I thought I'd lost you. It was horrible."

"I don't think you're going to lose me," he assured her, half smiling. "I don't think you've got a chance. Want to be stuck with a banged-up old Texan with trick knees and a bad shoulder?"

She took a deep breath. "Yes." She couldn't imagine wanting any other man in the world, ever. "I do."

He drew her nearer. "Then you've got me. Permanently, if you'll have me. I'm going to take you and Tony to Washington with me. I'm going to get a job behind a desk. I think I want to live in the suburbs and have a wife and a kid and stay out of trouble. Try life in a slower lane. What do you say?"

"I say it sounds wonderful."

His eyes searched her face. "I love you."

"I love you." She smiled. Her heart soared as she leaned down so that their lips could meet

He kissed her until she made him stop. "We've got a lifetime to do this, you know," she said. "I think right now you'd better save your strength."

He was about to object, but the door opened. He let his arm slide down around her waist. They both turned.

Tony appeared. He stopped when he saw that Nikolas was conscious. Smiling shyly, he held out a paper sack and an extravagant bouquet of wildflowers.

"Are you all right, Nikolas?" The boy looked somewhat awed.

"Great, slugger. I won't turn any cartwheels for a few days, but I'll live."

"I brought Mom some lunch," Tony said, shifting from foot to foot self-consciously. "Charmian sent it. She says you gotta eat, Mom. She sent you some flowers, Nikolas. She picked them herself so there wouldn't be a rose in the bunch."

Valery smiled at him. She still had one arm wound around Nikolas's neck. She wondered what the boy thought, seeing the two of them like that.

Tony just looked at them. They looked fine together to him. Just fine. Like they belonged. He went to Valery and handed her the sack.

She set it on the bedside table, then pulled Tony next to her and hugged him tight, keeping her other arm linked around Nikolas.

Tony clutched the flowers awkwardly, but couldn't keep his eyes off Valery and Nikolas. His mother looked happier than he could ever remember seeing her. The Grady guy looked happy, too, but serious at the same time.

"Tony," Nikolas said gruffly, measuring his words carefully, "I'm going to Washington when I get out of here. I want you and your mother to come with me. She's said yes. What do you think? Is that all right with you?"

Tony blinked at him, solemn as a little owl. "I think it's fine," he said softly.

The boy looked up at their faces again. He looked particularly hard at Nikolas Grady. He'd never known a braver man. This was the man who'd helped save his mother. This was the man so tough the bad people couldn't kill him. The man who'd made his mother smile again. Tony felt a swell of pride and admiration. He'd grow up to be just like him. Exactly.

He tried a word in his mind: Dad. He tried it again. Dad. Yeah. Dad. It sounded good. Somehow it felt right.

Yes, for the first time in a long time, things felt right.

He knew that his mother and Nikolas knew it, too. Things were right again at last, things had become whole. Valery hugged them both. She smiled first at Tony, then at Nikolas. They smiled back.

Nobody said anything. Nobody had to.